INTRODUCTION

From Halter to Altar by Cathy Marie Hake
Sociable Matty, who never met a stranger, soon makes far too many friends in James Collingswood's opinion. He is inadvertently responsible for the Craig sisters since he placed the original bridle order. Can he hitch these women up without getting lassoed by the openhearted one?

From Carriage to Marriage by Janelle Burnham Schneider
Shy Corrine, pregnant and still grieving her husband, came along because she cannot bear to be separated from her sisters. Luke Collingswood can tame every beast on the ranch. Will his gentle touch help heal and win her heart?

From Pride to Bride by JoAnn A. Grote
Bossy Bess cannot stop interfering in her sisters' romances or town life. She soon has Gideon Riker and the other men of Lickwind in an uproar because she's using his saloon as a classroom to rescue the soiled doves! Will Gideon's black heart be Bess's biggest reformation project?

From Alarming to Charming by Pamela Kaye Tracy
Tomboy Bertie never bothered to cultivate feminine wiles until she met Thomas Hardin. Suddenly, she's a whole new woman. This man is new money and old trouble. When his past catches up with him, can he protect this unpredictable contradiction of petticoats and pluck?

A Bride for a Bit

MISCOMMUNICATION STARTS A CHAIN
OF FOUR DELIGHTFUL WEDDINGS

JoAnn A. Grote
Cathy Marie Hake
Janelle Burnham Schneider
Pamela Kaye Tracy

BARBOUR
PUBLISHING

From Halter to Altar ©2003 by Cathy Marie Hake
From Carriage to Marriage ©2003 by Janelle Burnham Schneider
From Pride to Bride ©2003 by JoAnn A. Grote
From Alarming to Charming ©2003 by Pamela Kaye Tracy

Cover art: GettyOne, Inc.

Illustrations: Mari Goering

ISBN 1-58660-798-7

Published by Barbour Publishing, Inc., P.O. Box 719, Uhrichsville, Ohio 44683, www.barbourbooks.com

ечра Member of the
Evangelical Christian
Publishers Association

Printed in the United States of America.
5 4 3

A Bride

for a Bit

From Halter to Altar

by Cathy Marie Hake

Prologue

Littleton, Rhode Island—1868

Barney, anything interesting come in?"

"Ah-yuh. I posted them yonder." The young man jabbed his thumb at the wall.

Ellis Stack scratched his side and sauntered over to the collection of scraps of paper stuck on various nails lining the far wall. Squinting, he moved his thin lips as he sounded out each word. The middle post caught his attention.

> *L. S. Stocks*
> *Bridle Order: Sturdy, dependable, able to handle the stress of heavy labor. Plain ones only. Willing to pay fair price. Many needed.*
>
> *Contact: James Collingswood*
> *Lickwind, Dakota Territory*

His pale face lit up with glee. "Send a reply straight off!" Ellis scrawled some words on a paper, crossed out as many as he could to save money, then shoved it at the telegraph operator. " 'Bout time things went my way. Let me know as soon as you get a response."

As he turned to leave, he heard Barney's twitchy index finger hitting the telegraph key. Every single dot and dash sounded like cash falling into his pocket.

> *Collingswood,*
> *Regarding order: Four ready to ship. Suited to specifications, will serve well. One fifty, plus shipping, COD.*
> *E. Stack*

The next morning, Barney tracked Ellis down at the mercantile and handed him a folded slip. Ellis quickly opened the note.

> *Mr. Stack,*
> *Agree to price. Send what you have. As more are finished, ship as well.*
> *James Collingswood*

Ellis smiled. The four headaches he'd been suffering were about to end.

Chapter 1

Matilda Craig stepped down from the Union Pacific train and sighed in relief. She'd had enough of the dust and smoke to last her a lifetime. Ellis hadn't told them they were coming to the western edge of the Dakota Territory. She'd listened to the man behind her call the place they were stopping by an Indian name...Wyoming. The name paired with the train's endless chug—*Why am I roaming? Why am I roaming?*

Small pebbles rolled beneath her black high-top boots; and she tried valiantly to keep her balance, but her effort was in vain. Both legs slid forward, and she made a very unladylike *oomph!* as she landed in a sea of ruffled cotton petticoats. The horsehair bustle she'd hoped would make her appealing to her intended padded Matty's landing, but nothing would salvage her bruised pride.

"Here, Miss." A mountain of a man plucked her from the ground and set her on her feet as if she weighed no more than a pail of milk. Concern lined his craggy, tan face as glinting hazel eyes scanned her. "Are you all right?"

"Nothing damaged but my pride," she confessed. "Thank you."

His large hand continued to cup her shoulder in a proprietary, protective manner. "The town hasn't put in a boardwalk yet. After the rocking of the train, you'll be a mite unsteady."

"I noticed." Matilda couldn't resist smiling at him. He'd been an utter gentleman—even if he wore fringed buckskin like a rough saddle tramp, and a thin veil of trail dust covered unruly waves of dark brown hair. She probably looked no better after five days on a train.

"Matty!"

Matilda turned at the sound of her twin's voice. Mountain Man kept hold of her, and she wasn't sure whether to shake him off or cling for dear life. The knucklehead who put this gravel at the train stop obviously never wore heels. The last thing Matty wanted to do was decorate the ground again. In the past two minutes, a full dozen men appeared and gaped at her. Bouncing on her bustle again simply wouldn't do.

"Is this it? Are we really here?"

Matty tilted her face up to the buckskinned behemoth. "This is Lickwind, isn't it?"

"Yes, Ma'am." He shifted one hand to brace her elbow and reached out to help Corrine descend the slippery metal steps. "Careful."

"Thank you ever so much," Corrine murmured in her Sunday singing voice. Though always sweet and painfully shy, she had a way of adding a lilt when she sang or found herself near a handsome man.

Matilda felt an unaccountable spurt of irritation. She'd

found him first. Not that it meant anything. She wasn't going to get to choose her man, and neither would any of her sisters. Besides, Corrie hadn't done it on purpose; and she, more than any of them, needed folks to treat her gently.

With an air of expectation, Matty glanced at the rapidly growing collection of men who formed an arc around them. James Collingswood should step forward any minute now. He'd settle them in a boardinghouse until they courted a bit with their intended grooms. . .but if she could choose, Matty wouldn't mind a man like this one.

By the time pretty, dark-haired Bess descended, the men hurriedly started to preen. Hasty hands smoothed rowdy beards, hats came off, shirts were crammed into britches, and shoulders suddenly squared. By contrast, the mountain man calmly reached up to take four hatboxes, three valises, and a burlap bag and lugged two large steamer trunks from the disgruntled purser. Bess's beloved wooden hope chest came last, and her rescuer handled it with special care.

He set everything by Matty and her sisters, then shot the cowboys and horsemen an amused look. A smile split his tanned face, and he murmured under his breath, "Ladies, I ought to apologize for them. It's been years since Lickwind boasted such a fine display of femininity. You must all feel like the only apple pie at a church picnic!"

His words broke their tension. They still stood in a close knot. Matty threaded her fingers with Corrine's to give her a bit of much-needed reassurance. "You've already been so kind. Could I trouble you to please introduce us to Mr. Collingswood?"

"I'm Jim Collingswood." He gave her a surprised look.

"Imagine that! Well, Mr. Collingswood." Matty tried to give him a composed look, even though she really felt like her insides were skipping rope. "We're the Craig sisters. I'm Matilda. This is my twin, Corrine, that's Bess, and Bertie is at the end. I have the papers for you in my valise."

"What papers?"

"To finalize the arrangements."

His brows knit. "What arrangements, Miss Craig?"

"Why, we're the brides you sent for."

❧

"Just how many brides do you think you get?" Jim's brother, Luke, asked as he nudged alongside him.

Completely thunderstruck, Jim stared at the women. "Brides? I didn't send for brides."

The gal who'd quite literally fallen at his feet pinched her lips together in a firm line. The one next to her, who had no more color than a mashed potato, huddled close. The last two exchanged horrified looks as the train started to puff off into the distance.

"We're just what you asked for on the bridal order. Sturdy, dependable, plain—"

It was too outrageous to believe. Jim shook his head. "Ladies, something has gone terribly wrong. I ordered plain, ordinary bridles for my horses—not brides!"

"I see," Matilda Craig said. She pivoted a bit, and Jim instinctively reached out to keep her from falling again. The way her shoulders started to shake made his heart lurch.

"No need to cr—" He jerked away as he realized she wasn't in need of consolation. Of all things, the woman started to laugh.

"We should have known Ellis would mess this up," she said, her voice bobbing up and down with mirth. Jim stared at her intently, hoping she wasn't sliding into hysteria.

"What do we do now?" the youngest one huffed.

"Told you this wouldn't work out," Bess said. "Matty, this isn't funny in the least."

"Oh, no!" The gal who was a very pale copy of Matty lost that pretty lilt from a minute ago. "What is to become of us?" She continued to clutch Matilda's hand and leaned into her, nearly causing both of them to lose balance.

Jim reached out to brace Matty before the two of them toppled over. In the middle of this whole confusing mess, he wondered how in the world Ellis Stack ever described Matilda as plain. Sunrise gold hair was plaited on top of her head like a crown. It framed wide, expressive blue eyes that would always let a man know precisely how she felt. The feel of soft fabric beneath his hand and the mind-boggling scent of flowery perfume made him all too aware he hadn't been around anyone half this appealing in ages.

But he wasn't about to marry her. . .or any of her sisters. What was he supposed to do with four females?

The youngest one scrunched up her freckled nose and repeated, "What do we do?"

"We'll just have to make do." Matilda pulled away from his touch, disengaged from her sister, grabbed two hatboxes, and handed them to the pale one.

Jim swiped them right back. "Your sister isn't up to this."

In a bizarre tug-of-war, Matilda grabbed hold of them. "Sir, I understand this was all an honest mistake, but you're not making it any better. Right about now, it would be best if you'd go mind your own business and leave us alone." One of the lids popped off, and gobs of thin-as-air, lacy stuff fluttered in the air.

Corrine sat down on one of the trunks and burst into tears.

As he helped Matilda cram the wedding veil back into the hatbox, she hissed under her breath, "Now look what you did!"

"Whatever it was, Lady, I'm sorrier than you'll ever know."

Chapter 2

W "e'd best come up with a plan." Bess gave the town a disparaging look.

"Ellis already did that," Bertie grumbled as she flopped down on a trunk, "and look where it landed us."

"In the middle of nowhere, with no one to help us," Corrie whimpered.

Matty glanced at the odd collection of men and took their measure in a quick sweep. This lot rated more ragged than any group she'd ever seen. Most desperately needed to be reacquainted with scissors, a razor, and a tub. More than a few weren't refined sufficiently to keep from scratching like a hound with fleas. Even with all that counted against them, to the man, they'd all removed their hats and grinned. About half of them even boasted a full set of teeth. The minute one took a single step, the entire group trampled forward and formed a complete circle around them.

"Well." Matty injected a sunny tone to her voice and folded her hands in front of herself. "It's good to see so many strong, kind-looking men. My sisters and I seem to need to transfer our goods to the boardinghouse or hotel.

Could I trouble a few of you—?"

"Back off." Jim Collingswood's low snarl made the men freeze. "Miss Craig, Lickwind doesn't have a boardinghouse or hotel."

Bertie banged her heels against the trunk and propped her fist on her hips in a most unladylike way. "Isn't this a fine kettle of fish? Not that I cotton much to the notion of getting hitched, but being stranded without a place to lay our heads or a decent meal—"

"Hush," Bess clipped as she lifted her chin. "We'll simply have to take the next train home."

All of the men bellowed in denial.

Matty opened her reticule and pulled out the last seventeen dollars she owned. "Here. Bertie, give us your money."

"I spent it."

"It's at least forty dollars apiece for the tickets." Corrie's voice shook as she stated the terrible fact.

Matty gave Bess a questioning look. Bess's thin-lipped expression made her heart fall.

"This isn't a normal train stop." Jim Collingswood's comment carried the flavor of a mortician's announcement. "Probably won't stop here for at least another week."

At wit's end and worried about the way Corrie blanched, Matty finally gave into temptation and turned around to invite Mr. Collingswood to keep his tidings to himself. . .but she forgot about the gravel on the ground. His lightning-fast reflexes saved her from another humiliating fall, but the result wasn't any more desirable. He'd grabbed and yanked, so she landed face-first into his buckskin shirt.

"For a man who don't wan' a bride, he shore seems to be

stakin' a claim," one of the men said.

As several others hooted, Matty tried to summon a scrap of dignity and her balance. The minute she looked up into Jim's unblinking gaze, her tongue cleaved to the roof of her mouth.

"Easy now," he said in a strangely soothing tone.

"Whoa, there," another male voice said from a yard or so away. "Hey, Jim?"

Matty recovered her bearings enough to twist her head to the side and see who'd spoken. A man whose profile strongly resembled Mr. Collingswood's—good gracious; strong, handsome men were everywhere!—bent a bit. When he straightened, Matty realized he'd scooped up Corrie. Her twin drooped in his arms like a wilted daisy. He looked compassionate enough. . .until he curled his arms to hold her a bit closer. Then he looked as stricken as Matty felt.

"Hey, Darlin', I'm right here to catch you," a straddle-legged man with a tobacco-stained moustache declared from behind Bess. "Always did favor the fillies with dark manes."

Bess served him a withering glare that made him back up a step.

While a handful of men all argued over who ought to get Bess and Bertie, Matty shook free from her captor and gave in to the very unfeminine urge to exercise a trick the hired hand back home had shown her. She stuck two fingers in her mouth, let out an ear-piercing whistle, then smoothed her skirts to recover her dignity while all of the men gawked at her in utter amazement.

"This has gotten out of hand. Where is the nearest patch of shade for my sister?"

"The rough seas," James Collingswood stated in a curt tone.

"There's no need to be mean." Matty glowered at him.

"It's my ranch." Jim Collingswood clamped hold of her elbow and started to drag her down the street as he ordered over his shoulder, "You men load the women's gear into my wagon. Luke, do you need to take that one into Doc's office?"

"Doc's gone again. May as well haul her home and get her rested up."

Jim stopped by a buckboard and cinched his hands around Matty's waist, then hefted her up onto the seat without so much as a word of explanation. He boosted Bertie into the back as Luke laid Corrie in the wagon bed. Bess had managed to stop off at a pump somewhere and dampened her hanky. As she draped it over Corrie's forehead, Jim pawed through the possessions the townsmen hoisted aboard. The lacy parasol he pulled out looked ludicrous in his hands; and when he popped it open, Matty fought back the urge to giggle. None of this was funny in the least, but weariness and worry mingled to rob her of her manners. She started to laugh again.

As Jim turned to look at her, the rib from the parasol grazed through his hair and combed a furrow that stood at attention. His tawny eyes narrowed warily. "You're not going hysterical, are you?"

"No. Oh, not at all," Matty hastened to assure him. She smothered her levity and focused on Corrie out of concern for her as well as to keep from staring at his wild, parasol-framed hairstyle.

"Hold this over your sis," he ordered Bertie.

If Corrie hadn't been swooning so regularly in the past few months, Matty would have been far more alarmed. As it was, she fully expected her sister to rouse and feel mortified over all of the fuss, so she tried not to overreact. Clearly, what she needed to do was find someplace safe and cheap for them to stay until they could earn enough to catch a train back home.

Before she could pose any inquiries, Jim Collingswood swung up onto the seat beside her and put the buckboard in motion. "Sir, what are you doing?"

"I'm fixin' to clean up my mess." The angry glint in his eye made it clear just what—or who—that mess was.

❧

"Kicked clean outta my own home," Jim muttered as he pitched hay into a pile that would become his bed.

"Yeah, and we helped Pa build every last inch of that place," Luke repeated once again from the adjoining stall.

Jim stared at the hay and forked over a few more hefty heaps, then peevishly jabbed at a lump. "Propriety makes for an itchy bed. If Ma hadn't drummed respectability into us all those years, we could be sleeping in the study."

Luke let out a cross between a snort and a laugh. "Ma would skin your hide if she knew you'd sent for four brides."

"How many times do I have to tell you? I didn't send for brides; I sent for bridles."

Luke chortled as he flicked his wrists and the wool blanket fluffed out on the bed of hay. "If it weren't for that cute one feeling poorly, this would be a hoot and a half."

"She's feeling sickly? I thought only the one in the motherly way was under the weather."

Luke leaned across the stall and gave him an entertained look. "I was talking about the motherly one. Who are you so worked up about?"

"Not who. What. I made a close study of the ledger whilst you carried her up to a bedroom. A buck fifty for a bridle and shipping was fine—a hundred fifty apiece for four women is—"

Luke whistled. "More ready cash than we can scrape together. You know, maybe this was meant to be. That motherly one isn't in any shape to stick back on a train."

"Don't even think about it." Jim waggled his finger menacingly. "We lollygag around on this, and she'll be too far gone to travel. Spending the whole winter in the stable so's those gals can take over our house is just plain crazy. We have to come up with a plan."

"I'll concede that point."

"So I started thinking, maybe we can just send them back. You heard Matty: Tickets cost forty bucks. We'll do that and toss in an extra hundred so that brother-in-law won't have call to shove 'em outta their place this winter. It'll stretch our budget, but we can manage."

"Forty bucks is low-class accommodations. You couldn't possibly do that to those poor sisters, specially not the—" he patted his washboard belly, "one!"

"I suppose you have a better idea?"

"There's no rush. The next eastbound train won't stop here for nine days. Until then, you'd best cool your temper and figure on getting some tasty meals for a change."

Jim heaved a sigh as he flopped down on his itchy, makeshift bed. He stacked his hands behind his head and stared at the cobwebs adorning the barn's crossbeam ceiling. "I guess that's some consolation."

"Best meal we've eaten in years."

"Don't get used to it, Luke. No use compounding one mistake by making a bunch more."

Chapter 3

Matty sluiced water on her face and sighed with delight. Last night, she and her sisters made good use of the tub. After that dreadful five-day train ride, she'd been sure she'd never come clean. They'd acquainted themselves with the kitchen and whipped up chicken and dumplings. While they shared the supper table with the Collingswood brothers, no one had concocted a solution to their quandary.

The Collingswood brothers revealed their father had died four years ago, and their mother and sister now lived in Chicago. Jim looked at Matty and waggled his fork to punctuate his words. "No woman was made to live out here. Our ma and sis got out alive—two others came and didn't make it through their first winter."

James didn't ask them any personal questions. That notable omission made it clear he was unwilling to entertain any notion of honoring the mail-order arrangement—mixed up as it was. He held no responsibility for the predicament, and Matty almost felt relieved. She hadn't been happy about being sent out here to husband hunt. . .so why did she still feel a twinge of regret that this cowboy didn't want her?

He'd answered enough questions for the sisters to learn the Rough Cs Ranch ran cattle; but during the spring and summer, the brothers also captured and tamed wild mustangs. Clearly, they were ambitious men; and from the looks of the buildings and grounds, they were also very hardworking.

Luke managed to coax a bit of information from Matty and her sisters; but for the most part, he'd avidly eaten every last bit of food on the table.

Corrie fell asleep over dessert, and Jim Collingswood shot her a worried look. "Doesn't appear as though that afternoon nap did her much good."

"Corrie's a widow," Matty said as she rose. She'd rehearsed how to impart the news as delicately as she could, but now that the time was at hand, the words nearly choked her. "She'll make aunts of us all just before Christmas."

Both men stood when Matty rose. The table manners and genteel customs they displayed came as a very pleasant surprise. So did the fact that Luke bent and carefully scooped Corrie into his arms. "I suspected she was in the family way when I caught her at the train stop. I'll take her back upstairs."

As his brother carried Corrie to her bed and Bess followed along to tend her, Jim held Matty back. "And she came out here as a bride?"

Matty sighed. "My sister Adele's husband took over our parents' dairy farm after they passed on two years ago and made life for us unbearable. Corrie came back to live with us a couple of months ago, the day she became a widow. Ellis knew she was in a delicate condition, but it didn't matter to him in the least."

Jim shook his head in disbelief. "I suppose bringing her here was more merciful than leaving her in his care."

❧

More merciful. . . His words echoed in Matty's mind this morning as she braided her hair. Quietly so she wouldn't wake Corrie, she slipped into the blue delft-patterned dress she'd made from feed sacks and tiptoed out of the room.

"How's Corrie?" Bess whispered in the hall.

"Still sleeping like a baby."

"Good. I just woke Bertie. She was upside-down in the bed and still won't turn lose of that hatbox of hers. She's never suffered wearing a bonnet gladly. Do you suppose we've finally started taming her into womanhood?"

"I dearly hope so. Perhaps all of our prayers are finally being answered."

Bess shook her head as they went down the stairs. "I'm afraid not. We prayed for godly men to be our husbands. Instead, we're going to have to make our way amidst the rabble and roughs until we earn enough money to get back home."

"Or we could settle here. Ellis will marry us off to whomever he can just to get rid of us. If we make Lickwind our home, at least we can stay together."

"I declare, Matty, you're always making the best of a situation. Problem is, I can't see how we'll ever manage here on our own for any longer than it'll take to earn train fare."

"We'll consider it as a challenge. I was thinking last night—"

Bess shot her an alarmed look. "Oh, no."

"Now listen. It's a good plan. Only one of us needs to get married. Ellis had no right at all to sell us off as if we were his property. He put us on that train, and he's keeping the dairy farm."

"Adele didn't look very sad, sending us off," Bess grumbled as they entered the kitchen. "She and Ellis deserve one another."

"I figure they owe us for taking our share of the birthright; and this whole trip was Ellis's idea, so I don't feel bad that they're out the money for our train fares. We need to put together whatever we have left. That'll be enough seed money to set up a solid business in town."

"Town didn't look any too industrious. It's no more than a spit in the wind."

"Bess!" Matty laughed. "Mama would have a conniption if she ever heard you talk like that." While Bess *humpf*ed, Matty continued. "We could do mending and baking. I'm sure we could make it work."

As her sister lit a kerosene lamp, Matty stirred the embers in the four-burner Monitor stove and added another log. "I'll go milk the cow if you gather the eggs."

"You can't go into the barn. The men are there!"

"Which is why the cow is tied up by the coop." Matty grabbed a pail and scooted out the door. She'd managed to cajole one of the hands to find her a heifer that was fresh last night. He'd looked at her as if she were crazy as a loon for making that request, but he'd also been more than eager to please. As it turned out, Western ranches only viewed the cattle as beef on the hoof and ignored the dairy possibilities. Matty resolved to discuss that matter with whichever rancher married her.

The lavender predawn light allowed her to pick her way

across the yard. Matty patted the Rough Cs' brand on the heifer's hip. The three wavy, parallel lines with a tilted C riding them were both clever and would be hard to tamper with. It seemed the Collingswood brothers thought of almost everything except a milking stool. One would be nice; but since they didn't have one, she squatted down and set to work. Leaning into the warm side of the cow, she quickly hit a rhythm and filled the bucket.

"Forty-one eggs—half of them brown!" Bess declared as she exited the coop. "Can you imagine having such fine laying hens?"

"Beats frying lame hens," a man drawled as the sound of a shotgun being cocked clicked.

Both sisters jumped and yelped.

"Dear mercy!" Matty set down the milk before she spilled it.

"Sir, you have no business sneaking up on women." Bess clutched the egg basket closer and peered into the shadows.

The barn door crashed open. Jim and Luke Collingswood both bolted out with guns drawn. "What's wrong?"

"Found these two sneakin' round the henhouse," a gangly man said as he stepped from behind the privy. He bobbed his grizzled head. "Caught 'em red-handed. Cain't say I ivver seen prettier thieves."

"Thieves!" Bess stepped forward in outrage. "I'll have you know—"

"We were getting ready to make breakfast," Matty interrupted. "And we expect you'll be at the table in about fifteen minutes."

"Boss, is she givin' the invite to you or to all us hands?"

"Just us, Scotty," Jim growled as he cradled his rifle so it didn't endanger anyone. He looked as comfortable as a mother rocking a baby. The fact that his shirt hung wide open and he was standing barefoot on prickly straw and cold dirt didn't even seem to register.

"I heard tell you got yourself some brides from the train yesterday. Thought it was just Lanky's whiskey talkin'."

Luke shoved his revolver into his waistband and held his shirt closed. "I was wondering if I dreamed it myself."

Matty saw the impish sparkle in Luke's eyes, but the fire in Jim's made her decide to stick to the facts. "How many hands do you have, Mr. Collingswood?"

Jim closed the distance between himself and Matty. He scowled. "Don't you go getting any romantic notions about my men. I pay 'em fair, and they earn it; but not a one of 'em is marriage material, so you just stay away from them."

She nodded sagely. "I understand."

"Just what do you understand?" The muscles in his well-chiseled jaw twitched.

She turned away, dragging Bess along with her, and called over her shoulder, "You're a man who needs his coffee before he's ready to face the day. See you in a quarter hour."

❧

Fifteen minutes later, Jim figured his mind was playing tricks on him. He couldn't possibly be smelling coffee—not out here in the birthing shed when he needed to concentrate on the high-strung mare.

"Looks like you could use this," Matty whispered as she slipped up and pressed a steaming cup into his hands. She held a plate in her other hand—one with a mountain of fluffy scrambled eggs, biscuits, and gravy.

He hummed in appreciation as he took a bracing swig of the coffee, then accepted the plate. "Miss, you don't belong out here."

Her soft-as-flannel blue eyes twinkled. "Mr. Collingswood, we had a dairy farm back home. Indelicate as it may be, I've tended to the business end of plenty of farm animals."

"Is that so?"

Her calm demeanor surprised him. "Your mare's taking a minute to gather up her strength. Why don't you have a quick bite while I wipe her down with some straw?"

"You?"

Instead of being insulted, she looked at the mare. Her voice took on an amused flavor. "Well, forget your breakfast, Cowboy. This one's not going to wait."

A short while later, Jim stood by Matty's side and chuckled. "That foal's a hungry one."

Matty nudged him and giggled. "I'll bet you are, too. A dog ate your breakfast while we were busy."

He spun around and gave the empty plate a look of utter despair. "Dumb dog would try the patience of a saint. One of our hands went to town and, um—"

"Got lit?"

Jim could scarcely imagine this prim woman knew slang for a man making a fool of himself at the saloon. He cleared his throat. "Well, to make a long story short, he spent a whole month's wages on beer and what he thought was some fancy, purebred sheep."

"So now you're saddled with a poodle!" Matty's merry laughter filled the air for an instant, then she recovered her composure. "I apologize for making light of the situation. You're a good man to let him keep the dog, and at least he's one of the big ones so you don't have to worry about the horses trampling him."

Jim cocked one brow and drawled, "Are you trying to make me thankful to have that miserable beast?"

"It's not always easy to trust God when He puts odd circumstances in our lives, is it?"

"You talkin' about Ramon or about you and your sisters?"

"Maybe a bit of both."

The sparkle in her eyes warmed something deep inside of him. Instead of nagging or wailing, she acknowledged this wasn't a good situation.

"I'm sure you're still hungry. I'll be happy to fix you something."

Just as he opened his mouth to refuse, his stomach growled. Jim gave her a wry smile. "I'd be obliged."

They walked to the kitchen door. The whole way there, he kept getting a whiff of her flowery perfume. Nine days of this—then he'd have things back in order. He grabbed the doorknob, twisted, and pulled. . . .

And nearly got knocked over as the ugliest thing he'd ever seen cannoned out of the house. A second later, the poodle streaked past, making more racket than a stampede of wild mustangs.

"What was that?"

"Roberta Suzanne Craig!" Bess shouted from the kitchen as Jim turned to watch the dog tree a spitting ball of fur.

Matty sighed. "I guess Bertie didn't pack a bonnet in her hatbox, after all."

Chapter 4

Jim stared at the ledger and gulped the dregs of his coffee. A soft rustling at the study door made him look up.

"I thought you might appreciate a draught so you'd sleep well." Matty approached his desk and set down a teacup that exuded a pungent aroma. "I've no doubt you're hurting."

"It's not necessary." The stuff smelled worse with each passing tick of the grandfather clock. Then again, his leg ached like crazy and so did his shoulders.

Once he'd snagged Bertie's very ugly, very pregnant cat, Rhubarb, from the cottonwood, both animals massacred him instead of each other. Bess dragged the dog away, Bertie claimed her hideous fur ball, and he'd stomped off toward the pump.

Matty got there first and had already filled a bucket. "Come into the kitchen. I'll take care of you."

She'd been more than true to her word. Matty did a remarkable job of cleaning and stitching up the dog bite on his calf, and she'd applied a soothing salve to the deep cat scratches on his shoulders, too. To his surprise, she never batted an eye at the blood or the fact that he had to remove his shirt. She'd been soothing as could be and skilled enough to earn his respect. Better still, she hadn't chattered or expected him to be sociable.

Corrine sat by the kitchen window to mend his shirt, Bess made him a gigantic ham omelet, and Bertie mumbled an apology for her wayward, hideous cat after locking it up in her room. She'd then gone to the barn and polished five saddles to make amends.

Jim hated each and every kindness because he didn't cotton to owing anyone anything. Now, instead of them owing him for bending over backward to keep them, they'd gone the extra mile to make atonement. . .and it was for nothing more than a pair of lamebrained animals acting true to form. All day long he'd thought of how those Craig gals pitched in to make things right.

Now Matty was at it again. She still had that serene, comforting air about her, too.

"You're not poisoning me, are you?"

Her smile could light up the ranch on a moonless night. "I'm afraid I didn't bring anything toxic in my medical supplies."

He motioned for her to take a seat. "I didn't ask this morning, but I wondered what a gal like you is doing with a doctoring bag."

On her way to the leather wingback chair, she straightened the portrait of his parents that hung a bit askew. Oddly enough, she didn't act all fussy about it; she calmly set it to rights and even smiled at his folks as if she held pleasant memories of them.

"Back home, Dr. Timmons was stretched too thin. I'm handy with a needle, and I'm not goosey about changing dressings. Papa finally arranged for me to tag along with Doc for part of a summer so I could learn a few handy skills. I'm glad to see Lickwind boasts a doctor."

Jim winced. "Don't put too much store in Doc Mitchel. He didn't get formal training—he picked up whatever he knows on the battlefield. Best you and your sisters stay fit until you're back where you can get decent care. . .especially Corrine. A woman in her motherly condition doesn't belong out here."

"Believe me, Mr. Collingswood—"

"Jim. Two brothers sharing the same last name and four sisters sharing theirs will make formal address confusing."

"Three sisters. Corrine's last name is Taylor. Though I acknowledge that we'll avoid considerable chaos if we follow your plan."

He picked up the tea, gave it a wary look, and took a quick gulp. He half lowered the cup, squinted at the remaining fluid, and shuddered.

"I can see you prefer my coffee over my curatives."

Just to prove he wasn't a coward, Jim glugged down the rest and shoved the cup across his desk, only to discover a butterscotch candy on the saucer. "What's this?"

"It'll take away the dreadful aftertaste."

"Something had better." He popped the nugget into his mouth and said around it, "I haven't tasted anything that pitiful since—"

"I burned the chili two nights ago." Luke chuckled from the doorway. "Neither of us can cook worth a hoot."

Matty tilted her head to the side and looked downright sympathetic. "You gentlemen must tell us what you enjoy. We'll be sure to make it for you."

"Since you asked," Luke dove in without taking a breath, "cinnamon buns. Pork chops. A nice, tender roast with mashed potatoes and gravy. I'd think my mouth died and went to heaven if you'd boil up a batch of some kind of jam. Yes, that would—"

"Be far more than is necessary," Jim cut in. With each thing his brother listed, he'd been able to imagine the taste until he practically drooled. He slammed the books shut and stood. "It's past time we parted company for the night."

A sweet pink suffused Matty's cheeks as she backed up and left the room in a swirl of blue-and-white skirts. Her voice drifted back to them. "Just wait one more minute!"

Jim glowered at Luke. "Don't let your belly take over your brain. We've gotta get these women shipped out of here."

Luke shoved his thumbs into his pockets and rocked back on his heels. "I wouldn't mind sleeping in the stable if we got fed as well as we have all day long."

"Come December, you'll sing a different tune. Let's go hit the hay—" He paused, stretched, and winced. "Literally."

Matty and Corrine stopped them as they headed out through the kitchen. Matty shoved plates that held huge wedges of pie onto a tray. Corrine hastily added two cups of steaming coffee as she said, "Black for you, Mr. James. One spoon of sugar in yours, Mr. Luke—just as you like it."

Jim tried not to scowl at Corrine. Though she and Matty looked similar, Corrine seemed so fragile. One false step, one harsh word, and he feared he'd send Matty's twin into another swoon. "Obliged, Ma'am." He took the tray and lifted his chin. "Now you stop fretting and scamper off to bed. Best you take proper care of yourself."

Matty slipped up and curled an arm about her sister. The tenderness in her smile could bring a man to his knees. "Thank you for your concern, James. I'll be sure Corrie rests."

Jim lay in the barn with the sweet taste of Matty's canned-peach pie on his lips, the warmth of her coffee in his belly, and the smell of fresh hay for his pillow. A man could do worse. . . .

Luke cleared his throat in the dark and rumbled, "I was thinking—"

"That's always dangerous," Jim said wryly.

"If we married them, we could sleep in the house and eat like that all of the time."

"Luke, you whizzed right past dangerous and plum hit loco."

❧

"Tell me it isn't so!" Matty laughed as Bess and she held opposite ends of a sheet and wrung it out.

"Every last word is true."

"Will wonders never cease!" They pinned the last sheet to the clothesline, then hastily hung all of their small clothes between the bedding so the men couldn't see the unmentionables.

Men had dropped by all morning. The Hatch cousins—Oscar and Linus—stopped by to "swap howdies." The blacksmith, Amos Freeling, came calling to see if someone could read his latest mail and write letters for him. A shipment from the feedstore was delivered. James scowled at the fact that it had taken Keith Squires and two other men to bring out that one buckboard. In fact, one-eyed Gideon, the saloon owner, managed to dig out some long-forgotten requisition for medicinal whiskey that suddenly ought to be delivered in case of emergencies. Jim had already shooed his own cow-hands back to work when they'd been moseying around the barnyard.

"I'd best add this apron into the wash kettle," Bess mused as she pinned up one last petticoat.

"Better not. I already put the men's shirts in the pot. I won't be surprised if the dye on them runs."

"No telling what'll happen. I'm expecting them to fall to pieces. Dirt's probably all that's holding them together."

Matty looked at the ranch and nodded. "They're hard-working men."

"I grant you that. You'd be happy as a cow in clover, stay-ing out here. Me? I've had enough hay and fences to last me a lifetime. I'd rather settle in town."

"I've been gathering information."

Bess pushed the shirts around in the laundry pot with the paddle as Matty added another log to the fire beneath it. "And here I thought you were just making friends with every cowboy on the spread."

"Well, that, too." Matty accepted the truth with a small ache in her heart. She'd always managed to befriend the men in their congregation and the dairy hands. Each one ended up treating her as his sister. That was part of the problem, though—not a one ever actually looked at her as wife mate-rial. If she were dead-level honest, none of them seemed much like husband material to her, either. Never once had she felt the spark she'd seen between her parents. Still, she longed to be a wife and mother.

"Are you going to daydream, or will you tell me what you found out?"

"Oh." Matty smoothed back a few stray tendrils. "The only place in town that's empty is the jail."

"The jail!"

"It's not as bad as it sounds. They don't have a sheriff here. The building is completely empty. It's between the barbershop and the, um. . ." She knew Bess would be unhappy with the other business.

"Not a house of ill repute!" Bess lurched backward.

"No. The saloon."

"Lord, have mercy on us," Bess muttered as she fished out a shirt. "It's not as bad as it sounds. It's worse!"

Matty watched as a sleeve fell off the garment and plopped back into the pot. She could see Jim walking toward them. Even from this distance, she heard his moan. She quietly echoed her sister's prayer, "Lord, have mercy on us."

"Matilda Craig," he thundered, "did you go into the bunkhouse?"

"Only after Chico assured me it was empty."

"Woman!"

She smiled at him. "Really, James, I was very circumspect."

He folded his arms across his chest. "Just what is circumspect about a woman in a bunkhouse?"

"Rhubarb went in there. I didn't think the men would be very happy if she decided to have her litter on one of their beds."

"Chico could have gone in and hauled her out. Chico should have."

"I'd normally agree, but Chico sneezes around cats."

"Buckwheat—"

"Your cook isn't to be trusted around animals. He threatened to dice Ramon and Rhubarb and put them in a stew!"

Bess said, "They need to boil awhile before they'll turn out right."

"Bess!" Matty wheeled around and stared in shock at her sister.

"I was talking about these filthy shirts," she said as she dunked a pair of them. "Bertie loves that cat. Our sister has been dragged halfway across the nation and doesn't have a place to call home. The way she clings to Papa's old felt hat nearly breaks my heart. The last thing I'd do is let anyone touch a hair on that cat's—" Bess's voice died out as she searched for an adequate description.

"What happened to that mangy-looking creature, anyway?" Jim asked.

Matty stuck her hands in her apron pockets and looked Jim in the eye. "Ellis tossed a garter snake at her. She leapt off the fence and landed in a bad patch of tares. Bertie couldn't pull them all out, so she snipped out the worst ones."

Jim didn't say a word. He shook his head in sympathetic disgust of her story, then turned and strode off. When he got a few yards away, Matty heard him mutter, "Plumb loco."

Chapter 5

Matty sat out on the porch steps and savored a cup of coffee. The supper dishes were done, and she wanted to get away from her sisters for a few minutes. Though they got along well enough, five days on a train counted as enough togetherness. A little breather, and she'd be happy to go sit with them in the parlor.

"Ever seen such a sky?" asked a voice as velvety and rich as the star-studded, purple-black heavens.

Matty shook her head—partly because she hadn't ever seen anything as endless as the Western sky, but also because she felt unaccountably tongue-tied around Jim Collingswood.

He leaned against a post that held up part of the veranda and murmured, "Looks can be deceiving, Matty. It's so pretty and peaceful. Problem is, this land is wild as can be."

She took a sip of coffee and let silence swirl about them. "So you came from Chicago?"

He nodded. "Moved here in '62. Mama came because she loved Pa to distraction, but she rated the venture as pure folly. After one year, she sent my sister Annie back to a finishing school. Annie married within months. Pa, Luke, and I got the ranch started, but Pa fell off a hay wagon and got run over in '64."

"Oh, Jim, I'm so sorry."

"Accidents happen out here all of the time. It's why you don't belong. Women are too vulnerable." He stared at her.

"What about your mother?"

"Soon as Pa died, she went back to be with Annie. She couldn't wait to 'get back to civilization where a woman can be a lady.' Luke and I decided we had a good start on things, so we've been here on our own for the past four years."

Matty laughed briefly. "From what he said about your cooking, I suppose your survival is something akin to a miracle."

"If you're talking about marvels, explain to me why you're not married yet."

Matty gave him a weak smile. "Until I find a man who can hold me as dear as Papa held Mama, I don't want to marry. I didn't feel that special spark with any of the men in our church, but a handful of them turned out to be fine friends."

"Come on, Matty—there wasn't one special man?"

"No, but I played Cupid and matched a few of them up with my friends. I even introduced Corrie to her husband."

Jim squatted down and tilted her chin upward. "Matty, why didn't you marry one of those fellows? It was much safer than coming out here to a complete stranger."

The concern in his voice and eyes made her breath hitch. "Ellis made our lives miserable. Bess and he got along about as well as Rhubarb and Ramon, and Corrie needed to get away from all of her memories."

"Still, the man ought to be strung up for concocting the plan to send you here."

She sighed. "It's appalling. I'm not a husband-hunting kind of woman. I finally decided maybe it was a blessing in disguise—at least all four of us would still be together."

The muscle in his jaw twitched. He stood and pulled her to her feet. "I'll be sure you're all settled together, wherever I send you. Now go on inside."

❦

Oomph! Jim landed in the dust and nearly got the wind knocked out of him. Any man with the brains of a trout would know to keep his mind and eyes on the mustang, but Jim had gotten distracted. Amos and Keith had come from town and sat up on the patio, sipping cool drinks with Matty. He'd chased both of them off just two days ago. What were they doing back here again?

He stood, drew in a few steadying breaths, and decided to stomp over and demand the men leave and the woman stop acting like someone had hung a courting swing from his eaves.

"She's about to do something foolish," Lanky called to him.

Jim was ready to agree, but then he realized Lanky was talking about the horse—not Matty. Refusing to make a fool of himself in front of his hands and townsmen, Jim focused on the skittish mare. She danced sideways, pawed, and tossed her head.

"There now, Darlin', you got nothing to worry 'bout. I mean you no harm," he singsonged.

"She don't cotton much to being broke," Lanky said

from his perch on the corral's split rail fence.

Jim shot him a smile. "Not a female in the world who does."

"You shore got yerself a nice passel of gals in the house. And I'm a-tellin' you, the smells comin' outta that kitchen are nuff to make me pea green jealous over that dumb poodle dog for getting the scraps."

"If I'm lucky, I'll get them to take that stupid beast back home with them." Jim murmured a few soft words to the mare and managed to stroke her.

"Pity you can't find it in your heart to handle 'em with the same skill and kindness you show these here mustangs." Lanky spat a wad of tobacco off to the side and sauntered away.

Jim concentrated on the mare, singing to her softly under his breath as he let her get accustomed to his touch again. He didn't need to respond to Lanky's comment, but it rankled.

He'd tried to be considerate of the women. Why, he'd worn his buckskins out here to break the mustangs so he wouldn't cause more laundry and mending. Each day for the past week, he made sure he washed up properlike and put on a fresh shirt before he went to the supper table. Not only had he given up his bed, he'd made every effort to make life easy on Matty and her sisters.

Having women around was a mix of heaven and hardship. Their soft voices, laughter, and good cooking surely did make for pleasant evenings. Though he'd never confess it, he looked forward to those last-thing-in-the-evening chats with Matty out on the porch. Fact was, little Matty managed to put her hand to work out in the stable without anyone mentioning what needed to be done. When something came up that she didn't know about, she was downright eager to learn. Jim hated to admit it to himself, but he'd actually started looking around for her.

Then, there were times he wished she and her sisters had never stepped off that train. He'd died about ten deaths when a stallion tried to kick down a corral fence, and a splintered board went sailing toward Matty. How in the world was he supposed to keep her and her sisters safe? He'd gotten a nasty telegram from Ellis Stack, demanding money for these women. On top of all of that, playing the role of guard dog and chasing away all of the randy bachelors of Lickwind wore thin on his nerves.

No, the women shouldn't stay. He needed to send them off. Regardless of how sweet Matty smelled or how interesting her conversations were, she didn't belong out here.

The whole time he reasoned through the need to send Matty away, Jim kept pampering the horse and shooting wary gazes at the guys on the porch with her. To his everlasting relief, she stood and the men took their leave. It wasn't until Jim headed toward the gate that he realized what he'd been singing. "Nobody Knows the Trouble I've Seen. . . ."

❧

Bertie stepped on the lowest rung of the fence. The toe of her scuffed boot caught in the hem, and she impatiently yanked the skirts to the side. Her battered brown felt hat tumbled into the dust, revealing that her strawberry blond bun sat askew on her head. As usual, she looked like she'd slept in her rumpled clothes. From the expression on her face, Jim expected her to shout out her thoughts. Instead, she extended her hand toward the horse and spoke in a low tone. "Mr. James, have you seen Rhubarb?"

To his amazement, the edgy mare walked over and nosed Bertie's hand. "Careful," he warned. "She's feral. I've been working to break her."

"You're a beauty, aren't you?" Bertie caressed her muzzle and forelock, and the mare stood still for it. The girl then flashed him a smile that faded just as quickly. "Looks like you're doing a fine job with her. Have you seen Rhubarb?"

"Can't say as I have. Better keep her away from Ramon."

Bertie nodded, got off the fence, and continued her search. As she left, he thought about what her sister had said. Poor kid—she truly loved that creature. He hoped it hadn't gone missing. He worked a bit more with the mare, but his heart wasn't in it. After a few more minutes, he turned her over to a hand so she would be groomed and watered, then he went in search of the cat.

A short while later, he stared in disbelief at the sight before him. Rhubarb lay in the corner of his stall with three mewling still-wet kittens. . .on top of his favorite wool bedroll.

❧

"Matilda, get Bertie."

Matty looked up from the shirt she'd been mending and gave Jim a startled look. "Is something wrong?"

Bertie peeked around the kitchen door. "Did I hear my name?"

"Yup. You two come along with me."

Matty exchanged a nervous look with her youngest sister and followed Jim out the door. He headed across the yard, straight toward the stable. Both of them had to pick up their skirts and half-run to keep up with him.

"Where're you all headed to in such an all-fired hurry?" Buckwheat called.

"Leave the women be and go chop logs for the stove," Jim growled as he charged ahead.

Shafts of sunlight filtered into the stable. Silvery motes danced on them, and the smell of horses and hay filled the air. To one side, a mare nickered to her newborn foal. Matty jumped when Jim curled his hand around her arm and started leading her along the wide center aisle. He'd taken hold of Bertie's arm, too.

They went clear to the end, and he stopped. Pulling them both in front of himself, he settled a hand on Matty's shoulder and leaned forward so his breath brushed her cheek. "Look in the corner."

"Rhubarb!" Bertie cried with delight.

"Whoa now." Jim wouldn't let them go. "She's a new mama. She might not want anyone to bother her right now."

Matty spun around and tilted her head back to see his face. "Oh, Jim. On your blankets?"

He sighed and the left side of his mouth crooked upward in a rakish smile. "Never can predict the behavior of a female."

Unable to help herself, Matty started to laugh. He did as well, and the rich, deep sound of his chuckle warmed her as nothing ever had.

Bertie tiptoed over and knelt by the blanket. "Three, Matty—all gray-and-black striped like their mama."

"We'll be careful to keep the stall door shut so nothing

can get in here to rile her—specially Ramon," Jim promised. "Anytime you want to come check on her during the daytime, you feel free. She's a fine mama—grooming them already, and they're feeding well. Not a runt among them."

Matty listened to the gentle way he spoke to her sister. He must have taken Bess's words to heart about how much Bertie loved her pet. Instead of kicking up a fuss over the way the mess spoiled his bed, he squatted there, praising Rhubarb as if she'd won a prize at the county fair. Who would have ever guessed that beneath his gruff exterior, Jim Collingswood was gifted with compassion and mercy?

❧

"James, could you wait a minute, please?"

Jim stopped but didn't turn around. He didn't know why Matty whispered to him, but he figured he'd stay silent. She closed the door so quietly, he barely heard it latch.

"I have something for you." She pressed a bottle into his hand.

As he looked down, the muscles in his neck spasmed. He gritted his teeth against the pain. "What is it?"

"You're stiff. Bertie told me you were breaking an especially ornery mustang today; and when we went out to see the kittens, you grimaced when you knelt. I figured this might help out."

"I'm not a man to drown a few paltry aches in whiskey."

She covered her mouth, but he could still see her shoulders shake in silent laughter. Moonlight glowed on her fair hair and sparkled in her big blue eyes. When she lowered her hands, she whispered, "It's liniment."

Hmm. Later, when I hit the hay, I'll ponder on the fact that

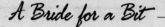

she's discussing my activities and watching me. For now, he lifted the bottle a bit higher. "It's red. It doesn't smell all flowery or girlie, does it?"

"No. Some of the hands back home tried it and claimed it worked well. Doc Timmons even said it's so good, he stopped mixing his own. If that's not enough, the company promises if you are dissatisfied with the results and only use it down to the 'Trial Mark,' you can return the bottle for a full refund."

"Who ever heard of a company promising to give you your money back?"

"I guess there's a first time for everything. The ingredients are sound—camphor, extract of capsicum, oil of spruce—"

Jim squinted and read, " 'J. R. Watkins Medical Company Red Liniment.' If they're as right about the effects as they are the color, it ought to do the trick just fine."

"You're a hardworking man, James Collingswood. I don't doubt your abilities for a minute, but I do hope you're being cautious."

Her concern warmed him, but he didn't want to feel that way. "Fretting doesn't get a job done."

"I suppose not."

His hand fisted around the bottle. "Don't think some good meals, cleaning, and a bit of doctoring are some kind of test like this try-it-for-a-bit cure-all, Matilda Craig. Sure as a coon has stripes, I'm not wife shopping. No matter what you do, you're not staying."

Chapter 6

The very next morning, Matty sat on the porch steps, humming and stitching. Jim thought about sauntering by to get a drink at the pump—maybe even tell her the liniment worked well—but before he could blink, Harvey and Mike ambled over to her. They stood there, jawing with her as if they had all day to talk and not a thing in the world to do. As a matter of fact, all of his hands were displaying the same bad habit. Every single time Jim turned around, one of them hovered over Matty.

It was her own fault, too. The woman was puppy-dog friendly. Why, she'd learn a man's name and greet him whenever he happened by. She could converse intelligently about important, interesting subjects—weather, livestock, repair work, and essential duties. She didn't fuss over fashions and simper silly things that left a man shuffling uncomfortably.

Luke nudged him out of his musings. "What are you scowling at?"

Jim nodded toward her. "That. The hands act like this is a Sunday picnic instead of a workday. That woman's setting out to find her a man, and I told her not to look for romance here.

Bad enough I have to ride our own men, but half of Lickwind keeps roaming here to try to court, too."

Luke shoved his hat back on his head and absently rubbed his jaw—a shaven jaw, Jim noticed. He used to shave every third day or so when the itch started to bug him. Now he did it every day.

"Seems to me you said you're not interested. You don't have any right to keep others from courting her."

"I'm paying them to work—not woo women. And as long as she's under my roof, she can good and well follow my orders not to flirt!"

"She doesn't flirt. Matty doesn't have wiles like that. She's like a butterfly—she flits. She doesn't show any favoritism, and she's been good for morale."

Jim jabbed his forefinger into Luke's chest. "If you're all that sold, then go claim her."

"She's not for me."

"Then ride into town and make arrangements for them to be on the next train. Take the money out of the bank and buy the tickets now. I want this settled."

❧

"I'll be going into town tomorrow," Luke announced after saying grace over supper.

"I'm going with you." Bess passed the corn bread to Luke.

"No need," Jim said as he snagged a pair of thick slices of tender roast. "We'll buy your train tickets. It's the least we can do."

"No need," Bess echoed back. She squared her shoulders. "We're not leaving."

Matty watched Jim's eyes widen in surprise, then narrow.

Before he could speak, she shoved the butter at him and said, "We've decided to settle in town, but we've appreciated your hospitality."

He stuck the butter plate on the table with a thump. "There's no place in town."

"There's the jail," Bertie chimed in.

"The jail!"

"We can sew and do laundry. Maybe cook or bake a bit," Corrie said with resolve.

"There's a laundry in town—not that it gets used much," Jim growled. "And what makes you think men want you to sew? We all buy ready-made clothes."

"There's been plenty of mending," Bess cut in. "Furthermore, there isn't a decent place for anyone to get a nice meal."

"The jail isn't big enough for the four of you to turn around in. You can't live there, let alone live and run a business out of it."

"I can't bear to get on the train again," Corrie said quietly.

"None of us can," Matty whispered to her. She looked Jim straight in the eye. "We've discussed it. This is the way it's going to be. We'll settle here in Lickwind."

"Luke," Jim barked, "explain to these women so it'll make sense."

Luke swallowed a bite and grinned. "Good roast beef. What're we having for dessert?"

The next morning, Jim demanded his brother buy the train tickets; the women stubbornly asserted they were going to rent the jailhouse. The breakfast table crackled with tension.

Bess rose and ordered, "Bertie, no going out to the stable to see the kittens until you've helped Corrie with the dishes.

Don't pester Scotty, either. And for pity's sake, don't take advantage of our absence to go gallivanting off to who-knows-where again. We all have enough on our minds without worrying where you've disappeared to. Corrie, after dishes, you lie down and nap awhile. Matty, get your reticule. We're leaving."

"Lickwind is not a town for ladies. I don't know where you came up with this absurd notion, but I'll not be party to it." Jim stood and tossed his napkin onto the table. "Luke, ride on in. The ladies won't be going."

Luke casually spread freshly churned butter on a fluffy biscuit and didn't even bother to look up. "Matty and I already hitched the buckboard."

Jim gawked at Matty. "You did what?"

She shrugged. "We're not frail flowers, James. Just as your telegram ordered, we're sturdy, dependable, hardworking, and plain. My father had no sons. We all learned to do what was necessary."

Jim glowered at her. "Three of you are sturdy. Dependable? The only thing I can depend on is that you're stubborn and vexatious. Hardworking? You can work hard someplace where you won't have every man for miles around trailing after you like a moonstruck calf. As for plain—" He shook his finger at her. "You can just forget blinking those great big blue eyes at me and trying to tell that ridiculous tale. I know a pretty woman when I see one." He slapped his hat on his head and stomped out the door.

Matty stared at the door in disbelief. Back home, men said her dress was pretty or she'd done a fine job at something, but Jim stared her right in the eye and spoke with such unwavering conviction, it made her go weak in the knees.

"Hard to imagine he's the same man who was singing to a fractious mare yesterday," Bertie grumbled as she started stacking the dishes.

"It won't much matter in a few days." Bess lifted her chin and stabbed a hatpin through her bonnet to keep it in place. "We'll be in town, so we won't be here to plague him."

Matty walked to the hall tree to fetch her reticule. *I don't want to vex him. . .but I don't want to move to town, either. He thinks I'm pretty!*

❧

"Trying to git yerself kilt?" Scotty stuck out his weathered right hand and yanked Jim to his feet. Instead of letting go, the old man tugged him close and said in a gravelly undertone, "Son, you gotta pay attention to the horse you're on—not the mares who went to town."

After taking his third bone-jarring, spine-crunching fall in less than an hour, Jim knew he couldn't deny the truth. He bent, picked up his hat, and smacked it against his thigh. Dust flew about him from that simple action—proof he'd spent more time out of the saddle than in it. He jutted his chin toward the mustang he'd been breaking. "He's about to see who's in charge."

Three hours later, when he'd broken the mustang and rewarded it with plenty of affection and soothing, Jim shot another look at the sun. They still weren't back from town.

Last night was sleepless and frustrating as could be. He should've been able to doze off in the stable—he'd slept on hard ground so much, it wasn't any skin off his nose. Though he'd never admit it to Luke, the sumptuous meals that the women served more than made up for sleeping out here. The fact was, Jim had come to the conclusion he liked having Matty around. In fact, he didn't even mind her sisters, either.

He knew they wanted to stay. He wanted them to, too—but he couldn't let emotions lead him from the path wisdom and safety dictated. This was no place for them. Why, if Matty left the house to go to the stable during the winter, a blizzard could kick up and she'd die from exposure. And what with her around the horses and all, one was bound to kick her sometime. He'd taken to having her shadow him most of the day so he'd be sure she wouldn't meet with any harm. Her companionship was all any man could ever hope for—but his conscience wouldn't allow him to keep her. The minute something happened, he'd never forgive himself. He was morally bound to send them someplace where ladies were sheltered from the harsh realities of life.

Bertie ran out of the house and skidded to a halt in front of him. She held a drumstick in her hand and mumbled around the bite in her mouth, "Lunch is on the table for you. Corrie's lying down, so try not to slam the door. Bess said you need to oil the hinges—they squeak."

As she dashed off toward the stable to see Rhubarb and the kittens, Jim didn't know whether to chuckle or grumble. Ellis Stack had to be blind and stupid to think Bertie was either old or mature enough to be a bride. Then again, Jim didn't particularly cotton to the notion of a kid telling him to stay quiet in his own home—or her bossy oldest sister deciding what he needed to repair. He headed toward the house, consoling himself with the fact that Luke was buying the train tickets.

Jim choked down the miserable excuse for lunch Bertie left on the table for him, then finished oiling the hinges on the screen as Luke drove the buckboard up to the house. He nearly squirted oil onto his shirt as he caught sight of the sun glinting on Matty's hair. Teamed with her green dress, that golden hair made her look pretty as the yellow flowers Ma used to favor each spring. Seeing her sitting next to Luke made Jim grit his teeth.

"Get everything settled?" he asked his brother as he absently helped Bess from the buckboard.

"Not yet," Bess said as she stepped aside and lavishly petted Ramon's springy gray fur. The dumb dog somehow decided he belonged to her, and Jim immediately made a mental note to pay off his ranch hand and give the dog to Bess when she left.

Jim grabbed for Matty before Luke could. He settled his hands around her waist and drew her toward himself. The breeze blew that beguiling perfume she favored toward him, and he tried not to be obvious in sniffing to catch another whiff. He forced himself to listen to what she was saying.

"—but they'll need to vote on it."

"What?"

Matty squeezed his shoulders and looked downward to remind him to finish setting her on the ground instead of hanging on and letting her toes dangle. Still, she spoke to cover the awkward moment. "Mr. Potter, the attorney at the land office, said the town owns the jail, so they'll have to put an announcement in the paper and hold a vote."

Jim glared over her shoulder, straight at Luke. Luke shrugged. "Ma taught us it was rude to argue with women."

"You mean you wasted the entire morning—"

"Hey. You want 'em gone, you do your own dirty work."

Chapter 7

Yes, I know how to smile and nod. What kind of question is that?" Matty gave Jim a baffled look. He'd let her sisters walk ahead toward the buggy, but he'd held her back.

"All you do is smile and nod to all of the men in town. It's Sunday. You're there for worship—not courtship."

"I refuse to be rude!"

"Good," Jim cut in. He grabbed her arm and marched her to the buggy. "Just remember that. No talking in church."

She stopped in her tracks. "You missed breakfast and are surly as a coyote with crossed eyes. Do I need to get you a cup of coffee?"

"Matty, we're going to be late!" Corrie called.

The whole ride into town, Matty stewed over Jim's orders. Who was he to tell her how to conduct herself? He had no call to monitor her behavior. She'd done nothing to earn his orders.

By the time they reached town, all of the Craig sisters huddled a little closer to one another. An entire cadre of men surrounded the buggy. Men, each in his very best bib and tucker, had come to attend the monthly service the circuit rider gave; but from the way they greeted one another, most never darkened the door of the church.

Or, in this case, never bothered to gather in the jailhouse—which was where the circuit preacher normally held services.

"Josh, you old coot, what're you doing, all fancied up?"

"Why, goin' to the Sunday meetin'!"

"That's two miracles," Luke murmured for the sisters' benefit. "In the five years I've known him, Josh hasn't ever bathed or attended church."

Bertie burst out laughing.

When the sisters got out of the buggy, what looked to be the entire population of Lickwind stood in a bedraggled line, like soldiers awaiting inspection. A tall one with his fair hair parted in the middle and pomaded into two slick halves stepped forward with his bowler pressed over his heart and a fistful of wildflowers. "I'll be proud to claim any of you as my bride. I got me a purty little start-up ranch with a good, sound cabin—"

"Hold your horses!" Jim roared above the crowd. "No one's getting married today. You can all forget proposing to these women and start paying attention to the parson."

"I can do both," a grizzled man announced.

"Not today, you won't."

Matty stayed with her sisters as the men decided services could be held outside, on the other side of the railroad tracks. Chairs and benches got dragged from the saloon and mercantile, and the men all argued over who got to sit next to the women.

Parson Harris handled the situation by simply announcing the Craig sisters would be the choir and sit behind him. Bertie actually sat still through the service for the first time in her life. Bess made a point of keeping a parasol over Corrie to protect her from the sun's heat. Matty remembered Jim's advice to smile and nod. . .but why was he glaring back at her the whole time the parson preached on loving your neighbor as yourself?

❧

"Just what is the meaning of this?" Jim took the paper out of his vest pocket and flung it down on the table. He'd been fit to be tied ever since the moment he spied the paper tacked to the Jones's storefront. He'd hardly heard a word the pastor said after he'd grabbed a bench for church.

"It's one of the invitations," Bess said matter-of-factly as she checked on the rolls in the oven.

"You." Jim turned and waggled his forefinger at Matty. "You're behind this. You're so gregarious, you want every man in the territory to drop in and be your friend."

"Actually," Luke said, "it was my idea."

"What?"

"It's just a barbecue. These women shouldn't have to go back to where they're not wanted."

Angrily tapping the toe of his boot on the floor planks, Jim shook his head. "They don't have to go back there, but they need to go somewhere safe and decent."

"There's nothing wrong with them meeting men who could make them happy here in Lickwind."

Jim plopped into a chair and stared at his brother in disbelief. "You must've hit your head one too many times while breaking that last batch of horses." Suddenly, Bess's words fully registered. He shot forward. "What do you mean, 'One of the invitations'? Just how many got posted?"

Matty sashayed past him with a platter of meat loaf. Aromatic steam wafted off of it and made his mouth water, but Matty's words made his mouth suddenly go dry. "Bess posted about six of them in town. I only handed out a dozen or so."

Luke snitched a roll as Bess took them from the oven. He tossed it from hand to hand so it would cool as he tacked on, "But I gave a stack of them to Jones in the mercantile, Squires at the feedstore, and Gideon at the saloon. They've been passing them around. We ought to have a good turnout."

❦

Jim, Matty thought, *looks and acts like a riled porcupine.* He'd barely spoken and not shaved at all since Sunday. It wasn't because he needed more of the Watkins Liniment, either. Each time someone said something about the barbecue, he'd bristled. Corrie sat on the edge of the bed and sighed. "After tomorrow, it'll all be over."

Matty heard the grief in her twin's voice. She set down her brush, sat beside Corrie, and squeezed her hand. "We'll manage better than you think. Bess has a good plan. Once the men all arrive, we'll get them to hold a vote to let us settle in the jailhouse until we can each have a chance to do some courting and decide on who suits each of us best. Don't worry—we won't send you off as someone's bride tomorrow."

Corrie gave her a watery smile. "Bess and her plans."

Matty nudged her shoulder. "Have you ever known

Bossy Bess to come up with one that didn't work?"

"Turn around. I'll braid your hair." As soon as Matty spun around, Corrie started to finger-comb her twin's hair and plait it into a loose braid that matched her own. "You seem much happier here than back home."

"Getting away from Ellis is such a relief. There wasn't a day that went by that I wondered if God sent him as a test for my Christian patience."

"Papa willed that farm to all of us. He'd be so sad to see how greedy Ellis got."

Matty traced a sprig of daisies on her lawn nightgown. "Ellis is going to fly into a rage when he finds out he's not getting any money out of this."

"Bess is right, though. We're not his legal charges, and it's illegal to sell people. He stuck us on that train, and we aren't even what the Collingswoods ordered. They don't owe him anything and neither do we."

"And our train fare is only a fraction of what he owes us for our shares of the dairy."

As she tied a narrow strip of ribbon on the tail of Matty's braid, Corrie quietly asked, "So if we're staying, are you interested in any of the men you've met yet?"

"They're all fine men. Some are a bit on the unpolished side, but they have good hearts." Matty hopped up, blew out the lamp, and crawled into bed. She snuggled under the covers. Matty waited as her sister wiggled to settle in next to her, then whispered, "I know no one will ever be like Brian—but is there anyone you think you might get along with yourself?"

"I know I'm going to need someone to provide for me

and the baby. . . ." Corrie's voice hitched, then she blurted out, "But I can't imagine ever loving another man."

Matty scooted over and hugged her. "If any of the men want me as a wife, I'll see if I can't have him take you as part of the bargain."

"You would?"

The tremble in her sister's voice cut Matty to the core. "After getting here and seeing all that needs to be done, I think it's a very reasonable idea. Especially if he's a rancher, my husband would know that having an extra woman around to help with cooking, sewing, and cleaning would be a bonus."

"There's a world of difference between an extra pair of hands and a widow with a baby."

Matty propped herself up on one elbow and gave Corrie's braid a playful yank. "The only problem will be fighting back all of the men who come to call. Sis, you can't believe the way all of the hands keep sneaking into the stable to check on the kittens. Big, tough old cowboys—down on their knees, bringing treats so Rhubarb will let them pet her kittens. If they're that way with kittens, I know they'll go wild over your little baby."

"You're spinning a yarn."

"You just watch the stable and see if I'm not right. Lanky, Pete, and Scotty have all swiped eggs from the henhouse for her. Chico gave up one of his prized graniteware bowls so she could have milk each day. Luke keeps taking over fresh hay to be sure the corner is soft and warm enough."

"Well, I'll be!"

"Yes." Matty flopped back down and stared at the ceiling.

"Jim gave up that blanket, and I saw him hunkered down, singing under his breath while he hand fed Rhubarb a rasher of bacon."

"Tilde?"

Matty started. Her twin rarely ever called her that pet name. "Huh?"

"Be careful of your heart. Jim's trying his best to get rid of us, but your voice softens when you say his name. You've never done that with anybody else."

"Nonsense. My heart's not in any danger."

"I'm not being silly. I sense a spark between the two of you, but he's every bit as stubborn as you are. You came here planning to be a bride, so your mind freed your heart to find love. The problem is—Jim's dead-set against marriage. I don't want you to get hurt."

"Corrie, when we set out, I told God I trusted Him to find me the right mate. I must have faith that He will direct my path." She tugged at the covers, then muttered, "But so far, it's seemed like a rocky path on a moonless night."

Corrie giggled.

"Hey, you!" Bess called from the room next door. "Hush up and go to sleep!"

"It's Matty's fault!" Corrie sang out.

When Matty stopped laughing at that ridiculous fib, she whispered, "You told a lie. You have to say the bedtime prayer tonight."

Corrie fumbled and grabbed Matty's hand. She said a sweet prayer and asked the Lord to bless her baby's health and for Him to provide good men as grooms for each of her sisters. "And, Father, please give each of them a sense of assurance when You put that man in her path."

After Corrie was fast asleep, Matty still lay there and remembered thinking she wanted to marry a man like the one who rescued her at the train—even before she knew he was James Collingswood. He was a good, solid man, strong and honest. From all of the time she'd spent with him, she knew his gruffness hid a heart of gold. Other men here had become her pals—just like back home, but James Collingswood was different.

Lord, what Corrie said is starting to ring true. I never felt this way about a man before. If Jim's the man for me, You're going to have to change his heart, because he's all but shoved me out the door.

∾

Clyde Kincaid rode up at the crack of dawn. Jim stood in the doorway of the stable and squinted at his neighbor as he dismounted. The wind carried the reek of his bay rum.

"Mornin'." Clyde swaggered over. "Gonna be some day, huh?"

"Not 'til noon. Men all have work to do before they socialize." Jim stuffed his hands into a worn pair of leather gloves. "I expect you'll be coming back after you've tended to chores at your spread."

"Naw. I can afford to take a day off. I'll marry up with one of the gals, and we can catch up on work tomorrow." Clyde tilted his head toward the house. "I seen them all at Sunday worship. Robust women. Able to pull their weight."

"They're women," Jim ground out, "not draft horses."

Clyde chuckled. "Soon as they're hitched, they'll be brood mares."

"Kincaid, you've got ten seconds to get clear of my property before I level you."

The dust hadn't settled from Clyde's hasty departure when Luke sauntered by. "I've seen friendlier-looking thunderclouds. What's gotten into you?"

"You and your idiotic barbecue, that's what."

"Come on, Jim. You don't want the women here. It's a good way to introduce them—"

"No." Jim glared at his brother. "If you think I'm happy about stuffing those sweet women back on a train, you can guess again. Fact is, it's the lesser of two evils. I'd never buy me a bride like I was bidding on livestock. This whole thing is a nightmare, but the best I can do is send them somewhere decent. There aren't a handful of men in the whole county who are fit to marry them."

"It's not up to us to judge that. You're gonna have a revolution on your hands if you interfere or send the Craig sisters away."

Jim took a step closer and gritted, "Clyde Kincaid was just here."

"He's about to lose his place." Luke roared in outrage, "What does he think he's doing, trying to get one of our gals?"

"Our gals?" Jim poked him in the chest. "Since when did you decide they were ours?"

"We can't let those kind of men around the Craig girls."

"That's the problem. Just you watch today. We're going to be overrun with every man in the county, and we'll be lucky if even one is able to provide decently. To take it a step farther, just how many of the leatherhands around here know how to treat a lady?"

Luke leaned back against the stable wall and banged his head on the boards as he moaned, "What have I done?"

"I started the whole mess, not ordering the bridles from the feedstore." Jim kicked at the earth and stared at Matty as the kitchen door banged behind her. Humming and swinging a bucket, she headed toward the milk cow. "Little brother, we're gonna have to bird-dog those women all day and scare off the undesirables."

"What a catastrophe."

"Here's the plan. . . ."

Chapter 8

Matty tried not to wiggle as Corrie used the curling iron to help her finish her coiffure. They'd studied the pictures in *Godey's Lady's Book* and decided this one would suit her.

"You look beautiful," Corrie proclaimed.

Matty laughed. "Somehow, it never seems quite right for us to say that to each other."

Bess finished pinning Mama's cameo to her bodice. "All we need is to convince the men to rent us the jail. Then we won't have to jump into any marriages."

"Jumping behind bars instead of over a broom." Bertie laughed as she swiped a finger around the base of a cake and licked off the icing.

The kitchen door opened. Jim stood at the threshold and scanned the room. He shook his head. "Bess, take off that jewelry. You don't want anyone thinking you're an heiress. Bertie, get your hair out of that–that—" He spiraled his forefinger in the air in a gesture of masculine hopelessness. "Put it in plaits."

"Plaits! I'm seventeen!"

Jim strode across the kitchen, his boots ringing on each plank. "Too young to get married, and that's exactly what we're telling the men."

Matty scooted free from her twin's fussing. "What about Corrie?"

Jim stared at her, then glanced at Corrie. He looked back at her. "Try your best to make Corrie look drab—plainest widow's weeds, and be sure she's wearing that mourning brooch."

Bess leaned against the table. "James, I do believe I like the way you think."

Still, he continued to keep eye contact with Matty. She felt her cheeks growing hot under his scrutiny. He growled, "Do you remember what I told you before we went to church?"

"Smile and nod?" she said in a strangled tone.

"Well, I don't want you doing either today. For once in your life, try not to befriend everyone who talks to you."

"But how am I going to find a husband if—"

"Woman, when God's good and ready, He'll put a man in your life. Until then, use sense instead of smiles. It'll keep you outta trouble." He started to walk away but turned back around. "One more thing: Wash off that flowery-smelling stuff you dab on. It's enough to drive a man daft."

The kitchen door closed behind him, and everyone stayed quiet for an embarrassing stretch of time. Matty drew in a breath, then tried to sound breezy. "Well, how do you like that? The oil worked. The door doesn't squeak anymore."

Corrie shot her a knowing look. "It's not the hinges that matter—it's a secure latch."

A secure latch. . . Corrie's words echoed in Matty's mind

as she wandered across the barnyard at noon. She'd never seen so many men in one place. Every last one of them tried to capture her attention.

"Miss, yore purdy enuff to make a man dizzy."

"Your collar's too tight, Nitwit," the man next to him said as he elbowed him out of the way. "Miss Matilda, I've got me a right fine piece of land and a good start-up herd."

"He's lucky if he's got a dozen head," Mr. Smit hooted. From what Matty gathered, he'd been an original settler and boasted a fair spread and a sizable herd.

Not five minutes later, Matty saw Mr. Start-Up over by Corrie. She hastened over to rescue her sister.

"A right fine place. Forty acres—"

"Excuse me," Matty interrupted. She got up on tiptoe and whispered, "My sister is newly widowed."

"Then I s'pose she's mighty lonesome."

To Matty's relief, Jim wrapped his arm around that persistent man's shoulders and led him off a ways. He murmured something, and the guy cast Corrie a terrified look, then hastened toward Bess.

If a man ever kept busier than Jim did, Matty hadn't met him. She saw him stride toward the knot of men surrounding Bertie, elbow his way in, and playfully yank one of her plaits.

"Okay, baby girl, you've had a chance to talk with the grown-ups for awhile. Scamper off to the stable now and go play with your kitties." He gave her a meaningful look. "Scotty's there. He'll keep an eye on you."

The men all complained. "She ain't no baby," one protested more loudly than the others.

"Why, Mr. Squires," Matty cooed as she hastened to Jim's side, "I'm certain you're not disagreeing with our host, are you?"

"She come out here as a bride," the feedstore owner groused.

"You're right," Matty agreed. "But that was before we understood what it would take to be a bride out here in a rugged man's world."

"You're not going to fight over me, are you?"

Matty wanted to pinch her sister for sounding thrilled over such an appalling prospect.

"You're worth a fight," the blacksmith, Amos Freeling, said as he twisted the end of his handlebar moustache.

Jim took Bertie by the shoulders, turned her toward the stable, and gave her a tiny push. "You run along now, Squirt." He glowered at the men. "Stop scaring her. Poor thing. How'd you like it if a bunch of men chased after your kid sister?"

Baffled and shamefaced, the men muttered to themselves. Matty took pity on them. "I do hope you men are helping yourselves to the barbecue. It smells delicious."

"I'd be honored to escort you to the table." Hank proffered his arm.

Before she could reply, Jim grabbed her. "Sorry. Go on ahead, and Matilda will try to catch up with you. Her sister needs her."

Matty craned her neck to look for Bess. Jim didn't wait. He started hauling her toward the pump. "What—?"

"Trust me," Jim gritted. "This man is a scoundrel. Bess deserves better."

"Matty, this is Clyde Kincaid," Bess said as soon as they approached. "He owns the cattle ranch next door."

"Mr. Kincaid." Matty nodded to him coolly.

"Collingswood, it's about time you let us all have a chance at these women." Clyde waggled his brows. "I know I'm not alone, saying I'm ready to take 'em off your hands."

"Actually, there is an alternative—an excellent alternative." Bess squared her shoulders. "My sisters and I have decided to ask you kind gentlemen to take a community vote since it seems the entire township is here today. We'd like to rent the jail and live in town. That way, we can have time to get to know all of you and—"

"Why bother?" Clyde slashed the air with his hand. "Only four of you. I say, those of us who speak up first get you."

"I agree." Jim gave a curt nod.

Matty almost fell over from the shock.

Jim reached over, snagged Bess by the waistband of her apron, and gave her a tug. At the same time, he clenched his arm around Matty and dragged her so close to his side, she couldn't have wedged a broom straw between them. "I spoke first. They're mine—all four of 'em. They're not going into town. Until I give my approval, they're not marrying up with anyone."

Clyde stomped off, and Bess turned on Jim. "Whatever got into you? How dare you foul up my plan?"

"Bess, look around. You're a capable woman, and I don't doubt for a minute that you'd be able to manage in town." As he spoke, Jim let go of Bess and absently stroked Matty's shoulder. She fought the urge to lean into him as he continued to speak. "But think of your sisters. Bertie's far too

70

naïve and will get into a peck of trouble, and Corrie needs to be sheltered."

"Matty and I can—"

"You will both stay here with your sisters until other arrangements—safe, wise arrangements—can be made. I—"

A commotion over on the porch made them all turn around. Luke smashed his fist into someone's face and knocked him clear over the railing. By the time Matty and Bess caught up with Jim, Luke already had Corrie in his arms and was carrying her to the door.

"What happened?" Bess breathlessly jerked open the door.

"Yahoos and idiots, the whole pack of them," Luke muttered.

"Corrie—" Matty rushed in and wet a cloth. She blotted her sister's wan face.

"Fainted again. I'll carry her upstairs."

"Bess, Lanky's right outside the door. Have him go alongside you to the stable and drag Bertie back in here," Jim ordered. "I don't want her out there with that pack of woman-hungry wolves."

Luke headed up the stairs, Bess scurried outside, and Jim stood with his arms akimbo as he glared at Matty. "I can't for the life of me figure out what I did that got God so all-fired mad at me that He dropped you in my lap, but He did. As long as He stuck you here, you're corralled here on the Rough Cs, and I expect you to keep your sisters reined in."

Matty shoved the damp towel in her hands at his chest. "If you're done listing your woes, I'll go see to my sister now." Without waiting for a response, she dashed from the room.

Jim tossed the wet rag onto the kitchen table, grimaced,

and headed outside. He stood on the porch and looked over all of Lickwind's residents. The savory smell of barbecue hung in the air, but Jim knew good and well the dishes the men wanted weren't on the table. Lanky strutted along between Bess and Bertie, trying to skirt around the edge of the yard; but even then, they couldn't go two steps without someone trying to waylay the women.

Jim had hated to leave Matty's side for even one moment today, fearing all of the men would flock to her. The woman didn't understand just how beguiling men found her. Just looking at her could make a man's heart gallop, but the sound of her laughter—well, his heart just melted then. Jim wouldn't allow it. No, he wouldn't. She deserved far better than any man Lickwind had to offer.

At least for the moment, she was in the house and safe. He found a scrap of relief in that fact as he waited for Bess to plow ahead and propel Bertie into the kitchen. Josiah stopped Bess for a moment. Now there was a handsome man who had land and money enough to support her—but Bess gave him a look that would curdle milk and kept Bertie marching.

Males couldn't leave the Craig females alone. Why, even stupid Ramon had managed to get into Rhubarb's stall and dragged in scraps from the pig trough for the mama cat. The kitchen door banged shut, and Jim refocused his attention.

"Men." Then he whistled loudly and fleetingly recalled Matty had done the same thing back at the train station the day she'd arrived. "Listen up." He curled his hands around the porch railing, scanned the crowd, and waited for them to grow quiet.

"How's the little lady?" Chico asked. "Heard she swooned."

"Matilda is tucking the widow in for a nap." Jim narrowed his eyes at a man nursing a bloody bandana over his nose. "I suspect by now, you've all heard tell the Widow Taylor is in the family way. After just burying her husband and finding out she's got a little one on the way, she's in no condition to take on a new husband."

"That still leaves three!"

"Jones, you always were fast with your figurin' at the mercantile." Jim hoped to lighten the tone for a moment so they'd take his news better. "Since you're so good with numbers, let me give you another one: seventeen. Bertie isn't even out of the schoolroom, and I won't let her wed for a full year yet."

"Her kin sent her out here. That's consent enough," Mr. Smit shouted.

"That would be the same lazy, no-good brother-in-law who stole their dairy farm."

The men began to scuffle their boots in the dirt.

Amos let out a gust of a sigh. "I got a good look at the youngest, fellas. She's got a crop of freckles that make her look cute as a speckled pup. We'd be robbin' a cradle if we took her to wife."

Relief threaded through Jim. Men might well argue with him over the issue because he looked downright selfish over the whole matter, but few men were foolish enough to cross the hulking blacksmith. Matty's kid sister ought to be safe for awhile. Now he could concentrate on sweet little Matty.

Luke stomped out of the house. He didn't even come to a stop before he thundered, "There are women, then there are ladies. The Rough Cs only has ladies. Do I make myself clear?"

"Well," Jones finally said, "that leaves two ladies. Now what're you gonna say, Jim?"

"I'm gonna say that since you're so good at sums and differences, I'll graduate to fractions." Jim widened his stance and lifted his chin. "Possession is nine-tenths of the law. The women are here. I sent for 'em, and they're mine."

Later that night, Jim slipped one last little bit of barbecued beef to Rhubarb and kicked hay into a pile for his bed. "Luke, you made quite a scene today."

"I was just protecting the gals."

"You went far past protective and hit possessive."

Luke folded his arms over the wall of the stall and gave him an amused look. "I did? You're not one to cast stones."

"Knock it off. I'm doing what Ma always taught us from the Bible—you know: taking care of the widows and orphans."

The stable rang with Luke's laughter. "If you're going to start quoting the Bible, I hope you don't hearken back to the Old Testament. Men back then had multiple wives, and I distinctly heard you announce the women were all yours."

❧

Matty looked at the neat rows of vegetables they'd planted and felt a twinge. Jim declared nothing would grow in the sandy soil, but for all of his grousing, he'd come out and plowed a nice patch for her. Soon, the seeds Bess brought from home sprouted. If only love would flower so easily.

"Wonder if we'll be here for harvest," Bertie said as she leaned on her hoe.

"I don't know. Still, Jim and Luke have been so good to

us; the least we can do is keep a garden."

Bertie snorted. "You pointed out how good they've been, so we're gardening and making cheese. Corrie felt thankful, so she had us making them shirts. Bess is glad, so we're going berrying and making jam. The only thing I'm grateful for is the fact that I don't have more sisters out here, or I'd have to do more work!"

"Cheer up. Jim said Rhubarb is ready to be moved back into the house. Ask Corrie for a feed sack. You can stuff it, put it in a box, and make a bed for the kittens."

Bertie started hoeing again. "Betcha she gives me that one with the purple zigzags on it. It's the only one of that pattern."

"Good thing, too. I've never seen an uglier pattern." Just last week, Jim had led Matty into the stable, opened the door on a huge wooden bin, and five years of empty feed sacks tumbled out. The memory of his generosity warmed her heart.

Bess and she had sneaked away with a few sweet little prints so they could sew baby clothes as a surprise and a few darker solids that would make much-needed maternity clothes for Corrie, who now wore her dresses unbuttoned beneath her loosely tied apron. Jim and Buckwheat carried the rest of the feed sacks over to the porch. It took a whole morning to wash them, but it felt like Christmas.

After all of the sacks were dry, Jim carried them into the house and watched for awhile as the sisters matched up all of the patterns. He shook his head at what a production they made of it, but Matty laughed and said, "You started this!"

"Doesn't take much to make you happy," he said.

"After watching you eat almost half a jar of gooseberry jam this morning, I could say the same thing."

"Thanks for reminding me." He paced off to the kitchen and started banging around. Matty knew to expect the jar to be scraped clean. Jim's mother must have brought jars when they started up the ranch; and as fast as Matty could fill jars with jam, he'd empty them.

Each sister had selected fabric to make a shirt for each of the brothers; then she chose a pattern to make a new dress for herself. Word was, the town planned to throw a celebration for Wyoming being declared a territory, and the Craig sisters figured it would be a good excuse for new dresses. Several feed sacks remained, earmarked for dish towels, quilts, and more clothing. Still, that purple zigzag didn't have a match.

Bertie managed to strike a small stone with her hoe and made it flip into the air. It hit Matty's skirt and pulled her back to the present.

"For all of the feed sacks I've ever seen, I never saw one like that purple one," Bertie said.

"I haven't, either."

God, am I like that feed sack—so peculiar that I'll never have a mate? Could it be that when You designed me, You had a specific pattern in mind so I'd suit only one special man? If that man were Jim Collingswood—

"So do we have a deal?" Bertie asked.

"Huh?" *I really need to stop daydreaming.* Matty stopped musing and gave her sister a questioning look.

"For true, Matty, you know how much I hate to sew. If I do the dishes for you for the next month, will you sew both of the shirts for me?"

"Laundry, not dishes."

Bertie glowered from beneath her brown felt hat. "I'm being more than fair, and you know it."

"You? Fair?" a familiar nasal whine said from behind her.

Matty spun around. "Ellis! What are you doing here?"

His beady eyes scanned the ranch. "I'm here, dear sisters-in-law, to collect on a debt."

Chapter 9

A saloon wasn't the most suitable location for a trial, but it was the biggest room in town. In honor of the auspicious occasion, Gideon Riker allowed all of the tables to be removed. Row upon row of benches and chairs filled the establishment.

Now that Wyoming had become a territory, no one was quite certain if the old circuit judge would be around next month. Then, too, Ellis Stack adamantly demanded money or the women at once. He had a return ticket on the next train. Due to his unyielding insistence, the town's only attorney, Donald Potter, now sat on a barstool behind the bar and acted as judge.

Jim winced. Whoever had draped a cloth over the oil painting didn't do a thorough job of it, so a delicate, bare foot peeped out from the right bottom corner. This was no place for a lady. . .and he had four of them sitting directly behind him. He didn't care what it took—he'd resolved before he got here that he'd do whatever it took to keep his sweet little Matty and her sisters.

A dozen men—all striving to look their best in hopes of

catching the eye of one of the Craig sisters—sat off to the side. None of them wanted Stack to cart them off; then again, everyone knew those men weren't exactly pleased with the fact that Jim had claimed them as his own. He couldn't decide whether they might have a slight leaning for or against him.

The "judge" didn't have a gavel, so he settled for pounding on the bar with the handle of a Navy Colt. The gun promptly discharged, shattering a glass on the shelf just off to the judge's left.

"Oscar, I thought you told me this thing wasn't loaded."

"He was probably loaded when he tol' you that," someone drawled.

It took the judge a moment to regain order in the court. He then raised his brows at Ellis. "Mr. Stack, suppose you tell us why you've dragged us all away from our work today."

Ellis Stack was a contradiction—a large, rawboned man, he possessed a high-pitched, whining nasal voice. He dressed with great precision and style, yet his motions were singularly ungainly. Jim couldn't help wondering if that duplicity extended toward his version of the "truth."

"Your honor, Sir, I'm missing work myself. It took me five days to get here from my dairy farm in Rhode Island. I've been waiting four days for this trial. Even catching the train back tomorrow, I'll have missed two solid weeks. You know what a loss that represents to a businessman."

"Nobody dragged you out here," Luke said.

Stack turned toward them. "I had to come because I've been cheated out of more money than any man can afford to write off. I have a contract with James Collingswood for six hunnerd dollars. He ain't paid a cent."

"You have a copy of that contract?"

Stack pulled a sheet of paper from a leather satchel. "This is the telegram he sent. He agrees to my price and says to send them at once."

"Them?"

"The brides." Ellis jerked his thumb toward the ladies. "Just like he ordered: plain, sturdy, dependable ones who could do hard work."

The judge inspected the telegram, then looked over the rim of his glasses at the jurors. "To my recollection, about four of you had schooling. I'll read this aloud so everyone in the jury and courtroom has the same information." He proceeded to do so and then passed the telegram down to the jurors.

Jim fought the urge to jump out of his seat and throttle Ellis Stack. The man twisted things about and slanted them something awful.

"Now, Collingswood, suppose you give us your version of the events," the judge finally invited.

Jim rose. "I'm calling Linus Hatch as my first witness."

Lickwind's telegraph operator came forward carrying a thick book. At Jim's urging, he produced the original telegraph message. "It says bridle here. B-R-I-D-L-E. The kind you use for a horse. A man who wants a mail-order woman spells it B-R-I-D-A-L. I looked it up in my dictionary before I sent it off, just to make sure I got it right."

Jim hummed approvingly. He wanted to be careful not to offend the jurors who were illiterate. Stack's mistakes were ones someone who couldn't read well would make.

Linus tilted his head to the side and studiously pointed toward the top of the page in his book. "I got it all right here.

James Collingswood's telegram was addressed to L. S. Stocks in Rhode Island. A few of the ranchers hereabouts order gear from that company. Anybody can see right away that Mr. Stack blundered and botched things up on his end."

Bess testified that Ellis made the mail-order arrangements before consulting with any of the sisters. Jim thanked her, then observed, "It's illegal in the United States of America to buy or sell human beings. By setting a price for each of these women and coming to claim the money, Stack is putting forth that he owned them and can treat them like chattel."

Unable to contain herself, Bertie stood up. "Yes, he treated us like chattel. And what about the cattle? Tell them about the dairy farm he said was his. It's ours, too, and he's sent us away so he can keep it for himself!"

"Your sister still lives there," Ellis snapped. "She agreed with me on this whole plan. None of the men in town would take any of you—Bess is bossy as a general, and Bertie is a tomboy. Corrine—well, no man wants to marry up with a widow who's on the nest, and then there's Matilda. She befriended every last man in town, so marrying her would be like kissin' his sister. We were doing them a favor, arranging for them to get married."

"Do you normally get paid for doing a 'favor' for a family member?" Jim shot back.

"Train fare was expensive!"

It didn't take long for the jury to huddle and come to a consensus. "Don—I mean, Mr. Potter—I mean, Your Judgeship, we done made up our minds."

Jim cast a look back at Matty. She held Corrie's hand and gave him a brave smile. Her courage impressed him.

Openhearted, sympathetic, sweet Matty—worried more about her twin than about herself. There wasn't a woman on the face of the earth finer than Matilda Craig. He winked, hoping his reassurance wouldn't be false.

"Me and the boys figured Jim sent off for horses' bridles and Mr. Stack made a mistake. Now, it's a mistake we can all understand."

Jim felt the air freeze in his chest.

"Them gals are right fine ladies—purty and nice, too—no matter what their brother-in-law said, and they deserve far better than they got. We don't care much that he paid their train fare—it's precious little compared to their share of the dairy when he booted them out."

The judge didn't risk using the handles of the Colt on the bar to quiet the noisy room. Instead, he smacked his palms on the countertop. "Order!"

"Me and the guys don't think Jim owes him anything since he didn't deliver what was originally ordered."

"Fine!" Ellis Stack jumped out of his chair and glowered at the sisters. "Bess, Matty, and Corrie can stay here and molder in this backwater place. Bertie, I've decided you're too young to stay here, and Adele needs your help. You're coming home with me."

"You can't have her!" Bess roared. She and Matty both leapt out of their seats and stood in front of their little sister like a pair of lionesses. The difference was, while Bess glowered at Ellis, Matty stared at Jim. Her eyes pleaded with him to do something—anything—to avert this disaster.

Jim turned to the judge. "Don, if I marry one of the sisters, wouldn't that give me as much say in whether Bertie stays in

Lickwind or goes back to Rhode Island?"

The judge thought for a second, then nodded. "Yes, it would."

Matty stared at Jim in amazement.

Ellis spluttered for a moment, then crowed with glee, "Then he's accepting shipment of the brides, and he has to pay me! You can marry up with whichever one you want, but you're gonna pay me full price for all four of 'em—six hunnerd dollars!"

Though Matty didn't know the state of the Collingswood brothers' finances, she could tell by the way Jim went white beneath his tan that shelling out six hundred dollars would be a huge blow. She couldn't ask this of him; she couldn't not ask this of him—not loving him the way she did.

He straightened his black string tie and squared his shoulders. Ignoring everyone else in the crowded saloon turned courthouse, he faced Matty, took her hand in his big, rough right hand, and went down on one knee. She stared into his earnest hazel eyes and could barely breathe.

"Miss Matilda Craig, would you do me the honor of becoming my wife?"

Chapter 10

"Yeeeehaw!" Lanky yelled. "The brides is stayin'!"

Jim remained on bended knee, awaiting Matty's answer. The poor woman looked completely flabbergasted. She blinked and couldn't quite manage to keep from gaping. Still, she gave no answer. Something jabbing at his shoulder made him turn his attention to the side.

"You owe me six hunnerd bucks. Pay up."

A man could afford to kneel to propose, but Jim surely wasn't willing to be groveling at Stack's feet while settling this distasteful business. He slowly unfolded and towered over the weasel.

"Wait!" Jones called from the jurors' seats. "You all jest hang onto yer hats a second." He and the other jurors all huddled together.

Jim pulled Matty to his side and held her tightly as he waited.

"Your Judgeship, we're the jury, and we're thinkin' we oughtta have some say here."

Donald Potter leaned forward on the bar and pinched his lower lip between his thumb and forefinger while he deliberated. "Suppose you tell me what you have in mind."

Jones strutted over near the judge, then turned to face Ellis. "Now it's true, if Jim Collingswood marries up with Miss Matilda, he's taking delivery on the brides."

Ellis let out a self-satisfied laugh.

"But—" Jones held up his hand to halt Ellis's celebration, "we looked at the telegram again. It don't say one-hundred-fifty dollars. It just says one-fifty. Me and the jury decided Collingswood's gotta pay Mr. Stack a buck-fifty for each of the Craig gals, and they're both settled fair and square."

"Done!" Potter banged both fists on the bar and stood.

Ellis turned purple with rage. "You can't do that!"

"I can, and I am." The judge pulled a silver dollar out of his pocket and tossed it to Jim. "Consider that part of my wedding gift."

Mr. Llewellyn stood and tossed a gleaming gold coin. "My bank is glad to see the community grow."

Doc did the same. "Me, too."

Soon, coins rained all around—nickels, dimes, and a few quarters pinged as they hit the floor. Bertie laughed delightedly as she scurried to pick them up. Bess held out her hands to accept them, then shoved a fistful at Jim. "Six dollars!"

Jim hefted the coins in his hand and listened to them jingle. "I haven't rightly counted them out, but I'd guess there are exactly thirty pieces in my hand. Seems fitting, somehow, Ellis, since you betrayed those you should have loved and protected. Take this and get out of town. We don't want your kind here."

"You haven't seen the end of this!"

Jim stared at Ellis and jutted out his chin. "This had best

be the end, or I'll be filing a lawsuit so's my wife gets her share of that dairy farm."

Nervously yanking at his collar, Ellis spluttered and started to leave.

Jim grabbed him and thrust the coins into his shirt pocket. "You're all my witnesses. Stack is paid in full."

"Best deal you ever made," Luke declared.

"Come on, Sweetheart," Jim said as he took hold of Matty's hand and gave her a gentle tug. "Let's take your sisters and go home."

More than half of the men in town accompanied them back to the Rough Cs. They said they wanted to help celebrate; but from the way they all jockeyed their horses to stay close to the buckboard, those men clearly hoped to get a chance to start doing a bit of courting with one of the other sisters. The rest of the men stayed in town—ostensibly to help put the tables back in the saloon. Bess muttered that they'd all be bending their elbows as soon as that task was done.

Matty and Jim didn't have a chance to say a thing to one another. They had no privacy, and everyone kept calling out to them. Amos Freeling shouted across the road, "Hey, Jones! I just had me a dandy thought!"

"Guess there's a first time for everything," Jones hollered back.

When the hoots died down, Amos shouted back, "Any of us who claims the other brides is only gonna have to pay Collingswood a buck and a half as a dowry."

Jim shook his head. "They're priceless women, not livestock. I never said they were up for bid."

"Never said they were forbidden, either," Luke piped up.

Jim groaned. He hoped he could ditch everyone and spend a little quiet time with Matty. Folks had jumped in so fast, she didn't even get a chance to answer his proposal. The half-hour ride home had never taken longer.

❧

The minute they reached the ranch, Matty mumbled an excuse and dashed to the outhouse. As a hiding place, it left lots to be desired, but she couldn't think of anyplace else where she'd be left alone. She shut the door, latched it, and then buried her face in her hands.

This is all my fault. I gave Jim that pleading look in the courtroom. I asked him, just as plainly as if I said the words aloud. I've humiliated myself by forcing a man to propose to me so I could keep my sister. He's such a good man. He'll never say otherwise, but I've forced him into a marriage he doesn't want.

Tears blurred her vision.

Lord, what am I going to do? You gave me what I asked for, what I longed for—but now, I don't want it. I don't want a husband who proposed just because he was being gallant. I don't want a man who marries me because of a mix-up. When I prayed for a husband, I figured You understood I wanted a man who would love me the way Papa loved Mama. Now, Jim will have every reason to resent me instead of love me.

"Matty."

Jim's whisper stopped her prayer cold.

"Matty darlin', come on out here," he said in a quiet, gentle voice.

"Leave me alone."

"If I thought for a second you needed a private moment, I wouldn't bother you; but your skirt's caught in the door, and I can see the back of your pretty sunshine hair through the half-moon cutout on the door."

She moaned in acute embarrassment, then felt him give the tail of her skirt a few jerks.

"We need to go for a walk. I'll make everyone leave us be."

I can't stay in here forever. I'll have to face him eventually.

It took every scrap of courage she could summon to open the door. Even then, she didn't look Jim in the eye. He took her hand, steered her around toward the north pasture, and fished a bandana from his vest pocket. As he offered it, he said, "You don't have to marry me."

Those words raked across her soul. Matty tried not to react, but she couldn't help herself. She stopped dead in her tracks and tried to muffle her wail in the bandana.

"Aw, Matty." Jim leaned against the split rail fence and pulled her into an embrace that only made her cry more.

She didn't know how long they stood there. The bandana was a soggy mess, but Jim still held her. "I'm sorry," she mumbled.

He tucked a wisp of hair behind her ear and gave her a tender smile. "I learned long ago, sometimes I've gotta let a filly wear herself out before I can work with her."

She closed her eyes. "But you chose which fillies you catch and work with."

"I think I caught me a fine one." He snuggled her close and pressed a kiss on her hair.

Matty let out a sigh. "You're being noble. I don't want to marry you—a marriage shouldn't be an obligation or a rescue. It should be because a man and a woman love and respect each other. This whole mess—"

"Isn't a mess at all."

She sniffled. "The day we arrived, you called it a mess, and now I can see how right you were. Once Ellis leaves, we can tell everyone it was just an act. My sisters and I will move to town."

He tilted her face to his. Three deep furrows creased his brow. "Matty, is there someone else you want to marry?"

She choked back a nearly hysterical laugh and shook her head.

"Is there something about me that bothers you? I thought we got along."

"We do get along, but there's a world of difference between being acquaintances and being married."

"I thought we'd become much more than acquaintances." He cupped her jaw in his rough hand and brushed his thumb back and forth on her cheek. "We've shared a table for two months now."

"My sisters were there, too."

"You've worked by my side to deliver a colt, stitched my leg, and pulled out my splinters. They weren't around then."

She shrugged. "Those were just everyday things."

"Marriage is made up of days filled with 'everyday things.' I figure if we can find contentment in the commonplace together, we should be able to forge a happy union."

"A union—like our country after the Civil War?"

He chuckled. "I don't doubt we'll have some skirmishes now and then, but who wouldn't? Mild women won't survive out here. I didn't think any woman could until you came along. My sis was miserable, and once Pa died, Ma headed right back East. Only two other decent women have come out, and neither survived a year. Everything inside of me said I ought to send you back for your own welfare. Your gumption and fire changed my mind. If anyone could stand by her man and make a go of it out here, it's you."

"Hey, Jim!" Luke shouted. "Bring that gal back to the house. Everyone's waitin' to congratulate you!"

Matty wanted to sink under a fence post, but she just ducked her head and tried to hide her tear-streaked cheeks.

Jim cradled her close. "You're being a pest, Luke. Sweethearts deserve a bit of time alone."

"You're as bad as Pa was with Ma."

"It's the Collingswood way, and you know it. When we fall, we fall hard."

Matty leaned into his warmth and strength and wished his words were more than pretense to salvage their pride.

"Now that he's gone, I have a few things to say to you," Jim whispered against her temple.

Each word made her tremble.

"My parents had a solid marriage. No one could look at them for more than a heartbeat without knowing they loved each other. Luke wasn't teasing—he sees that same spark between us."

"Luke's a nice man, but his opinion doesn't count for much in this matter."

Jim chuckled. "Matty, my darlin', I fought tooth and nail against falling in love with you because you deserve better than living out here in the wilds with a bunch of rough men. Problem was, my heart didn't pay any attention to my mind.

"You can't begin to imagine how many sleepless nights I've spent in the stable, wrestling with God over this. The day of the barbecue, I made an utter fool of myself because I couldn't bear to think of you leaving here, let alone think of you leaving here with another man."

"You were simply being protective."

"I was protective—of your sisters. You? Oh, Matty, I was downright, unashamedly possessive of you. Haven't you noticed the way I've been assigning chores, just so we could be together?"

"I didn't know what to think. Corrie told me to guard my heart since you were trying to get rid of us."

He groaned. "I was an idiot. I went to that trial today, ready to do whatever I had to, to make up for my foolishness and keep you here. I'd sell every last horse and cow to pay off Ellis, get down on my knees, and beg you to stay. And if all of that failed, I was going to bribe your sisters so they'd nudge you into my arms. If you don't have the sense to run from me, I'm going to lasso you and drag you to the altar."

"You don't have to."

He cupped her chin and growled. "I want to." Before she could reply, he branded her with a toe-curling kiss. When he lifted his head, he whispered, "Matty, God knows the desires of our hearts even better than we do. Why can't you trust Him to do a work in your heart so you can learn to love me back?"

His words made her heart sing. Matty nestled close and confessed, "I already do love you."

"It's about time!"

After they kissed again, Jim put his arm around her waist and started to lead her toward the house. "Jim?"

"Yes, Darlin'?"

"You don't have to lasso me."

He threw back his head and started to chuckle. "I suppose not. I should have seen it from the start. I ordered a halter. Instead, God sent you to meet me at the altar. You can't escape His will any more than I could."

"I don't even want to. You're every wish and prayer I ever had for my husband."

Epilogue

Ten days later, it was the Sunday for Parson Harris to complete his circuit and preach in Lickwind. Instead of a standard service in the jailhouse or one out by the railroad tracks, he and the township all went out to the Rough Cs. Bess made it quite clear no sister of hers would ever get married in a saloon, and the porch would make a nice setting for a wedding.

Bertie didn't want to wear a fancy dress and carry flowers, so the Craig sisters managed to compromise as only they could. Bertie agreed to wear a new blue-and-green-striped dress and carried Rhubarb, who sported a ribbon to match. Next came Bess, looking somehow softer than usual in a violet dress with lavender trim. Ramon trotted by her side with great dignity in spite of the fact that his fur had been trimmed so it looked like a bunch of cotton bolls. Corrie was maid of honor in an appropriately sedate gray and mauve gown. Rhubarb's kittens filled the beribboned basket she carried, which managed to hide her tummy quite discreetly. The sisters lined up on the veranda and watched as Jim tried not to look impatient.

The open windows allowed the strains of "The Wedding March" to filter out. Harry, the barkeep, knew the tune and had volunteered to play it on the piano. Matty appeared on Luke's arm. She wore a wondrous, white satin creation that sounded like the brush of a thousand angel wings as she walked toward Jim.

He could see her bright smile beneath the sheer veil. Over the past days, they'd not had to hide their feelings for one another, and she came to him now with her eyes sparkling with joy.

"Dearly beloved," Parson Harris began.

Matty and James exchanged a tender smile and mouthed the words to one another. Indeed, they were dearly beloved of one another and of the Lord.

GOOSEBERRY JAM

Gooseberries - 3 lb slightly underripe,
    stemmed and washed
Water - 1 pint
Cane Sugar - 3 lb
Butter - ¼ oz

Gently simmer gooseberries and water for about 30 minutes until really soft and reduced. Pulp with a wooden spoon or potato masher. Remove from the heat and add the sugar to the fruit pulp.

Stir until dissolved; then add butter.

Bring to a boil and boil rapidly for about 10 minutes. Stir to keep from scorching. When the setting point is reached, take the pan off the heat and skim the surface with a slotted spoon. Pour into freshly boiled jars and seal.

CATHY MARIE HAKE

Cathy Marie is a Southern California native who loves her work as a nurse and Lamaze teacher. She and her husband have a daughter, a son, and a dog, so life is never dull or quiet. Cathy Marie considers herself a sentimental packrat, collecting antiques and Hummel figurines. She otherwise keeps busy with reading, writing, and being a prayer warrior. "I am easily distracted during prayer, so I devote certain tasks and chores to specific requests or persons so I can keep faithful in my prayer life." Cathy Marie's first book was published by **Heartsong Presents** in 2000 and earned her a spot as one of the readers' favorite new authors.

From Carriage
to Marriage

by Janelle Burnham Schneider

Chapter 1

Luke Collingswood dragged himself out of the bed that had proved no friendlier in the past six hours than it had in the past fifteen nights. He grunted as he pulled on long underwear and then a worn flannel shirt. Now that he had his own room in the ranch house, rather than sleeping in the barn with his brother, his sleep should be more restful. But warmth and comfort weren't enough to settle his mind.

Jim and Matty's marriage had sealed the destiny of the four sisters. The thought terrified Luke. He couldn't wish Matty gone. She'd brought too much light and joy to his solemn brother's life. And Bess would thrive no matter where she found herself. The woman wouldn't permit it any other way. Young Bertie had enough of the wild mustang in her that she'd likely do right well in Wyoming. But the little widow with the baby on the way caused Luke enough concern for all four of them. He just couldn't see how Corrie would survive in this harsh place.

He tried to push the thoughts aside as he poked kindling into the cookstove and waited for the banked embers to turn to flame. Once the fire caught, he added some larger chunks of wood to ensure the stove would be hot and the kitchen warm when the sisters came down to begin breakfast preparation. Quietly, he grabbed his coat and slipped out the back door toward the chicken coop. Gathering eggs was definitely women's work, and Jim would rib him severely if he caught him. But Luke knew gathering eggs was Corrie's chore. He also knew from the shadows under her eyes each morning that nights proved no more restful for her than they did for him. The least he could do was save her the trip out into the cold.

Such a wealth of sorrow lay in the widow's blue gaze.

Luke had always been drawn to the wounded creatures on their ranch. He'd even developed a knack for healing them—so much so that neighboring ranchers often asked for his assistance. However, it would take a lot more than warm mash or Matty's special liniment to set little Corrie to rights.

He'd seen what this country did to fragile women. He'd helped two neighbors bury their wives. His own mother, sturdy of both soul and body, had returned east as soon as possible after Pa's death. He'd pondered writing to see if Ma would take in the Widow Taylor but dismissed the idea instantly. One had only to spend a day around Corrie and Matty to see the bond between them. Corrie simply wouldn't survive separation.

As he left the henhouse with a full basket of eggs, he noticed a figure walking swiftly toward the barn. Jim? While Luke loved early morning hours, Jim was rarely at his best until he'd had his coffee and his breakfast. Something of importance must have enticed him out of his bed so early. Luke set the basket of eggs just outside the chicken yard, then quietly followed his brother. He pulled the barn door open slowly so the hinge wouldn't squeak, then almost let it bang shut in his delight at what he saw. His brother, who had strongly resisted the sisters' plea for a milk cow, now hunched on the milking stool, sending streams of milk into the tin bucket. Luke backed away from the barn, grinning. In the tradition of Collingswood men, Jim had obviously given his heart away in full. Only love would put Jim to work milking, rather than herding or butchering, a cow.

❦

Corrie turned over in her bed yet again, seeking an ever-elusive position of comfort. In recent weeks, her pregnancy had mounded her belly to the point that lying on her stomach was no longer comfortable. But it wasn't this physical change that disrupted her nights.

For the first time in her life, she slept alone.

From the day of her birth, a stronger person had shared her bed. First, it was her twin, Matty. Whereas Corrie felt intimidated by life, Matty embraced it with delight. Events of the day often penetrated Corrie's nights, waking her from troubling dreams. Matty had always been able to talk the troubles away with her cheerful common sense.

Then Brian entered their lives. The day he professed his love for her, Corrie felt as if the most impossible of dreams had come true. She'd always feared the day Matty would marry, leaving her to stumble through life alone. Instead, this handsome, smart, and personable young fisherman had chosen Corrie, ensuring she'd never be alone.

Corrie turned in her bed yet again, grabbing the coverlet, which seemed determined to slide onto the floor. Fall had come to Wyoming, bringing cold nights. She tugged the covering firmly over her shoulders and settled onto her side, hoping her memories would carry her back into sleep. The babe within gave a sharp kick, as if to tell Mama that her tossing and turning wasn't helping. Corrie grinned to herself in the darkness. From the moment she'd begun to suspect her pregnancy, the thought of being a mama had delighted her. She just knew this little one would have Brian's charm and intelligence and her own depth of devotion. Perhaps being a mother would help her find her own place in life. As much as she loved being Brian's wife and Matty's sister, she secretly hoped to find an identity all her own.

But that dream belonged to happier days. Just two weeks after Doc Timmons confirmed her impending motherhood, a freak Atlantic storm turned Corrie into a widow. Matty immediately rushed to Corrie's side and stayed with her night and day. The bank repossessed the cheery little home Brian had worked so hard to provide for his bride; so Corrie moved back to the family farm, back to the bed she and Matty had always shared. Less than two months later, their brother-in-law, Ellis, had announced he was sending them and their other two unmarried sisters, Bess and Bertie, to the wilds of Wyoming to find husbands.

At least for her three sisters, the enforced adventure had worked out well. Bertie loved the freedom of the ranch, spending more time outdoors with the animals than indoors learning how to be the woman her sisters wanted her to be. Bess thrived on the constant work and activity.

And dear Matty. Corrie couldn't help but sigh over her twin's happiness. Jim Collingswood certainly wasn't the kind of husband Corrie would have chosen. Taciturn and sometimes downright grumpy—when Matty was around, the man turned to butter. One of her ever-present smiles softened him up for hours afterward.

But now Corrie was on her own for the first time ever. Yes, she had a roof over her head and good food to eat, but she couldn't depend on Jim and Matty's generosity forever. In a mere four months, the babe would be born, which would result in an endless list of needs to be met for many years to come. Corrie simply had to find a way to begin providing for herself and the little one. Marrying again might be the easy solution for some, but the mere thought gave Corrie shivers. She'd given her heart to Brian, and he'd taken it with him when he died. Some of the men hereabouts—that sleazy Clyde Kincaid for one—would quite happily accept a loveless marriage just to get a woman. The mere memory of his smell turned her stomach.

She shifted to her other side, untangling her flannel nightdress from around her legs. Ever since Matty's marriage two weeks ago, Corrie had spent night after night like this, unable to get comfortable, unable to come up with a solution for her own future. Useless as it was, she fervently wished she could set the calendar back six months and keep it there.

Slumber eventually claimed her, only to be nudged aside by faint daybreak. It took her a moment to realize she'd overslept again. She knew her sisters would be understanding, but she hated not pulling her own weight. If milking were her duty, the cow would be bellowing in discomfort by now. With a groan, she pulled herself from her bed. Her black dress lay draped across a nearby chair, frequent washings having dulled it to a muddy gray. She hated the thought of putting it on again. Though cut generously, it no longer fit properly. Besides, she'd been wearing it almost every day. Part of her longed for a more cheerful color, even while her conscience accused her of disloyalty. The love she and Brian had shared deserved at least a full year of mourning.

She firmly turned her thoughts away from the sadness. She'd never stop loving her husband, but one thing she'd learned in the past four months—if she let the grief dominate her thoughts upon waking, the entire day would be shrouded.

She pulled her fingers through the braid that she had plaited in her hair for sleep. Then she combed her hair smooth. With the speed of much practice, she rebraided it and wound the braid into a simple bun at the back of her head, not letting herself dwell on the memory of how Brian had loved to let her hair sift through his fingers. She carefully pinned her mourning brooch in place. The feel of its weight on her dress brought a fragment of comfort. Though she could no longer embrace Brian himself, this brooch made her feel as though he were still near. As she opened her bedroom door, the scent of coffee lured her downstairs.

As she expected, Matty stood at the stove, a steaming pail of milk on the counter beside her and a basket of eggs near the sink.

"You've been busy, Matty."

"Good morning." Matty's usual cheerful smile looked softer these days, even as her eyes narrowed with intense observation. "You look pale, Corrie. Are you okay?"

Corrie shrugged off her twin's concern. "I'm okay. Just slow waking up this morning, I guess."

Matty crossed the kitchen to put a hand on each of Corrie's arms as she continued her inspection, looking intently into Corrie's eyes. The twins had few secrets from one another; those that Corrie tried to keep, Matty could often discern with a mere look. But this time, Corrie refused to let her grief shadow Matty's fresh happiness.

Matty still saw more than Corrie wanted her to. "It's okay, little sister. I'm not going to pry. I just worry about you. You have more than yourself to take care of, remember?" She patted the as-yet-small bulge of Corrie's abdomen affectionately.

Though she wouldn't have appreciated anyone else touching her so intimately, Corrie cherished Matty's hands on her. They soothed, and she liked to think they pleased the baby, too. She wanted her little one to bask in Matty's abundant love even before birth. Matty moved her hands back to Corrie's shoulders. "Promise me you'll try to nap after lunch, okay?"

Corrie favored her with a small nod. "I'll try." She let herself relax in Matty's embrace for a moment, then she moved toward the counter. "Thanks for gathering the eggs."

Matty grinned. "That wasn't me. I think Luke must have done it while Jim was milking Betty."

Corrie exaggerated her gasp of surprise. "The grumpy cowboy actually did wimmen's work? Marriage must be making him soft."

Matty's face took on a pink tinge. "He'd be terribly

embarrassed if he knew I told you. Please don't tell the other two."

"As long as you don't let on that I didn't do my chores, either," Corrie promised with a wink. "Perhaps I should stir up a batch of Mama's coffee cake as a thank-you."

"I've no doubt they'd leave nothing but crumbs," Matty assured her with a laugh. "How you do it, I don't know. I use the same recipes you use, but my baking turns out like bricks while yours is as light as anything Mama used to make."

This time Corrie's cheeks warmed. She would never say so out loud for fear of sounding boastful, but she knew she'd inherited her mama's touch with baked goods. Baking always made her feel connected to the mother she still missed, especially now that she was in a motherly way herself. She continued cleaning eggs in silence, wiping each shell carefully with a damp cloth, then setting the cleaned eggs in a cloth-lined basket. The chickens Matty had talked Jim into buying were obviously settling in well. Every few days, egg production increased. Thankfully, with cooler weather coming on, they'd be able to keep the eggs for more than a day. Still, they'd need to think of ways to use the bounty. It would be a sin to have to feed the eggs to the pigs.

Then as she stirred ingredients together for the coffee cake, an idea began to form. Neighboring ranchers often dropped by, much to Jim's disgust. With the only three unmarried women for miles living at the Rough Cs, it wasn't hard to figure out what drew the male visitors. Corrie had noticed the way the men inhaled the home-baked goods. What if she made extra bread and cookies to sell to them? It seemed inhospitable to think about luring money out of guests at their table, but circumstances gave her some leeway, she felt sure. She wasn't at all interested in being courted, and neither was Bess, as near as she could tell. Bertie was just plain too young. So, if the men persisted in coming, why not turn the visits into something profitable? She'd have to start out using the supplies the Collingswood brothers had already purchased; but if her business did well, she'd be able to re-pay them.

Jim and Luke's response to her coffee cake provided the perfect opening for her to mention her thoughts. "I can't remember the last time I had a treat like this for breakfast," Jim pronounced, stabbing his third piece from the platter.

Luke snorted. "Perhaps the cinnamon rolls from two days ago? As I recall, you ate four for breakfast, two at cof-fee time, and stole the last one at lunch. Marriage is making your memory go."

Corrie loved to watch the men banter. They looked much alike, with their hazel eyes, broad shoulders, and tall frames. Yet, while Jim tended to be gruff, Luke had a gentle way about him. Solid affection lay beneath their frequently barbed comments to one another.

"And who was it that grabbed the last biscuit off my fork just last night?" Jim inquired. "I can't believe my younger brother would steal food from my very mouth."

"Sometimes it's the only way to get my fair share," Luke retorted.

As the laughter around the table faded, Corrie voiced her thoughts. "I had an idea while I was making the coffee cake this morning. I'm thinking I might turn the baking into a business, if you men don't object." She gave Luke and

Jim each a glance but knew it was Matty she'd have to convince. "I could sell bread and cookies to the neighbors who come calling. Once I have a bit of profit, I'd pay you back for the supplies I've used."

Jim nodded. "Not a bad idea, Corrie. Might as well get some use out of these louts who seem to have nothing better to do than gawk at pretty women."

Bess also wore an encouraging expression. "That is a good idea. You have a real touch with baked goods. I'm sure the men hereabouts would pay well for whatever you could make. Just be sure you charge a fair price for what you do. You do tend to undervalue yourself."

Corrie warmed from the unexpected support, particularly in light of the matching expressions on the faces of Luke and Matty. She couldn't address Luke directly, so she made her appeal to Matty. "You know I love to bake, Matty. It wouldn't be hard. I'd feel good to be doing something practical. I'm going to need to be able to support the babe and myself eventually anyway."

The sound that came from Luke's throat sounded like a cross between a growl and the beginning of speech. But Matty beat him to it. "There's plenty of time to worry about supporting yourself after we get that little one safely here. In the meantime, you mustn't overdo. There's nothing more important than keeping yourself and that baby well."

"But I do feel well," Corrie protested. "I'd feel even better if I could do this. You have the cow and the chickens to look after. Bess has the garden."

She saw the softening in Luke's eyes before Matty's, but slowly Matty relented, as well. "If Jim and Luke don't mind you using the supplies, I suppose it wouldn't hurt. But you have to promise me you'll spend at least an hour per day resting."

At that moment, Corrie would have promised anything. For the first time since Brian's death, she felt as if she were no longer just drifting on a tumultuous ocean of circumstances. Might the day come when she'd actually have dreams again?

Chapter 2

The first day of her venture, Corrie made four loaves of bread. She knew her plan would succeed only if she could show Matty it wouldn't require too much work. The next day, she found some dried apples in the pantry and, after cooking them, turned them into cookies, which filled the house with their spicy scent. She made sure a full dozen were available for Jim and Luke's afternoon coffee time, and both pronounced them better than the coffee cake.

Just as she expected, Clyde Kincaid, Josiah Temple, and Amos Freeling showed up in the late afternoon. None of them seemed to want to visit with any sister in particular, much to her relief, but all were willing to consume more than their fair share of the cookies. Rather than hide in her room as she often did during these visits, she forced herself to stay and make her business pitch. She waited for yet one more fulsome compliment on the goodies, then took a deep breath. "As a matter of fact, Mr. Temple, if you'd like to take some home with you, I'm selling them for ten cents a dozen. I also have bread for sale if you like."

Clyde Kincaid let out a particularly nasty-sounding guffaw.

"Now if that don't beat all. Not only is she purty, but she's got a business head about her. I'll take two dozen cookies and two loaves of bread, Miz Taylor. Looks like I'm gonna have to marry you after all, so I can get all these goodies for free."

Corrie didn't know how to respond. She wanted to flee, but she knew she had to learn how to handle situations like this on her own. But before she could think of a reply, a gruff comment from the back door surprised her. "Glad you appreciate our hospitality, Kincaid, but Miz Taylor doesn't have stock for more than one dozen cookies and one loaf of bread per customer. We'll try to have more for you next week at this time." With that, Luke scooped a loaf of bread and a handful of cookies into a square of muslin Corrie had set out on the counter. He wrapped the bundle, then held out his hand. "I'll take your money, and you can take your goods and be on your way."

Clyde dug a grimy hand into his pocket and produced coins, which he dropped into Luke's palm. "I'll tell you, it's a good thing your mama ain't here to see how you boys have become downright inhospitable. She'd give you both a whuppin', I'm sure." He released that annoying hee-haw laugh of his that showed more gaps than teeth. "No need to rush me; I'm on my way." He tucked the cloth-wrapped parcel under his arm and tromped through the door, which Luke held ajar for him.

The two men remaining eyed the baked goods still on the counter. Mr. Temple stood and rummaged in his pocket, which looked a good deal cleaner than Kincaid's had. He looked from Luke to Corrie and back again, as though not sure whom he should address. "I'll take one of those loaves, if you don't mind, Collingswood, and here's an extra penny for the lady's trouble."

Amos Freeling also bought a loaf, as well as some of the cookies; and he, too, added a penny to the purchase price. With goods in hand, the two left together, as if the purpose of their visit had been business only.

Luke handed the money over to Corrie, then left the house without comment. She couldn't decide whether she resented his actions or appreciated his intervention.

Word of Corrie's venture spread quickly. Two days later, four neighboring ranchers showed up to buy fresh bread. "It's been months since we've had anything this tasty, Ma'am," one of them informed her as he cradled the muslin-wrapped loaf as gently as he might a sickly calf.

Corrie felt delight push her lips into a smile. "Thank you for the compliment. I'll have more for you next week."

He tipped his hat to her and rode back the way he'd come.

Corrie cradled the coins in her palm. Her venture was working! It wouldn't be easy to keep up with demand right after the baby came, but she'd find a way. She had to. No matter what the men around here thought, she wouldn't marry again. She'd have to work hard to provide for herself and her child, but any amount of hard work was preferable to marriage.

That thought kept Corrie going over the next days. It motivated her out of bed in the mornings and gave her energy for kneading batch after batch of bread. She made sure she always had plenty on hand for Jim and Luke so they'd never have cause to complain about her fledgling business. By working steadily, she found herself able to make up to eight loaves of bread every other day, with cookies and muffins on the alternating days. Some mysterious signal seemed to let her rough-edged customers know when new baked goods were available. A steady stream of buyers carried her products away almost as quickly as she made them. An equally steady stream of coins trickled into the old sock she used to store her earnings. Before long, she'd have to ask Jim or Luke to bring home more sugar and flour, and she'd be able to pay for them herself.

The other advantage of her work came each evening at bedtime. It took only moments after falling into bed before sleep claimed her. Most nights, she slept soundly until dawn. If she woke feeling less rested than she would have liked, no one else noticed.

As autumn progressed, the pace of life on the ranch increased. Bess and Bertie spent most of each day outside, gathering vegetables from the garden and preparing them for storage in the root cellar. They foraged for berries, which Corrie happily incorporated into her baked goods and Matty turned into jam. Corrie even found time to put together a gooseberry pie for the family's dinner. Not so much as a trickle of berry juice was left by the time Matty started clearing the table.

"That was a fine supper, ladies," Jim commented as he stood. Though his words addressed them all, his eyes remained fixed on Matty, whose cheeks blushed prettily.

In typical fashion, she turned the attention away from herself. "Corrie always has had the touch for baking," she said, laying a gentle hand on her twin's shoulder. "Our mama was that way, too."

"We're most grateful." Luke's gaze sought Corrie's across the table. "You're not working yourself too hard, are you? No dessert is worth making yourself sick over."

His concern warmed her through, and she smiled reassuringly, glad he couldn't feel the deep ache in her lower back from standing all day. "It feels good to be useful. Besides, Matty makes me take a rest every afternoon. I can't so much as sneeze without her fretting."

He didn't look convinced but said nothing more. As if his concern had infected the entire room, her sisters wouldn't let her help with the dishes. When she refused to retire to her room like an invalid, Bess waved her toward the parlor. "Then just sit with your feet up," she ordered, affectionate concern underlying her tone. "You have the baby to think of, remember?"

As if Corrie could forget. The little one seemed to move continuously. Most of the time, she relished the sense of companionship. But at times like this, when her entire body ached from weariness, the movements within increased her tiredness. She lowered herself onto the settee in the parlor, then propped her feet on a nearby footstool. It felt good to get her legs up. She leaned her head against the back of the settee and let relaxation ooze through her. The chatter of her sisters in the kitchen and the rumble of the men's voices as they thumped around on the back porch provided soothing background noise. For the first time since Brian's death, she felt at home. She belonged here, on this ranch, with these people.

She awoke from a dreamless sleep to feel Matty tucking a quilt around her. Matty stroked her cheek with a gentle, though rough-skinned, hand. "You looked so peaceful here. I was hoping I wouldn't wake you."

"I don't mind, although if I'm going to sleep, I probably should go upstairs. I'd hate for the men to see me like this."

Matty's smile was tender. "I'm sure they wouldn't find a thing wrong with it. Luke seems quite concerned about you."

Corrie shrugged. "He's just protective. He can't help worrying about anything or anyone he thinks is hurting or fragile."

Matty raised her eyebrows as if preparing to argue with Corrie's conclusion, but instead she rested her hand on Corrie's abdomen. "How's the little one?" She rubbed in gentle circles, which eased the stretched, achy feeling.

"Busy as always." Corrie couldn't help but grin. "I think this one is going to have Bertie's energy."

"We can hope it's more easily channeled," Matty commented, then paused her rubbing to trace her fingers along the center of Corrie's apron where it covered the gap in her dress.

"It's not a problem," Corrie assured her. "My apron covers it, though the space seems to get wider by the day."

"For someone whose blessing was almost invisible for so many months, you're certainly advertising your condition now." Matty put a hand on either side of Corrie's stomach. She stretched her fingers wide, as though trying to encompass the entire width in her open hands. The babe squirmed. Matty's eyes widened. "Does the little one often kick on both sides at the same time?"

Corrie nodded. "Especially when I'm trying to rest."

A secretive smile came into Matty's eyes. "I wonder—"

Before she could say the words, Corrie comprehended. She felt her eyes widen with shock. "Two babies?" she whispered. "Twins?"

Matty caressed Corrie's stomach again. "Wouldn't that be wonderful? I've always loved being a twin."

Tears pooled in Corrie's eyes. For the first time since Matty's marriage, she felt as if the special bond she'd shared with this sister might not be broken after all. She hugged her twin fiercely. "It would be special for them, but how am I going to take care of two babies at once?"

Matty pulled back from the hug to look deeply into Corrie's eyes. "You won't have to do it alone, Corrie. We're all here for you, and nothing will change that, whether you have one baby or two." She must have seen the doubts that still swirled in Corrie's mind. "Sis, there's no way to know for sure until the baby is born. You fretting isn't good for the little one—or ones. Try not to worry, okay?"

Corrie tried to smile reassuringly, once again hoping her twin wouldn't read her thoughts. How could she tell Matty that being dependent on her sisters wasn't what she wanted?

Chapter 3

In the following weeks, Corrie found herself alone only at night. Bess and Matty took turns staying in the farmhouse while the other did outside chores. Even Luke seemed to always be nearby, ready to lift, reach, or bend for her. Rarely did she have to gather eggs anymore. No matter how early she awoke, when she came downstairs, the full basket sat on the counter, awaiting her attention.

Her girth continued to increase and movement became more difficult. "If this baby gets any bigger, I'm going to explode," she complained to Matty one afternoon as she sat near the table with her feet up on a stool, as Matty had instructed. No longer were daily naps adequate. Matty now insisted Corrie stop her work every hour and put her feet up for at least ten minutes.

"I shouldn't tell you this, but you'll get a lot bigger, especially if there's—"

Corrie cut her off. "Don't say it. I don't want anyone else to know until we're certain." She couldn't confess that hearing the word "twins" out loud would make her intuition too strong to ignore. The mere thought of being responsible for two little lives, rather than just one, felt overwhelming. The bakery business expanded along with her waistline, and Corrie could see hope of supporting herself and her little one eventually. But she felt herself slowing down daily. By the beginning of December, she wouldn't be doing much baking at all and likely wouldn't be ready to resume until February. If she had twins, she knew it would be much longer before she'd be able to do anything but care for her little ones.

She rubbed her belly with one hand, while using the other to hold a glass of water to her lips. That was another of Matty's edicts. Corrie had to drink one full glass of water during each of her breaks. "I declare, I feel as if I don't do anything but take breaks and go to the necessary," she often complained.

But Matty remained firm. "It wouldn't hurt you a bit if that's all you did do. Just be grateful I don't ban you from the kitchen entirely."

So Corrie sat and sipped her water. She already felt an indescribable bond with the little one—or ones—she sheltered within her body. Impatient though she felt with Matty's restrictions, she wouldn't, for a moment, do anything to harm this new life.

She saw the minute hand on the clock tick past the ten-minute mark and pushed herself to her feet again. A large bowl of dough awaited her attention. "Should I make buns or sweet rolls?" she wondered aloud.

"Sweet rolls are tempting," Matty admitted, ladling hot jam into jars. "But with Jim and Luke leaving in two days to herd cattle, buns would probably come in more handy."

Corrie agreed. "You're right. I'd forgotten about them leaving. If I have the energy tomorrow, I'll do up some sweet rolls to send with them."

"You spoil those men!" Matty declared with a laugh.

Corrie just shrugged and changed the subject. "How long will they be gone?"

Matty's expression turned sober. "Jim says maybe as long as a week. He says it takes awhile to round up all the strays and check the herd over for problems. This will be the first time we've been apart since we married."

The words brought a rush of memories. How well Corrie knew Matty's feelings! Just a month after Corrie and Brian's marriage, Brian left for a week on the fishing boat. The pattern for their marriage had been established then. Weeks away and days at home. Not once did Corrie find it easy to say good-bye to her husband, even though she knew his departure was necessary. She knew nothing she could say would make the separation any easier for Matty.

The morning the men left, she woke early to be with Matty. Silence hovered between them as Matty closed the door. It was a silence that went deeper than lack of conversation, the silence they'd shared at many other moments in their lives when words simply wouldn't express the emotions they felt. Corrie pulled her sister near in a tight embrace. With a firm prod, the baby protested being included.

"Goodness!" Matty laughed, even while wiping tears from her eyes.

"Tell me about it," Corrie groaned, moving slowly to the counter where the basket of eggs awaited her. Even on this morning, Luke had done his bit to ease her load. "His favorite time for exercise is just when I'm trying to fall asleep. Sometimes it actually hurts."

"Poor mama," Matty said in the tone that never failed to make Corrie feel utterly wrapped in love. She massaged Corrie's shoulders, then worked her way down to Corrie's lower back. "Does that help?"

"Oh, yes!" Corrie hadn't realized how stiff those muscles were. "Too bad you can't just spend the day doing this."

As the days of the men's absence passed, Corrie voiced her discomforts more than she usually did. Pampering Corrie seemed to take Matty's mind off her husband's absence. For her part, Corrie enjoyed being alone with her sisters. Even the ranch hands, with the exception of Scotty, had gone herding with Jim and Luke. Other than a knock on the door and a quiet, twice a day, "You ladies okay up here?" Scotty kept to himself. The duties of autumn still demanded the sisters' attention, but the pace seemed slower. Meals didn't have to be as extensive, and thus cleanup happened more quickly.

Corrie's baking customers were also conspicuously absent. She hoped it meant because they, too, were gathering up their herds, not because they'd decided to do without baked goods.

A third possibility revealed itself the third day after the men left. Corrie decided to give the parlor a good dusting, and she happened to look out the window as she worked. A lone rider approached the ranch.

She called to her sister in the kitchen. "Matty!"

"What?" Matty hurried into the room, wiping her hands on her apron. "Are you okay?"

"Yes, I'm fine. But it looks like we have a visitor and not one I'm eager to see."

Matty peered out the window. "That Kincaid man. I know he's one of your best customers, but I don't think it's a good idea for him to be here when Luke and Jim are gone."

Corrie agreed. "What are we going to do?"

"Maybe we don't have to do anything." Matty pointed toward another rider approaching from the barn area—Scotty. Conversation seemed to pass between the two men. Clyde became visibly upset, and Scotty pointed back the direction from which Clyde had come. A bit more discussion followed, and then Clyde left the ranch.

"Well, I'll be!" Matty declared. "Looks like Scotty's doing guard duty. I don't know whether to be flattered or insulted."

Bess was less ambivalent. Hunched over a washtub on the back porch, she listened as Matty described what they'd seen. "I appreciate the thought, but I do wish those men would realize we can take care of ourselves! We're just as strong as those bridles they ordered!"

Matty and Corrie giggled at the reminder of Jim's blunder, and slowly a grin spread across Bess's face. "I wonder how Ellis feels about owning the entire dairy now that he doesn't have us around to keep things running."

Corrie didn't even want to think about it. Hard as it had been, getting sent to Lickwind and thus the Rough Cs had been the best thing to happen to her since Brian's death. At least here she had half a chance of making it on her own, regardless of how fragile everyone seemed to think she was.

The next day, Matty decided to clean and organize the pantry. "I guess it's my own now," she announced after breakfast, her diffident shrug very much out of character. "I might as well know what's in every nook and crack."

Corrie quietly slipped into the small room to assist. With her baking temporary halted, she had to find something to do. Bess wouldn't think of allowing her to help pick the last of the vegetables from the garden, though she and Bertie were working tirelessly to bring the produce in before a hard frost damaged it. Matty had suggested Corrie try some needlework to keep herself busy, but Corrie found it too frustrating. While she sewed, her mind wandered into memories better left untouched. With each day of Luke's absence, she found herself recalling more vividly Brian's last day alive. Why Luke and Brian would share space in her thoughts, she didn't even want to consider. Far better to keep herself busy.

It took them two full days to finish, but Matty looked highly pleased with herself at the end of it. "Doesn't it look beautiful, Corrie? I can't believe I actually have my own pantry. I still have to pinch myself to be sure I'm not just dreaming I'm married."

Corrie advanced on her with a grin, fingers held as if to administer the pinch, but Matty quickly circled the table. "Now, now, Corrie dear. You mustn't get yourself all stirred up."

The baby kicked just then, strong enough to make Corrie gasp for a breath. Merriment vanished from Matty's face. "Are you okay?"

Corrie nodded. When she was able to draw a full breath, she explained, "Every once in awhile this little one kicks hard enough to hurt. With legs like this, it's got to be a boy."

"Or one of each?" Matty's words were teasing, but her eyes took in every detail of Corrie's condition.

"I'm not listening." Corrie stalked away with as much

dignity as she could muster and set herself to washing the dozens of canning jars they'd found in a back corner of the pantry. Bess and Bertie's efforts in the garden had produced heaps of fresh peas, beans, and tomatoes. Corrie guessed they'd probably insist on her shelling the peas and snapping the beans, since both jobs could be done sitting down.

But the next morning that proved impossible. No matter which chair she sat in or how she arranged her work around her, she couldn't get comfortable. Her back ached unrelentingly. She did as much as she could while standing, but she finally asked Matty to let her peel the tomatoes or blanch the beans—anything to allow her some movement around the kitchen.

Matty's eyes narrowed. "You're not feeling contractions, are you?"

"No more than usual." Corrie dismissed the concern. She really didn't want to be fussed over today.

Her twin sensed her resistance and said nothing more. But throughout the morning, Corrie felt her sister studying her. Corrie watched the clock and sat down for her breaks before Matty could say anything. She sipped water faithfully. After lunch, she lay down on the settee in the parlor, unable to find the strength to climb the stairs. When a knock came at the door, she forced herself not to answer.

But Scotty's quiet tones carried clearly to where she lay. "Mrs. Collingswood, Ma'am, would you mind coming out to the barn for a few minutes? One of the yearlings has cut hisself on the fence wire. Mr. Jim told me if any of the animals was sicklike, to let you tend them."

Corrie felt Matty's rush of pleasure at her husband's

secondhand compliment. The delight in her voice made Corrie grin. "I'll be right there as soon as I grab my kit."

With her twin out of the way, Corrie returned to the kitchen. Reclining on the sofa hadn't helped. Bess looked at her sharply. "Are you sure you rested enough?"

Corrie silently gave thanks Bess wasn't as intuitive as Matty. "I'm fine. I feel better when I'm busy."

If the mountain of vegetables hadn't lay between them, Corrie knew Bess probably wouldn't have given in so easily. But the work had to be done. Their winter meals depended on it.

By the time dusk closed in, neat rows of cooling jars displayed their contents. Quarts of tomatoes, tomato sauce, and green beans stood ready to feed the four sisters and two brothers throughout the months until the garden would produce food again. Shelled peas lay on the drying racks above the stove. Matty still hadn't returned from the barn, so Corrie prepared a sandwich to take to her.

"No, you don't," Bess informed her. "You worked harder than you should have today, and Matty would have my scalp if I let you walk down to the barn. I'll go."

Corrie didn't argue. Now that the vegetables no longer occupied her attention, she felt every muscle in her back and abdomen protesting the three days of work she'd done. She lowered herself onto the settee again to rest for a bit before going upstairs to bed. But just as she felt sleep beginning to overtake her, a cramp around her middle jolted her to full alertness.

Chapter 4

Luke's bay splashed across the stream, and Luke resisted the urge to nudge his stallion into a trot. It would take another half hour of steady riding before they reached the ranch yard. If he showed his impatience now, Jim would have plenty of time to tease him. He'd done a good job of concealing his concern over leaving the four women with only Scotty to turn to if things went wrong. If Jim had perceived his uneasiness, he would have known in an instant that it had nothing to do with the ever-practical Bess, the capable Matty, or even the irrepressible Bertie. All Luke's concern focused on just one of the sisters—the one most likely to succumb to the harshness of the frontier, the one with the most to lose, the one for whom he'd never be able to provide enough protection. She still grieved for her husband. Luke saw it in her eyes every time he thought about courting her. As much as he longed to have the right to love her, he refused to take advantage of her wounded spirit. Should he ever be blessed enough to become a permanent part of her life, it would be because she wanted the love as much as he did. Though he worried often about her physical safety, her emotional well-being concerned him just as much. He could tell she worried about being a burden. What if one of his less scrupulous neighbors decided to take advantage of her vulnerability? He'd given Scotty instructions about visitors to the ranch during his absence. Now that they were back, there wasn't much he could do to keep other men away. Her bakery business drew them like flies, as well as the appeal of her two unmarried sisters. It was an impossible situation.

As soon as the ranch house came into view, he knew something was wrong. Matty's cow stood by the barn door bawling to be milked. The garden, at which Bess toiled continuously, lay unattended. No laundry flapped on the clotheslines. The place looked deserted.

As if reading his thoughts, Jim pulled his horse alongside Luke's. "Doesn't look right, does it?"

Luke shook his head. Though every cell in his body screamed at him to gallop full speed to the house, one of the brothers had to stay with the ranch hands to help get the small band of sickly calves to the barn and the horses unloaded and brushed down. As Matty's husband, it was Jim's right to forego the chores. "You go on in. I'll take care of things outside."

The speed with which Jim spurred his horse into a gallop told Luke they shared the same sick fear. Never before had emotion gripped him so tightly. Though he'd often been concerned about his parents or his sister, never had he felt the burden of responsibility that clung to him now. He realized as he slid from his horse and opened the corral gate that, no matter what happened with any of the sisters, each of them would always be a part of his heart. He took care of the animals, even milking the cow, which was obviously well past her usual milking time. His hands ached when he finished the job. Whoever had dubbed milking cows "women's work" had obviously never done it. He couldn't imagine how the sisters had managed the dairy alone after their parents' deaths. Of course, Ellis had been around; but after meeting the man, Luke strongly suspected he hadn't been of much practical assistance. With the cow once again released to her fenced pasture, he noticed the colt occupying the far stall, his leg neatly bandaged. Luke entered the stall, murmuring calming words to the colt just as Scotty came into the barn. "Howdy, Boss."

"Hi, Scotty. What happened with this fellow?" Luke ran his hands down the colt's leg, noticing how neatly and firmly the bandage had been applied.

"I think he snagged his leg on some fencing wire. Miz Matty fixed him right up. Didn't even need me to hold him while she worked. As soon as she started talkin' to him, he settled right down."

"There's no fever in the leg. That's a good sign."

"Yessir. She cleaned the cut real well. Sent me to the cook shack for clean water three times. She don't do things by half measures."

Luke grinned briefly to himself as he left the stall. Scotty could give no higher praise. Conscientious and thorough, he strongly admired anyone who did a job as well as he would have done it.

"Ever'thing okay up at the house?" Scotty's inquiry told Luke what had brought the weathered cowboy to the barn.

"I don't know," Luke answered. "I figured Jim had more right than I did to skip out of chores."

"For now anyway," Scotty replied cryptically. "I haven't seen a-one of the ladies since last night, other than when I knocked this morning and Miss Bess told me they was okay."

The knot in Luke's middle tightened. If one of them had been injured or fallen ill, Bess likely would have told the cowboy. Only one thing he could think of would keep all of them indoors without explanation. Corrie's baby.

"Anything I can do for you, Boss, so you can go on up to the house?"

Luke could have hugged the older man for his understanding, but it would have embarrassed them both. "Thanks, Scotty, but I think everything is done for the night. We'll need to check out the animals we brought back from the range with us, but that can wait until tomorrow."

"Okay then." Scotty turned toward the door, then paused. "If there's anything wrong, let the ladies know that us at the bunkhouse will be sayin' a few prayers."

Luke nodded in acknowledgment. Scotty might not be the most refined of men, but he had a heart as big as the range and a faith as durable. When Scotty prayed, Luke knew God heard and responded.

The thought made him realize he hadn't yet turned to God with his worry. A pile of hay in a back corner of the barn had often been his place of prayer. He now dropped to his knees. "God, I'm sorry I didn't turn to You sooner. You know how Corrie is on my mind so much, to the point I'm not even thinking straight anymore. Please, Father, help me keep my mind on You and Your goodness. Whatever is wrong with the sisters, please provide us with all we need to meet their needs." He continued kneeling for several minutes in silence. He felt familiar peace slip into his soul. With the peace came the assurance that he needn't hide his feelings from his heavenly Father. Trying to hide from God, in fact, was a waste of time, since God knew his heart anyway. "Father, I want to be able to court Corrie and to win her heart, but both You and I know she's not ready for that. I couldn't bear to watch her marry another man for anything less than love, and yet I simply can't approach her with my feelings when she's so fragile. If she's the one You've designed for me, I trust You to bring us together in Your way and Your time. Until then, help me be patient and leave our hearts in Your care."

The burden of past weeks eased from his heart. He had no more assurance of the future than he'd had an hour ago, but now he felt able to leave the unknown with the only One who knew how it would turn out. With lighter steps, he strode toward the house. A lonely figure sat slumped on the steps.

"Hi, Bertie," he greeted her, playfully knocking askew the battered brown felt hat she so often wore. "Are you okay?"

A kidlike grin flitted across her face as she jammed the hat back in place. Then the somber look returned. "Corrie's sick, Luke. Matty won't let anyone else into Corrie's room, and Bess won't tell me anything. I know the baby is trying to come early, but they think I'm too young to talk about it. I'm not too young. I love her just as much as they do." She swiped at her eyes with a fist.

Luke lowered himself to the step beside her, holding

back the urge that made him want to charge up the stairs. Even if he did get past Bess, Matty would bar his access to Corrie. He simply didn't have the right to be at her side. With a clarity that wouldn't have come to him a day ago, he realized the sister who needed him most at the moment wasn't the one who occupied his thoughts so frequently. He glanced sideways at Bertie, not wanting her to know he was studying her. Her reddish blond hair hung in braids always on the verge of coming loose. While the eyes of the other three sisters spoke of feminine understanding, Bertie's told of dreams of adventure, lively imagination, and a spirit that refused to be confined by convention. He rarely knew how to relate to her, with her mysterious combination of womanly appearance but childlike enthusiasm. At this moment, however, he felt an unexpected bond.

"I know how you feel, Bertie."

The girl's gaze snapped to his, disbelief, then disdain written across her face. "You can't know. She's not your sister. You're boss of your own ranch, not the youngest of five sisters."

"No, Corrie isn't my sister," Luke acknowledged slowly, hoping he didn't inadvertently reveal more than was appropriate. "But I've come to care a lot for the four of you. However, since I'm not a woman and not related to any of you, they won't tell me any more than they're telling you. That doesn't mean God won't let us talk to Him about her."

Bertie played with the end of a braid, seemingly thinking about what he'd said. Then with a defiant expression, she looked into his eyes. "I don't pray. Not since Mama and Papa died."

Luke's heart twisted with the hurt this child-woman couldn't express. "Well, Bertie, I think God knows exactly what you're feeling, and His heart hurts with you. When you're ready to talk with Him, He'll be ready to listen. In the meantime, you can be certain He understands what you can't say." After a few moments of silence between them, he rose and tiptoed through the front door.

Chapter 5

Luke's reception inside the house was pretty much what he expected. Jim sat at the table nursing a cup of coffee. If the look in his eyes hadn't warned Luke the situation was grim, the expression on Bess's face would have told him everything. Bess wasn't given to the abundance of smiles Matty usually displayed, but tonight her face looked pinched and tight. Luke knew she wouldn't tell him much, nor would she welcome any direct comments from him.

He didn't think she'd welcome a hug, either. He contented himself with pulling out a chair across from Jim and seating himself with the comment, "I've been praying, Bess."

He couldn't be sure, but it seemed tears might have shimmered in her eyes as she looked briefly at him. "Please don't stop," she said as she disappeared into the pantry.

It was just the opportunity Luke was waiting for. Having removed his boots at the door, he slipped soundlessly toward the stairs in his stocking feet. Jim's eyes both twinkled and warned Luke the ploy wouldn't work. Luke didn't expect to get far, but he had to attempt it. He had no intention of trying to see Corrie. Such a thing simply wouldn't be proper. But perhaps he could get a word with Matty. Just maybe she would tell him something—anything—to ease the knot in his gut. He sensed Bess's presence at the bottom of the stairs, but he refused to look back. If she wasn't going to say anything, he wasn't going to give her an opportunity. At the top of the stairs, he turned left down a hallway. At the end of the hallway stood the doorway to what had been his parents' room and had recently become Jim and Matty's. Corrie's smaller room lay just to the left. He wouldn't knock on the closed door. If Corrie was sleeping, he didn't want to disturb her. He just planned to wait around until Matty appeared.

He felt Bess's presence behind him even before her whispered admonition. "Luke, this isn't proper."

She wasn't saying anything he didn't already know. "I just want to hear Matty say she's okay."

Bess moved to stand between him and the door to Corrie's room. "I can't let you disturb—"

Before she finished the sentence, the door opened and a haggard Matty appeared. Locks of her normally tidy blond hair hung around her face. Worry lines radiated from her red-rimmed eyes. She shook her head. "Luke, I can't let you in."

"I'm not asking for that," he assured her though he wished with all his heart he had the right to ask. "I just want to know how she is."

Bess shook her head as though to indicate Matty should say nothing, but Matty just laid one hand on Bess's arm and another on Luke's. "We need a miracle," she said frankly. "The baby is still moving, which is a good sign, but the longer the labor continues, the more dangerous it is for both Corrie and the baby."

"How long has she been laboring?" Luke asked. He knew from working with animals how a long labor exhausted both mother and offspring.

Bess's mouth tightened, but Matty answered. "We don't know for sure. She hasn't been feeling well for a couple of days, but she didn't tell us how bad it was. Last night it got serious enough for her to tell me the details."

As long as she was willing to talk, he had one more question. "It's too early for the baby, isn't it?"

The shadows in Matty's eyes deepened as she nodded. "Yes, by at least a couple of weeks. That's why I'm worried. Pray, please, Luke. That's all you can do right now, but it's what we need more than anything."

"Ma—a—atty!"

The pained cry from the bedroom sent Matty scurrying back inside, and it made Luke's heart feel as if it were breaking. Bess steered him toward the stairs, though without reproof. He felt somewhat better for having heard directly from Matty, even though the information was not reassuring.

Jim looked up from the kitchen table when they returned. Luke explained, since Bess didn't seem ready to say anything. "Matty says things don't look good right now, but there's still time for a miracle."

"Maybe we should fetch Doc Mitchel." Jim looked from Luke to Bess and back again.

Bess's face brightened as soon as she heard the word "Doc." When Luke growled "No," she whirled on him. "Why not? Corrie needs all the help we can get her."

"Doc Mitchel would be more trouble than help." Luke tried to keep his voice calm, even though he wanted to strangle his brother for opening the subject. "Jim, you know the doc is barely adequate for basic stitching and bandaging. I don't want his grubby soldier hands within a mile of Corrie." He stalked out of the kitchen and reached for his boots. Hanging around here would only get him in trouble.

Bertie still sat hunched on the steps. She turned at the sound of his steps, her hopeful eyes shining in the light that spilled from the doorway. "Is everything okay?"

"I wish I could say yes." Though every muscle in his body screamed for movement, some kind of action to distract him from the fear in his soul, he forced himself to sit once again on the step beside Bertie. "There's no way to know how things will work out."

Even in the dusk, fear shone vividly in the young woman's eyes. "Is Corrie dying?"

Luke draped his arm over her shoulders and drew her close. Propriety didn't matter nearly as much as giving what comfort he could. "I don't know as much as I'd like, Bertie. There are some things that just aren't appropriate for us to know." He felt her stiffen beside him. "I know it's not fair, but it's the way things are. Right now, what matters is Corrie. Even though we don't know details, we can be sure that God does. All we can do is trust Him to take care of her and ask Him to give Matty all the wisdom she needs."

"God didn't keep my parents alive."

Luke hadn't given much thought to the amount of loss Bertie had already experienced in her short life. How could Ellis have sent this child-woman away from the only home she'd ever known? On the other hand, getting away from him was probably the best thing to have happened to her. He knew of nothing he could say that would remove her fear or make up for the losses she'd already endured. He chose his words carefully. "Bertie, I can't explain why God let your parents die, just like I can't explain why He let my dad die. He's too big for us to understand all His ways. But no matter what heartache He allows, we do know for sure that He loves us with a love that's far beyond our ability to comprehend. No matter how big the heartache, His love is even bigger. He loves Corrie more than we do; I can promise you that."

Bertie sat in silence, appearing to ponder his words. Finally she spoke. "Do you love Corrie, Luke?"

In all his thinking about Corrie, he'd carefully avoided that particular word. Hearing it spoken aloud gave him a jolt, even while it felt exactly right. Yet, he didn't know how to answer the question. His feelings shouldn't be put into words until Corrie was ready to hear them. He sent up a quick prayer for guidance. Then before he could form a reply, Bertie spoke again.

"You don't have to say it. I can tell you love her. I hope she says yes when you ask her."

It surprised him how quickly her mind changed directions. At least she was no longer contemplating the possibility of Corrie's death. She apparently didn't realize the danger to the baby as well, and he had no intention of alerting her. "I need to ask you a favor, Bertie."

"Sure." The customary lilt was back in her voice.

"Corrie isn't ready to hear how I feel about her just yet. Can I trust you to keep it a secret?"

She studied him with an expression of womanly wisdom, which seemed to imply she knew more than he did.

"She wouldn't believe me even if I did tell her."

"That doesn't matter." Luke made his tone firm. "Corrie trusts me right now, and that's very important to me. If she discovers my feelings too soon, it could destroy her trust. That would hurt more than if she never is able to love me back. I need your promise, Bertie."

"Okay, I promise."

He still didn't feel comfortable with her knowledge, but the matter had been wrested out of his control. In some ways, she might have not yet matured into womanhood, but her intuition was obviously full-grown. One of these days some besotted young man was going to take young Bertie for granted and end up with the surprise of his life. Luke grinned. Men liked to think of women as the weaker sex; but the more time he spent around women, the less he thought of that theory. They might be physically less strong; but in matters of the heart and soul, they had more going for them than most men could ever hope for. "Are you ready to go inside yet, little sister?"

"No."

"It's probably not a good idea for you to sit out here alone, and I need to go down to the barn."

"I'll come with you."

"I wish you could, but young ladies don't hang out with men in barns."

She giggled. "Now you sound like Bess."

Her lightning-swift changes between womanhood and girlhood made him smile. "Your sister is right more often than we'd like her to be." He mentally debated for a moment as to whether his next thoughts should be spoken; then he surrendered to the impulse. "I'll tell you what, Bertie. If you go up to your room, Bess will probably just be relieved you're inside where it's safe. Stay quiet, and you might hear Matty out in the hall. When you do, slip out and ask her about Corrie. She might be able to help you feel better."

Bertie grinned and disappeared indoors.

Luke trudged down to the barn. There wasn't much he could do in the dark, but he couldn't tolerate being in the house and unable to do anything to alleviate Corrie's suffering. In the corner by the workshop, he once again dropped to his knees. "Almighty God," he whispered into the hay-scented night, "Your Scripture tells us that You know the plans You have for us. While I want Your plan for me to include Corrie, at this hour what I want even more is for her to live and for You to spare the life of her little one. You know Matty is doing all that can be done humanly. With Your mercy, do more than we can do." His words ceased, but his heart remained focused on his heavenly Father. Peace enveloped him. He continued in wordless prayer, even as his legs cramped. The burden in his soul made his physical discomfort negligible by comparison. He couldn't have said how long he knelt before the burden eased, but when he stood, his legs shook. Lighting a lantern, he made his way into the workshop, where an idea began to take shape. Work on the ranch had kept him away from the woodworking he loved. He knew sleep wouldn't come readily tonight, so he might as well do something he enjoyed. The pile of fine-grained, smooth wood under the bench would make a fine cradle. Through the rest of the night, his hands shaped and smoothed the wood while his soul sent prayers heavenward.

Chapter 6

Corrie woke to daylight streaming through the window. She felt sticky, achy, and still tired. She stretched, feeling the baby kick at the same time her leg cramped up so severely she let out a quiet cry. Instantly, Matty was by her side.

"Another contraction, Sweetie?"

Corrie could barely speak but managed to shake her head while straining to reach around her swollen belly to rub the cramped muscle. Matty read her body language and rubbed Corrie's leg with firm, experienced strokes.

"Ah, that's so much better." Corrie sighed as the pain abated. "I keep forgetting I can't tighten those muscles without penalty."

Matty massaged for a few more minutes, then lightly stroked Corrie's belly. "How's the baby?"

Corrie grinned. "Busy as ever."

"That's a good sign. Any cramping?"

Corrie pondered. "I don't think so. I feel sore but not crampy."

Matty's eyes shone with delight. "That's good news. You

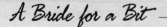

fell asleep around midnight and seemed to sleep peacefully, which tells me the contractions may have stopped."

"When can I have a bath?"

"I'll have Bess bring up some warm water, and I'll give you a sponge bath."

"I can do it."

"No, you can't." Matty's voice rarely took such a firm note with Corrie. "Sweetie, you're not moving out of this bed except to use a chamber pot."

"Matty!" Corrie heard the whine in her own voice and hated it even while she felt powerless to get rid of it. "I'll die of boredom up here!"

"No, my dear one, you won't. You'll save your baby's life."

The bald statement jolted Corrie. She felt the shock widen her eyes.

"I'm not exaggerating, Corrie. If the contractions hadn't stopped, if your baby had been born today, he or she wouldn't have had a chance. You need to do everything you can to keep that little one happy inside you for at least another month. That means you need to stay relaxed and quiet. The slightest bit of exertion could start your labor again, and it might not stop."

Corrie felt despicable tears fill her eyes. She turned her head toward the wall so Matty wouldn't see. If she lost this baby, her own life might as well end. But a month of being cooped up in this little room?

The first few days weren't as difficult as she'd expected. Her body seemed to crave sleep. Now there was no reason for her to resist the urge. Her naps frequently broke with the baby's activity or by her own bodily discomfort, but a change of position usually allowed her to drift back into slumber.

By the end of the week, however, her need for sleep became less acute. She had time to miss the rhythm of family life. Matty came in every morning with her breakfast and a sponge bath. Either Bess or Matty brought lunch and dinner. Matty usually stayed to chat while Corrie ate. Bess always inquired as to how Corrie felt, but she didn't linger.

In those hours of aloneness, Corrie couldn't help but contemplate the difference between her life as it was and the life she'd anticipated when she'd married Brian. He'd been a charming, jovial man. In fact, it had been Matty who had introduced him to the family. Corrie fully expected the two of them to make a match of it. But after only two visits, Brian started singling out Corrie. Thinking back, she shook her head at her own naïveté. She'd thought he was just being polite. Though she felt attracted to him, she'd kept her feelings out of sight, in deference to her sister. The night Brian had asked her permission to court her, she'd felt as though someone had tipped her world sideways. She'd refused to give him an answer until she'd talked with Matty.

Matty had assured her there was nothing romantic between her and Brian. "He views me like a sister," she'd said. "I can't think of anyone I'd rather see courting my other half."

Six months later, Corrie and Brian were married, Corrie wearing a gown stitched by Matty. Their marriage was better than anything Corrie could have dreamed. Occasionally, she wondered if she'd stolen happiness from Matty. She knew now that wasn't the case. Brian had never put the sparkle in Matty's eyes that Jim Collingswood had created almost from the first moment he and Matty met.

The only flaw in Brian and Corrie's marriage had been the lack of children. Corrie had so wanted to start a family right away, but month after month passed with no pregnancy. At long last, two years after their wedding day, Corrie knew her prayers had been answered. Three days after she'd told Brian their good news, an Atlantic storm swept him off the fishing boat and out of her life. A scant two months later, she was on the train with her sisters, history's most reluctant mail-order bride.

Tears flooded her eyes again and ran down her cheeks. She hadn't wept much over her loss. The pain had been too deep for tears, and the future too frightening. Now as she lay in a warm bed, surrounded by her sisters' tenderness and without the distraction of work, her pent-up grief began to flow freely. She couldn't lay facedown to weep into her pillow, so she pulled the blanket up to her face and stifled her sobs in the scratchy wool. She allowed herself to weep until it felt as if every drop of moisture had been wrung from her body. Matty would probably say she shouldn't cry so hard, for the baby's sake, but her sorrow refused to be denied its rightful release.

When the storm abated, she carefully eased herself out of bed. Matty had left the washbasin on the bureau. Corrie dipped a cloth in the now-tepid water, wrung it out, and then buried her face in the soothing coolness. The raw knot in the vicinity of her heart felt less tangled, less stabbing in its pain. Tears still ran but less intensely. It likely wasn't the last time she'd weep over the loss of her mate, but she felt a small measure of healing. Returning to bed lest Matty catch her upright, Corrie snuggled down into the covers and let a peaceful sleep claim her. She didn't wake until Matty brought her lunch.

The days passed, and Corrie came to relish her imposed solitude. She remembered, she wept, and she felt herself become stronger. One afternoon as she reminisced over her wedding, she recalled a private moment with Mama.

"I decided years ago I'd give this to whichever one of you girls married first," Mama had said, placing her big black Bible in Corrie's hands. "May it give you as much wisdom in raising your family as it's given me."

Corrie had treasured the link with her mother, especially after Mama's death a mere three months later. Still she'd spent little time reading the Book itself. Her life had been too full of Brian and new love. Yet, when gathering her meager belongings for the trip west, Mama's Bible had been the first thing she'd put in her trunk.

Devoutly hoping Matty wouldn't make a surprise visit, Corrie waddled to the trunk, which sat under the window. After just a few moments of digging, her fingers encountered the smooth, hard outlines of a book. She closed the trunk and carried the Bible back to her bed. She had no idea how long she lay there, tracing the edges of the Bible with her fingertips, remembering Mama. This had been one of her most treasured possessions. Though Mama had worked long hours every day, helping Papa in the dairy and raising her five daughters, each morning and each evening found her cradling the Book in her lap as she sat in her rocking chair. From an early age, her daughters knew not to disturb Mama when her Bible lay open before her.

Corrie had made her own profession of faith at ten years

of age, mostly in response to Mama's strong, yet quiet, faith. Corrie wanted to be like Mama in every way, and faith was part of the package. But it had been an inherited faith, not her own. When her parents had been killed and then when news of Brian's death had come, faith wasn't where she turned first. It had been Matty who had bolstered them both, whose faith had kept them going.

Now Corrie felt a longing for a personal faith. She opened the Bible, not sure where she should start reading. One passage, then another, caught her attention, the words familiar from the many times Mama had read Scripture aloud. But nothing made her linger until some underlined words in John's Gospel beckoned. "Let not your heart be troubled: ye believe in God, believe also in me."

She couldn't remember a time when she hadn't had an abstract belief in God. But Jesus Himself was saying it wasn't enough. She scanned the surrounding verses and realized He was talking with His disciples, and yet it felt like a message designed for her personally. The verses that followed talked about keeping His commandments and then about Him sending the Comforter to be with them.

She gazed unseeingly at the wall across from her. A prayer formed deep within, though she didn't speak the words aloud. *Father God, I feel like I've known about You all my life, but now I want to know You personally, the way Jesus said we can. I need Your comfort, and I also need Your wisdom as I prepare to raise this child. . .* She paused. It was time to stop hiding from the truth. . .*these children alone. Please use these coming days of solitude and rest to help me learn to know You as my personal heavenly Father.*

❧

Luke once again dismissed the urge to prop a ladder on the side of the house and crawl up to Corrie's window. It had been almost a month since he'd seen her, counting the week he and Jim had been out herding before the crisis. It was practically unbearable knowing she lay just up the stairs and around a corner but as remote from him as if she'd returned to Rhode Island. Matty had assured him Corrie and the baby were doing well, but she had been adamant that Corrie would not be getting out of bed for any reason anytime soon.

He tried to hide his loneliness in work. After putting in a full day on the ranch, he spent evenings in the barn and workshop mending tack, sharpening tools, and his favorite activity—painstakingly crafting the cradle. He couldn't recall why his dad had originally purchased the wood. It was fine-grained, smooth, and straight, so it must have cost a fair bit. Perhaps he'd been planning a storage chest for Mom or a hope chest for Annie. Whatever the original intent, Luke was sure Dad wouldn't mind the use he'd found for it.

Still, suppertime remained the worst part of the day. For some reason, it was then that he missed Corrie most intensely. Perhaps it was seeing the tender glances between Jim and Matty and knowing that an entire evening of togetherness stretched before them. Maybe it was just knowing that only a layer of wood and two strong-minded women separated him from the woman who'd unknowingly claimed his heart.

Whatever the cause, he'd even contemplated eating his supper at the bunkhouse. But that would stir up questions he preferred to leave unspoken. He pushed the beans around on his plate, knowing he'd better eat them or explain why he couldn't.

Jim's teasing tone interrupted Luke's mental dilemma. "Hey, little brother, if your lower lip were any longer, you could just use it to scoop your food into your mouth."

Luke looked up to see not only Jim but Matty and Bess grinning at him. Okay, so maybe he wasn't as inscrutable as he wished, but did Jim have to draw attention to it? "Speaking of big mouths," he tossed back, not sure whether his animosity was genuine or part of the sibling habit of communication he and Jim had developed.

"I'm just worried about you." The grin on Jim's face belied the serious tone he tried to maintain. "You look lonely, even though you're sharing a table with your favorite brother and three beautiful women."

Though repartee usually flowed freely between the two of them, on this occasion, Luke couldn't think of a single reply. Anything he wanted to say would only invite more teasing or, worse, solicitous inquiry from one of the women. He just wanted to be alone in his misery.

As Bess stood to serve slices from a cake that ordinarily would have had him licking his lips in anticipated enjoyment, he stood as well. "If you ladies would excuse me, I need to make a final check on a couple of ailing heifers."

The look in Matty's eyes could have rivaled the expression on Rhubarb's face as she stalked Ramon. "If you happen to be finished in an hour, Corrie has said she'd like some company for a few minutes."

Chapter 7

Since Luke's "chores" in the barn had been merely an excuse to get away from the table, he stayed outside only as long as he felt necessary to maintain his deception. As soon as he returned indoors, he stepped into the small wash-up room just off to the side of the entrance. Mom had insisted on the small room when they were building the house. "I want to make it easy for you guys to wash the barnyard grime off before coming to my kitchen table," she'd stated firmly.

Even when they were the only ones in the house, he and Jim still adhered to the standard she'd set. But tonight, Luke took even more care with his cleanup. He shaved, praying he wouldn't nick himself in his haste. After changing the water, he washed his hands again, even scrubbing under his nails. In his room, he selected his "going to town" shirt and a clean pair of pants. Jim would likely tease him about "going courtin'," but Luke didn't care. He wasn't going to pay even a short visit to Corrie's domain while looking and smelling like a ranch hand. He paced as much as his tiny room would allow until enough time had elapsed that no one could tease him about being overeager.

Jim was seated at the kitchen table with a cup of coffee, apparently keeping Matty company while she washed dishes. Luke could hear the other two sisters discussing a difference of opinion in the parlor. Jim opened his mouth as if to say something, but a look from Matty quelled the comment.

She dried her hands, then moved toward the stairs. "I'll just go up to make sure Corrie is ready for company."

Thankfully, Jim's silence held in his wife's absence. Only after Luke had been given permission to go upstairs did he whisper, "You've got it bad."

Jim's brotherly needling evaporated from Luke's mind as soon as he saw Corrie. Her hair hung loose and shining. She sat up in bed, leaning against the wall for support, clothed in some sort of dark blue, thick garment. Maybe it was what his mother would have called a dressing gown. She looked pale, but her eyes held more vibrancy than he remembered.

"Luke, you can sit here." Matty gestured toward a steamer trunk situated under the window and covered with a cloth. "I have a few things to do in our room, so you two enjoy your visit." She left the door wide open as she departed.

Luke didn't know what to say. He wanted to take Corrie's hand in his, enfold her in an embrace, any physical contact just to assure himself that she really was well.

"I won't break if you say something," she teased.

He chuckled to hide his surprise. The Corrie he remembered was too wounded and fragile to tease. What had happened up here in the past three weeks? "You're looking well," he managed to say.

She smiled in acknowledgment. "I am well, better than

I've been in a long time. The rest has been good for me." Her hand lay on a large black Book by her side.

"You've been doing some reading?"

This time her smile glowed. "Yes. This was my mama's Bible, and I inherited it when I got married. I've finally been reading it."

Suddenly Luke understood the changes he detected in her face. Peace and healing had come to this fragile woman. Whatever had transpired between her and God had given her a strength he'd never guessed lay below the surface of her heartache.

"Isn't it amazing what God can tell us when we're finally able to listen?"

"Oh, it is!" The wonder in her voice caught at his heart. "Do you mind if I tell you what I've been reading today?"

"Not at all!" In fact, it would be a relief if she did most of the talking. He felt entranced by the changes he saw in her, his feelings intensified by the weeks of their separation. If he had to sit here just making conversation, he might say something that still needed to wait.

She opened her Bible to John's Gospel. Her gentle voice read a few verses, and then she went on to describe what the verses had come to mean to her. "I've never realized before how deep God's love for us is. I keep reading this one Gospel over and over. It seems every time I read it, I understand something new. Even the miracles Jesus did reflect His love for the people involved. Somehow, I'd always thought of Him as remote from human daily life. But He's not. He really cares!"

Luke couldn't help but grin in response. "I can't think of anything better to think about whether one is busy or confined to bed. I've been reminding myself often of how much He loves us. It helps to know He cares as much about my loved ones as I do."

Pink tinged her cheeks as she rubbed her huge belly. He could see in her eyes reflections of myriad thoughts chasing one another through her mind, but the blush gave him hope she'd heard, and maybe even accepted, the hint he'd just given her.

Before any more could be said, Matty bustled back into the room. "I hate to say it, but time's up. We need to get the little mama lying down again."

However, each night thereafter, Matty invited him upstairs again. The visits were always short, yet Luke felt a one-hour Bible study couldn't have encouraged his spirit more. Corrie obviously spent her hours alone not only reading Scripture but also in making its message practical. In his most private moments, Luke also hoped he wasn't imagining the development of an emotional bond between them.

The day before Thanksgiving, Matty pulled him aside. "Would you be willing to carry Corrie downstairs tomorrow so she can spend the day with us?"

He gaped at her while a multitude of disjointed thoughts tumbled through his mind. Delight at being given a reason to hold Corrie in his arms. Joy that her health was stable enough to allow her to participate in the holiday. Anticipation of having her around all day. Concern that the excitement might be too much for her. "Bringing her downstairs won't cause a relapse?"

Matty shrugged. "It's impossible to predict. At this point, though, if the baby does insist on coming, I think he or she would be big enough to make it. The benefit to Corrie of being part of the family celebration outweighs the risk."

"Have you talked with her about it?"

"Not yet. I thought I'd wait until after she eats breakfast in the morning. If there have been no complications in the night, then I'll tell her what we have planned. However," Matty looked sternly at him, though twinkles in her eyes softened the look, "I will count on you to help ensure that she doesn't overdo. I don't want her taking more than three steps by herself, and I don't want her sitting upright for more than half an hour."

Luke hadn't felt this elated since his dad had allowed him to drive the family buggy the first time. Of course, Jim had some observations to make as they did evening chores together. "I hear my wife has given you your assignment for tomorrow."

"Yup." Luke refused to say anything that would give Jim added ammunition.

"It seems significant to me that she didn't ask me, her husband, to help care for her sister. She asked a nonrelative, if you know what I mean. It's almost as if I smell romance in the air."

Luke focused on portioning just the right amount of hay for the horses they would keep corralled throughout the winter. "Perhaps she knows that you'll be so busy making moon eyes at her that you wouldn't be trustworthy for the job."

"Married men don't make moon eyes," Jim protested, as Luke had known he would.

Luke looked pointedly at the pitchfork Jim was aiming

at the back corner of the stall in question. "They usually don't muck out stalls for milk cows, either."

❧

No major activities were ever planned for the Rough Cs for Thanksgiving Day, so Luke was able to finish his routine chores before breakfast. He even cajoled enough hot water away from the bunkhouse to take to the barn for a bath in an old laundry tub he set up in the workshop. He didn't want any scent of sweat or animal to be clinging to him when he held Corrie in his arms. A shave followed. Thankfully, the women had done laundry earlier in the week and ironing yesterday, so his best shirt and jeans were fresh.

Bess grinned at him as he entered the ranch house. He couldn't recall ever having seen that expression on her face before. She looked delighted with what she saw as she looked at him, as if he'd passed some test he hadn't known about. "Matty said you can go upstairs whenever you want."

Bertie stood at the counter stirring something and not looking happy about it. But as soon as she saw Luke, her countenance changed. "For true, you look fine, Luke. Corrie's sure to be impressed."

"Bertie!" Bess protested, though her eyes twinkled with laughter.

Luke felt heat creep up his neck, but he held Bertie's gaze. "Thank you for the compliment, but let's allow Corrie to make up her own mind, okay?"

Her eyes told him she understood his unspoken message. Bess looked back and forth from Luke to Bertie as though knowing there was more communication than she was privy to. But she didn't pry. "Go on then. I'm sure Corrie's impatient."

But impatience wasn't what Luke heard in Corrie's voice as he reached the top of the stairs.

"Matty, you can't ask Luke to carry me." She sounded embarrassed. "I'm sure I weigh more than one of his horses."

"No, dear one, you just feel like you do." Matty's voice was gentle. Luke could envision her stroking Corrie's hair as she did so often. "For your baby's sake, let him do this, okay?"

"I just hate being so helpless." Luke now heard tears in Corrie's tone. The sound twisted his heart. He paused, both to give Corrie time to collect herself and to give him time to think of a way to ease the situation for her.

Jim probably would have had a wisecrack to make her laugh. But Luke didn't want her to feel as if he were making light of her distress. Slowly he made his way toward her room, thumping his freshly cleaned boots on the floor slightly to ensure the women heard his approach. Before he reached her doorway, he called out, "Is the queen ready?"

The giggle from within reassured him, though it was Matty who answered. "I believe she is."

The view that greeted Luke as he stepped through the doorway almost made him trip over his own feet. Corrie sat on the edge of her bed, clad in a long, flowing dress of some soft gray material that brought out the blue of her eyes and gave her maternal figure the look of elegance and grace. Braids encircled her head, though tendrils of hair dangled around her face. He couldn't help the words that fell out of his mouth. "You're beautiful!"

Corrie's cheeks turned deep rose. "That's stretching a

compliment, but thank you. Are you sure you're up to carrying me down the stairs? I'd never forgive myself if you injured yourself."

"Corrie." He spoke her name gently, then waited for her to look into his face. "I promise you as your friend that if you're too heavy, I'll tell you. Can you trust me to be honest?"

She studied his eyes, then sighed and nodded. "Okay."

"So if I don't complain, you promise not to give in to any sneaky feelings of guilt or embarrassment?"

"I'll try."

Before she could anticipate his actions, he slid one arm under her knees and the other around her waist. Instinctively, she curled one of her arms around his neck. "See? There's nothing to you. I've lifted feed bags that are heavier."

She giggled.

As he turned toward the door, he caught a glimpse of Matty's glistening eyes. What could he have said to make Matty cry? She was still smiling, though, so it must be all right.

Chapter 8

C orrie couldn't remember a more joyous Thanksgiving Day. She did feel awkward lounging in the parlor while her sisters did all the bustling and preparing, but the feeling didn't last long. Luke pulled a chair and a small table close to where she lay, then set up a checkerboard.

"It's been ages since I played checkers," she informed him. "I probably won't be much of a challenge."

"It's been ages since I played, too," he replied with the gentle, just-for-her smile that sent shivers all the way down her spine.

"And even when we played every day, he still wasn't very good," Jim offered, setting a plate of fresh-baked rolls on the table beside the checkerboard. "Bess sent these in to tide us over until lunch."

Corrie played a game with Luke, then watched the brothers compete against one another. The banter and affectionate insults didn't pause throughout the game. Bertie then joined them to play against Jim and then Corrie. Corrie felt as if her youngest sister spent more time studying her than the checkerboard, and she kept trying to reassure Bertie with smiles. Then she'd catch Bertie studying Luke, then seeming to try to study the two of them together. She'd never had the instinctive understanding of Bertie that Bess seemed to possess, but today's behavior was even more inexplicable than usual. Still, Corrie reached out to give Bertie a hug after the game was over. "Thanks for helping keep your useless big sister entertained."

The girl's gray-blue eyes flashed. "You're not useless!" With that, she left the room.

Corrie looked at Luke to see if he'd noticed the exchange. He nodded. "She's had a rough time of it while you've been laid up. She's been really worried about you, and Matty and Bess didn't explain much."

"It wouldn't be proper to tell her," Corrie explained in a rush of defensiveness.

"I know." Luke's tone became soothing. "That's what I told her, and I explained that I get told even less than she does. I'm not sure I helped, though. She's lost a lot in the past few years."

Corrie instantly felt ashamed. "I've been so absorbed in my own troubles, I haven't given much thought to how she feels."

"She's doing fine," Luke assured her. "She just needs a bit of reassurance now and then, like we all do."

It took Corrie several minutes to realize she was staring at him. She simply couldn't imagine him in need of reassurance about anything. Before she could pursue the thought, though, Matty called them to lunch. Just that quickly, Luke scooped her up. He held her so lightly she could almost believe that he didn't notice her weight. It felt good to be supported by his strong arms, to have her arms around his shoulders. It felt as if they were pieces of a puzzle designed for each other. Before the thought could disturb her unduly, the rest of the family assembled around the table.

"Before I ask the blessing, I'd like to begin by stating what I'm thankful for," Jim said, reaching for Matty's hand. "I'm thankful that, before I even realized I needed a wife, God sent a perfect helpmate to me. . .dropped her at my feet, so to speak."

Matty turned pink, and her three sisters laughed aloud at the memory of Matty's ungraceful introduction to Jim. When she could make herself heard, Matty spoke. "I'm thankful for Corrie's continued good health."

Corrie thought she heard a quiet, masculine sounding "amen" from Luke's place beside her. "I'm grateful that God has given Matty the joy of marriage and the four of us a place to live," she said.

Bess spoke next. "I'm thankful the four of us are able to continue to be together and that we've come to a place where women's opinions matter."

There was a pause until Luke prompted gently, "Bertie?"

Bertie looked at her hands in confusion, then at each of her sisters before speaking. "I'm glad, too, that we're together and that Corrie is okay."

"I think we're all in agreement on that, Bertie," Luke replied. "I'm also grateful God sent the four of you to share our home for as long as He leaves you with us. I know I'm stuck with Matty for the rest of her life, but I hope the other three of you never feel you have to be in a hurry to leave here. Our home is your home for as long as you like." His words addressed the three of them, but his gaze never left Corrie's.

"Thank you, Luke," Bess responded, saving Corrie the trouble of forming a reply that wouldn't embarrass her. "Now, Jim, if you wouldn't mind asking the blessing so we can eat before the food gets cold."

Corrie grinned to herself. Emotion would never get out of hand with Bess around to remind them all of practicalities. Jim's prayer was short, as usual, and then the serving dishes began to make their way around the table. Corrie felt she couldn't possibly do justice to all the wonderful food. She took just a dab of this and a bit of that, hoping to be able to sample everything. Still, she felt uncomfortably full by the time the meal ended. The babies had grown so big that her stomach didn't have room for much more than a snack. In a couple of hours, she'd be hungry again.

Luke carried her back to the parlor, and Matty followed them. "How are you feeling, Corrie? Not too tired?"

"I think I'm ready for a rest," Corrie admitted, "but, no, not too tired. It's been wonderful being back with the family."

"It's been wonderful having you back," Matty assured her with a hug. "Now just don't overdo so we can keep you here."

By the time Luke carried her upstairs that evening, Corrie felt ready for the quiet of her room. It had been a day full of fun, laughter, and family togetherness, but her very bones felt tired. Her back ached. Her stomach still felt overstretched from lunch. She let Matty help her into a sleeping gown; then she settled gratefully into bed. But sleep didn't come easily or linger long. She kept feeling Luke's arms around her. Had she ever felt such safety in Brian's embrace? She tried to recall a time Brian had carried her, but no such memory surfaced to banish the memory of Luke's arms. Was she falling in love with the gentle-eyed rancher? Had she loved Brian as truly as she ought if she could replace him so quickly?

It took Matty only a single glance the next morning to declare Corrie bedridden for another day. "We must have worn you out, dear one," she said. "Your eyes look like burnt holes in a blanket."

Corrie didn't object. While she doubted how much sleep she'd get, she needed time alone to get her emotional bearings again. After a restless nap, she turned once more to John's Gospel and to the verses that had first caught her attention. "Let not your heart be troubled. . .I will not leave you comfortless. . . ." The words brought peace, if not physical comfort.

It seemed no matter how she lay on the bed, her back ached. When Matty brought lunch, Corrie refused it. "I feel like if I eat anything, I'll throw up."

Matty's eyebrows knit with what Corrie termed her "doctor frown." "Any cramps?"

"No, but my back aches miserably."

Matty helped Corrie turn onto her side, facing the wall, then rubbed the lower part of her spine. "Right here?"

"Ahhh, yes," Corrie breathed. But the relief didn't last long. "Oooh, now that hurts worse."

Matty instantly stopped rubbing Corrie's back, moving her hands to Corrie's arm instead, where she stroked gently. "How about if I get a hot pack?"

❧

Luke was just finishing his second cinnamon roll after lunch when Matty came back downstairs from taking lunch to

Corrie. A single look at her face put knots of tension in his shoulders. "She's having trouble again?"

Matty nodded. "Bess, we need some tea towels dipped in water as hot as you can stand, then wrung out. Luke and Jim, we need the water reservoir on the stove filled, as well as a large potful to heat on the stove." She studied Bertie for a moment, as if deep in thought. "Bertie, I need you to go through what's left of the flour sacks. We're going to need lots of cloths, so I'll need you to take the seams out. Choose patterns that we can't do much with. That purple one would be a good start."

Through the haze of his concern, Luke was glad to see Bertie's eyes brighten. Apparently, all she needed was to feel useful. He pushed back from the table, pocketing the remnant of his cinnamon bun. He'd lost interest in eating it, but Ramon usually enjoyed the table scraps he sneaked out of the house for him. On the way to the pump, he tossed the bun to the dog, who gobbled it. With energy brought on by worry, Luke had two buckets filled with water before Jim joined him. No words were exchanged as the brothers passed one another. Luke read in his brother's eyes the same concern he felt.

Once inside the kitchen, though, he found Matty waiting for him. "I need you upstairs."

Undeniable fear gripped him. "What's wrong?"

A skeleton of a smile crossed her face. "Corrie's asking for you. It may not be socially acceptable, but if your being there will help keep her calm, I won't stand in the way."

Luke stayed by Corrie's side throughout the afternoon and long after night fell. He lent his support when she insisted on pacing the hallway and helped Matty keep fresh hot packs against Corrie's back when she lay down. As the hours passed, Corrie's discomfort increased. It tore at his heart to hear her moans. When she squeezed his hand until it went numb, he willed the gesture to impart some of her pain to him.

Just as dawn was beginning to lighten the sky, he helped Corrie to her feet once more. She draped her arms over his shoulders and leaned against him as another spasm gripped her. Without warning, a gush of water poured over their feet. Matty instantly banished him from the room. "Go get Bess."

"Luke!" Corrie's voice was hoarse.

"He can't stay, dear one," Matty informed her tenderly. Though exhaustion ringed her eyes, not a trace of it showed in her tone.

Corrie looked up into Luke's face as she still clung to him. He marveled that she seemed to draw strength from his presence. He felt the bond between them, even though propriety didn't yet allow them to acknowledge it aloud. "Corrie," he whispered, "I'll stay right outside your room, okay? I won't stop praying until this is all over."

She nodded and allowed him to loosen her grip on his shoulders. He and Matty eased her onto the bed, and he left the room quickly before another spasm could take her. If he heard her pain-filled cry, not even his respect for Matty would keep him from fighting to stay by Corrie's side.

Bess responded instantly to his call. It seemed forever before she came out of the room again, her arms full of sodden-looking clothing. "Matty says it shouldn't be long now," she whispered. In moments, she reappeared, this time carrying a chair. Without comment, she positioned the chair outside

Corrie's doorway, then vanished back downstairs.

Luke couldn't have said whether minutes or hours passed. The chair stood watch as he paced the length of the hallway, sending wordless appeals from his heart to his heavenly Father. All at once, his absorption was broken by a small cry, hardly louder than Rhubarb's kittens. Then Matty appeared in the doorway, bearing a hastily wrapped bundle. "Take her, quick, and call Bess to come clean her up." She vanished back into the bedroom and closed the door.

He peered down at the squalling infant barely filling his two hands together. What could he possibly know about how to hold a baby? The thought had only a moment to register before the tiny eyes fluttered open. They gazed at him without recognition or focus, but Luke fell instantly in love. "So you're a girl, Matty said," he murmured, tucking the little one closer to his chest. "Welcome to the Rough Cs. You're most welcome here, little princess."

Before he reached the head of the stairs, Bess came barreling up, taking them two at a time. He wanted to grin at the uncharacteristic behavior, then at the joy of what he held in his hands, then at anything at all. "Matty say she's a girl and to get you to clean her up."

Bess reached for the baby. "Where's Matty? Is Corrie okay?"

Luke suddenly recalled Matty's haste in returning to the bedroom. Fear seared him once again. "I don't know. She seemed—"

The squalling of the infant Bess held suddenly became amplified. It took him a moment to realize a second cry had joined the first. Bess understood first. "Twins?" she asked, her voice cracking with amazement. "It's obviously a family thing." She headed down the stairs with her little bundle while Luke hurried to respond to Matty's second appearance in the doorway.

"Twin girls," she announced, surrendering the second bundle to Luke. "Ask Bess to get her cleaned up, too, then bring them back for Corrie to see right away."

"Is Corrie okay?" This time Luke's attention wasn't going to be stolen by feminine wiles, no matter how tiny or inexperienced.

Matty smiled broadly. "She is. She's tired but in good shape."

Relief flowed through him so strongly he felt his legs tremble. Matty placed her hands beneath his as he held the baby. "Careful, don't drop her. When you bring the babies back, I'll let you see Corrie for yourself."

It seemed to take forever for Bess to get the little ones cleaned up and wrapped in blankets. He held the first as she took care of the second. Then she placed the second little one in his other arm. He relished the armful. "Go ahead," Bess said, her eyes shining. "You deserve the honor of delivering them both to their mama."

He'd never taken the stairs so carefully, yet so joyously. The longer he held these little ones, the more he felt his heart being overtaken by them. He'd witnessed birth many times in the barn, but nothing could compare to the wonder of the human life he held.

Matty held the door open for him as he approached. Then he was beside Corrie's bed, where somehow he managed to kneel in spite of his cherished burden. Her face was still lined with the agony and effort of the night, but she'd never looked more beautiful to him. "Corrie, I'd like you to meet your daughters," Matty said as she helped him lay first one, then the other, on Corrie's chest. She looked down at the babies, radiance replacing the night's imprint on her features. "They're beautiful," she whispered. "Twins, just like us, Tilde. Thank you." She looked first at her sister, then held Luke's gaze for a long moment. "Thank you, too." Her attention returned to her daughters. Luke slipped out of the room and made his way quickly outside to the barn. He needed privacy before the tears of relief, joy, and love escaped.

Chapter 9

orrie floated for days on the euphoria of love for her babies, whom she named Brianne and Madeline, after their father and their aunt. Though her body was sore and unbroken sleep seemed but a distant memory, she couldn't get enough of watching them, touching them, feeding them, caring for them. She had no idea how she would have managed without the ready assistance of her sisters. They kept the never-ending pile of laundry from taking over her room, brought her meals, and cuddled one fussy baby while she nursed the other.

In the evenings, she ventured downstairs. There she found both Jim and Luke eager to take their turns with the babies. She turned to mush inside every time she saw one of the big ranchers so tenderly cradling one of her daughters. One night, she caught tears in Matty's eyes as Jim cooed to Madeline. Though Matty had a tender heart, she was rarely moved to tears. Was something amiss? Corrie studied her twin and decided the little ones had turned them all to mush.

Almost before she could catch a breath, Christmas arrived. The celebration wasn't the rollicking noisy time she remembered from her childhood, but the quietness of it suited her mood this year. She was surprised to find that each of her sisters had made gifts for her daughters, as well as for her. Matty and Bess had sewn her loose, front-opening dresses. Each garment came with a belt, which would pull in some of the fullness as she regained her figure. They'd also sewn a pile of baby nighties, which they presented, wrapped in two soft blankets.

"Wherever did you get such soft fabric?" Corrie asked as she fingered the edges.

Matty and Bess exchanged smiles. "We bought it before we left Rhode Island," Matty explained, "knowing you'd need baby-type Christmas presents. There's enough fabric left for two larger blankets for when they're older."

Bertie had carved a lovely wooden plaque with the babies' names and birth dates. "That's all I had time to do," she explained. "I hope you don't mind having them share it."

Corrie embraced her younger sister, touched by the uncertainty in her eyes. "It's a perfect gift, Bertie. I'll treasure it always."

She hadn't noticed Luke leave the room, but now he appeared, lugging a large, burlap-wrapped object. "My present is mostly for the babies, but I hope you'll like it, too." He set it in front of her.

Corrie slowly pulled the burlap away. "Ohhhh," she breathed in wonder, running her fingers over an intricately carved wooden cradle. "It's even wide enough for both of them."

He grinned. "I did have to expand it after they arrived. Now that winter is here, I plan to make another so they can each have their own bed when they're too big to share this one. For now, though, I thought they'd be happier sleeping together."

Her eyes filled with the tears that never seemed far away. She'd noticed the girls did prefer to sleep not only together, but touching one another. That he'd so accurately perceived her children's needs touched her more deeply than his ever-present concern for her. As she blinked away the tears, she noticed a cutout carving at one end of the cradle. Four intertwined hearts. She counted them again to be sure the tears hadn't warped her vision. Four.

She looked into his eyes. His steady gaze held hers, and she knew. As always, he wouldn't press his suit. The cradle was his declaration just the same. If she wanted his heart, he was ready to give it. Not just to her, but to all three of them. She smiled her thanks, then held out her arms for her babies, who were being cuddled by Bess and Bertie. "Time for mama and babies to have a rest." Her emotions had suddenly become too much for her, strangling her thoughts. She needed to get away to collect herself.

"May I bring the cradle up?" Luke asked softly.

She nodded and then made her way upstairs. It took a bit of shifting around to get the furniture arranged in such a way that she wouldn't bang her legs on something every time she moved, but eventually they found a solution. She settled the sleeping little ones in their new bed and nudged the rocker with her foot to set it in motion. "It's beautiful, Luke. Thank you."

"I enjoyed making it," he answered softly, one large finger tracing the hearts as the cradle rocked.

When the door thumped closed behind him, somehow his gentle presence lingered behind.

❧

As the New Year unfolded, the babies grew and Corrie regained her strength. She delighted in returning to the routine of the family life the six of them had established. Her life still centered around the babies, but there was always an extra pair of arms ready to cuddle them while she finished kneading a batch of bread or baking a panful of cookies.

Her connection with her twin didn't suffer, either. Though no one else commented on it, she noticed Matty's pallor in the mornings. Sensing what might be the trouble, Corrie did her best to make sure coffee was ready before Matty came downstairs so she wouldn't have to smell it being prepared. If there were meats to fry or other strong-smelling foods to prepare, she did what she could to relieve Matty of the chore. She wondered when Matty would be ready to announce her happy news to the rest of the family.

In addition, there was always an undercurrent of awareness shimmering between her and Luke. Their gazes often locked over the supper table or across the room. She no longer wore her mourning brooch because it tended to get in the way while she was feeding the little ones. Somehow, she didn't miss its weight.

One evening in early February, Corrie stood at the sink washing supper dishes. The chatter of the family swirled around her, and she reveled in it. She just was happy tonight, and it felt good after so many months of mourning and uncertainty. Bess sat at the end of the table with Brianne in her arms. Luke sat beside her, holding Madeline.

"Aren't you just the prettiest girls," Bess cooed. "You look just like your daddy, but you're still pretty, pretty, pretty. Your hair is curly like his, and you have his twinkly eyes."

Embarrassment and shame sliced into Corrie like twin knives. She hadn't noticed the resemblance; but now that Bess mentioned it, how could she have missed it? She hadn't been looking for their similarity to Brian. She'd been so caught up in the pink haze of her attraction to Luke, she'd not even considered her daughters' father, the one whose love had helped bring them into being. Hot tears filled her eyes as she rinsed the last few dishes and placed them on the counter to dry. Then, still blinking back the tears, she gathered Madeline and Brianne into her arms and carried them to her room. Tears dripped on their little heads as she nursed them and on their bellies as she changed their diapers. When she settled them into the cradle, she reached for her brooch on the bureau, and her weeping began in earnest.

She worked hard to keep her crying silent, both to avoid disturbing her daughters and to keep Matty from hearing her distress. There was no way she could discuss this with anyone. Yes, she cared deeply about Luke, but how could she do so if she'd truly cared about Brian? It hadn't been even a year since his death.

She forced herself to remember the awful day when she had become a widow. Her heart still ached over the loss, but she no longer felt emotionally crippled by it. Should she be able to recover so easily? She opened the brooch to stroke the lock of Brian's hair within. The hair could have belonged to anyone, for all the comfort it brought her.

Sleep eluded her, even in the hours when her daughters

slept. Every time she tried to slip into slumber, her thoughts chased one another in endless tangles, never creating a solution. Her love for Brian still caused her heart to ache. Yet her growing love for Luke demanded equal attention. What kind of woman could love two men?

The next morning, she didn't even try to go downstairs. As she expected, Matty came to check on her, looking no better than Corrie felt. "Are you okay, dear one?"

"Just a rough night." Corrie tried to manage a small smile. "You don't look so great yourself. When are you going to announce your news?"

Matty enfolded Corrie in a delighted, though shaky, embrace. "I should have known I couldn't hide it from you. Jim knows, but we're waiting another few weeks before we say anything. We like having our own secret."

Tears again pushed at Corrie's eyes, remembering hers and Brian's similar feelings not so long ago. "Don't push yourself too hard, okay? Remember what you told me—if something makes you sick, don't do it."

"Yes, Mother," Matty responded with mock resignation. "Would you like me to bring you some breakfast?"

"Only if it won't make you lose yours," Corrie answered, reaching for Madeline, who'd begun yelling for her own breakfast.

Just that easily a new routine established itself. Matty brought Corrie's meals and carried out the laundry. Corrie and her daughters remained ensconced in the bedroom, the one place where Corrie wouldn't have to face Luke or deal with her feelings. Without the distraction of his presence, her grief for Brian settled back into place, comforting in its familiarity and yet, if she were completely honest, feeling like a shoe that had worn through the sole.

Three days passed. Corrie's grief spent itself. The babies grew restless, having become accustomed to more company than just their mother. "You need to get used to this," Corrie told both herself and them. "The day will come soon when it will just be the three of us."

The conclusion had come to her slowly but settled in with certainty. As soon as the girls were eating solid food, she planned to move to town and resume her bakery business. She and her sisters had planned to make the jail habitable. Why couldn't she do it for herself and the babies? She knew it wouldn't be easy to meet their needs and support all of them financially, but it was what she needed to do. If, by the twins' first birthday, the attraction between her and Luke remained strong, then she would allow herself to put Brian's memory to rest.

A knock sounded on the door. "Come in," she said, expecting Matty.

Instead, Luke answered. "Are you decent?"

Panic coursed through her. She hadn't expected him to breach her hideaway. "No, I'm not. Just set my food out there, and I'll get it when I'm finished with the girls."

But the babies had heard his voice, and both started howling. She rocked the cradle, trying to settle them, but to no avail.

"Sounds like you need a hand."

At the repeated sound of his voice, the babies wailed even louder, and he had the nerve to laugh. "Sounds like they won't give you any peace until you let me in."

"Okay, come in, then." Corrie had to raise her voice to make herself heard.

Luke pushed the door open with his foot, carrying a plate in one hand and a tall glass of milk in the other. "Why don't I entertain the ladies while you eat?"

Corrie's stomach rumbled. One penalty of her self-imposed exile had been having to wait for food until Matty brought it rather than snacking whenever she felt hungry. Her appetite seemed insatiable these days. Gratefully, she accepted the plate.

Luke took a seat on the trunk and somehow lifted both babies into his lap. They stopped fussing, and both gazed at him intently. The shadow of Brian's memory threatened to fade in the bright light of the moment. Corrie forced herself to remember her grief.

Then she became aware of Luke talking. She focused on her food, but his words trickled into her consciousness. "What have you little girls been doing to make your mommy look so worn out? You shouldn't work her so hard, you know. She's a wonderful lady." The babies cooed at him, and Corrie couldn't suppress a smile. "I'm glad you agree. You see, I need to tell you a secret. Your mommy loves a man whom I know must have been one of the best God ever created. She wouldn't have loved him if he weren't. He was your daddy. Then he had to go live in heaven and left your mommy all alone and very sad. I'm hoping one of these days, when she's less sad, she'll let me love her and you, too. I hope she'll tell me more about your daddy so I can help you get to know him at least a little. I wouldn't blame her if she didn't have room in her heart for more than one man, but I'm hoping that she will." He paused, leaned close to the girls, and whispered, "Someday."

Madeline let out a giggle and then Brianne did the same. Corrie looked at Luke in astonishment. "Do it again! See if they'll laugh."

He leaned close and whispered again, "Someday."

The girls grinned and then giggled again.

At that moment, Corrie gave up the struggle to keep her heart barricaded against Luke. There before her was the evidence. Her daughters needed a living man who could cuddle them, tell them stories, and, yes, make them laugh. She couldn't be everything to them; and with the bounty of Luke's love being offered to her, there was no need for her to try.

The passage from John's Gospel, which had sustained her through the long days of her bed rest, came to mind again. "Let not your heart be troubled."

She reached out to trace the hearts on the cradle's headboard. "Babies, tell Luke that someday is here."

Prepare your favorite bread dough recipe. Let rise until double. Punch down, and separate out the equivalent of one loaf. Flatten this portion of bread dough to about ¼ inch thick. Spread thickly with butter, then with enough sugar to cover well. Sprinkle with plenty of cinnamon. Roll dough together to form log shape.

Melt two tablespoons of butter in the bottom of a baking pan. Slice log into ½-inch slices, and place slices cut-side down in the baking pan. When pan is full, let buns rise until doubled in size.

Bake in moderate heat in oven until buns are golden brown on top. Remove from oven and turn pan upside-down over cloth to let cool.

JANELLE BURNHAM SCHNEIDER
Janelle published her first five books with **Heartsong Presents** under her maiden name of Janelle Burnham. She put her writing aside during her own true-to-life romance, wedding, and the birth and infancy of her two children. Writing soon became a desire she could no longer ignore. As a military wife, she has lived various places across Canada, including British Columbia, New Brunswick, and Alberta, collecting new story ideas and learning much about real romance.

From Pride to Bride

by JoAnn A. Grote

Chapter 1

May 1869

From the hay-filled back of the Collingswood brothers' spring wagon, Bess Craig looked out at the crowd gathered in front of the Lickwind jailhouse for the Sunday service and bit back a groan.

Luke Collingswood looked back over his shoulder from the wagon seat and chuckled. "Looks like your usual admiration society is gathered, Bess."

"I'd be more impressed if I thought even one of those men came to worship the Lord instead of to ogle Bertie and me."

Beside her, Matty laughed softly. "Maybe the Lord's using you and Bertie to bring these men to hear His Word."

"Perhaps, but I doubt their ears are open."

The Craig sisters had been in Lickwind almost a year, and the bold attentions of the male population still amazed and unnerved Bess. A number of men had asked for her hand during that year, not even bothering to suggest the civilized tradition of courting. The winter months at the ranch had offered some, but not total, respite.

As Luke reined the horses to a stop, Bess glanced at the sky. Gray clouds rolled over each other. They'd been a mere shadow on the horizon when the group left the Rough Cs Ranch an hour earlier. No one had expected to encounter rain. Lickwind seldom saw more than a foot of rain in an entire year, as the area's sand and sagebrush testified.

"May I assist you, Miss Craig?" The portly banker extended his hand as Bess moved to climb down from the wagon.

"Thank you, Mr. Llewellyn."

As soon as her high-buttoned shoes touched the ground, she removed her hand from his and turned back to help her sisters. She didn't want to give Mr. Llewellyn any reason to believe she'd welcome his company at the service.

"I'll take the baby." Bess reached for Brianne bundled in Matty's arms, then waited while Jim gently helped Matty from the wagon bed. Even such simple things as climbing down from a wagon were difficult for Matty with a babe expected to arrive in another month.

Luke rounded the back of the wagon. "Thanks, Bess. I'll take Brianne now."

Bess couldn't keep back a smile as she handed the baby to her father. He so obviously loved holding his children. She found it endearing.

She started toward the jail, her sisters and brothers-in-law close behind her. Immediately, the wind caught her gray cape and her dress's black-and-gray-striped skirt. In spite of her attempts to keep her skirt vertical, it danced about, revealing more of her ruffled petticoat than modesty allowed. Her face heated. The Wyoming wind waged a constant battle with the

Craig sisters for their skirts and propriety.

The men who crowded the street between the jailhouse and the railroad tracks stepped back to make a path for Bess and her sisters. Men pulled their hats from their heads. Their greetings mixed into one. "Morning, Miss Craig."

"Good morning." Bess nodded at no one in particular, keeping her gaze on the open door.

When she reached it, she discovered more men filled the one-room building to capacity. Lean, dark-haired Parson Harris stood just within the doorway. "Good morning, Miss Craig. I believe I'll need to hold the service outside. Wonderful the Lord brought so many people." He smiled broadly.

"Certainly is, Parson," agreed Mr. Llewellyn, who had followed right behind Bess. "Afraid your congregation is going to get a mite wet, though."

A rumble sounded overhead as if to confirm the statement. A moment later, a large raindrop splashed in the dirt at Bess's feet.

Bess stepped quickly aside to clear the doorway. "Corrie, Luke, you'd best get inside. We don't want those babes getting wet."

There was barely room for the four, even after Parson Harris stepped outside to allow more space.

The clouds opened and the rain filled the air with a *sh-sh-sh*. Men slapped their hats back on their heads. Bess and her sisters pulled their capes tighter and ducked their heads so their hat brims kept the worst of the rain from their eyes.

"Some of you gentlemen move outside," Parson Harris called into the building, "and make room for the ladies."

"We need someplace larger." Bess raised her voice to cover the sound of rain and restless men's shuffling feet.

"There isn't anywhere else," Luke reminded her.

Bess nodded briskly. "Yes, there is. Follow me."

The crowd parted again as she started through it. As soon as there was enough room, she broke into a run, one hand clasping her bonnet to her head, the other hand clasping her skirt to keep it from tangling with her legs. She knew from the sound of boots hitting the earth behind her that others followed.

"Where are we going?" Bertie asked from beside her.

Bess didn't answer. They'd already reached her destination. The heels of her shoes clunked against the saloon's boardwalk when she stepped onto it. The wooden awning offered welcome relief from the rain, which came down harder every minute.

"Bess?" Jim Collingswood's voice held a note of trepidation.

The saloon's large wooden doors were shut tight, hiding the batwing doors that offered customers easy access and tempted them with sounds of piano music and revelry during business hours. Bess pounded her fists against the door.

"Bess Craig, have you gone loco?" Jim grabbed one of her hands. "We can't hold church services in a saloon."

"We're closed," an angry voice announced from the other side of the door.

Bess continued beating with her free hand.

"Hold your horses," the voice demanded. The door swung open, revealing an unshaven man with wavy, golden brown hair, which reached to his shoulders. A black patch covered his left eye. It took all Bess's courage not to step back at the sight of him.

Anger spit from Gideon Riker's unpatched eye. "Can't you see we're—?" Anger changed to confusion when he saw Bess, then the crowd behind her.

"We need to use your saloon—that is, would you allow us to use your saloon for church services?" Bess amended.

Gideon's incredulous gaze met hers. "Church services?"

She lifted her chin and met his brown-eyed gaze un-flinching. "Yes. It's raining, and yours is the only building large enough to accommodate everyone. Since you're not open for business, I was certain you'd wish to offer your premises."

Gideon hastily slid brown suspenders up over the shoulders of his gray Union Jack top, as if suddenly aware he stood before the entire town.

Behind Bess, Parson Harris cleared his throat. "We'll understand if you don't want us here, Mr. Riker."

Bess sidled past the saloon owner and into the building. "Of course he'll allow us to use his establishment."

The eyebrow above Gideon's patchless eye rose slightly as he watched Bess. She lifted her chin higher, silently challenging him to deny her statement. A drop of water fell from her hat brim and splashed onto her nose. She blinked in surprise.

Gideon's lips twitched into a smirk. He stepped back, opening the door wider. "I will not only allow it, Parson, I insist." He invited the crowd inside with a wave of one hand.

The matter decided to her satisfaction, Bess turned to survey the temporary chapel.

A boy of about ten, his long red hair falling over his forehead, stood beside the bar. He stared at her with wide eyes.

Was that Gideon Riker's boy? She hadn't heard Gideon had a son, but then, there was no reason anyone should have mentioned the child to her. She flashed him a brief smile and continued to scan the building. She'd been inside for Ellis's trial, but she'd been too worried about the outcome to pay much attention to her surroundings. Besides, the room had been cleaned and rearranged before the trial.

The yeasty odor of beer filled her nostrils. The room was dark, even with the light through the windows and door. The walls were unpainted and the floor bare. Round tables surrounded by chairs stood about the room. A couple of chairs lay on their backs. Empty bottles and glasses stood on the tables and on the bar, which stretched across the opposite wall. A man appeared to be sleeping at one of the tables, but she couldn't be certain since he wasn't facing her direction.

"Amos, get Doc out of here," Gideon ordered the blacksmith. Bess caught her breath in surprise. The man sleeping off a drinking spree was Dr. Mitchel. Thank the Lord, Luke hadn't allowed that man near Corrie when she delivered her babies.

"Harry, where are you?" Gideon called, searching the crowd. The barkeep who'd played piano at the Craig sisters' weddings—a young man who looked about eighteen—stepped out. "Clean off these tables," Gideon ordered. The boy jumped to business.

The crowd trailed in. Some of the men seated themselves at the dirty tables. Some stood along the wall. A number of them chuckled and snickered at the situation.

Gideon, his hands full of bottles, waved toward the room. "Could use a little help here. You don't expect people to worship before the place is cleaned up, do you?"

Looking shamefaced, men stepped forward to help.

Bess noticed her sisters and brothers-in-law stood near the door. Jim gripped one of Bertie's arms, as though to make sure none of the town's rowdy men walked away with her. Probably wise.

Ever-helpful Matty reached for an empty glass on the table in front of her. Jim grabbed her elbow. "I don't want my wife's hands smelling like liquor."

Matty flushed and stepped back beside him.

Corrie, with daughter Madeline in her arms, slipped up to Bess's side to whisper, "Bess, are you sure this is a good idea?"

Bess started to respond, but something in the corner of her vision stopped her. She turned for a better look. "Oh, my."

"Oh, my," Corrie repeated.

Bess hurried across the room to where Gideon was noisily piling used bottles and glasses behind the bar. She leaned across the bar, not wanting the entire room to hear her. "Mr. Riker, shouldn't you do something about that. . .that. . .painting?"

His face grew dusky as he darted a look at the painting of a scantily clad woman. He muttered something she felt it just as well she couldn't make out. A moment later, chuckles from the crowd resounded as he removed the gild-framed painting and set it on the floor behind the bar.

Chairs scraped along the wooden floor as people found seats. There weren't enough chairs for everyone, so many of the men remained standing along the walls. Bess started toward her sisters.

Mr. Llewellyn stood, blocking her path, and indicated a chair he'd managed to keep anyone else from claiming.

"Would you honor me with your company, Miss Craig?"

"Thank you, but I'll sit with my sisters." She hurried on, glad that thoughtful Corrie had kept a chair free beside her. Bess couldn't grow accustomed to attention from some of the area's most upstanding citizens. The banker back in Rhode Island wouldn't have given the daughter of a dairy farmer the time of day.

A piano stood along the wall at right angles to the bar. Parson Harris stood beside the piano and led the congregation in prayer. Then Harry sat down on the piano stool.

"Do you know 'Come We That Love the Lord'?" the parson asked.

"No, Sir."

" 'My God, How Wonderful Thou Art'?"

Harry's face brightened. "Yes, Sir."

With a relieved smile, Parson Harris started the song. The congregation joined in. Bess and her sisters and the Collingswood brothers sang out strong against the background of male voices that stumbled over the words.

After the hymn, Parson Harris announced, "Mrs. Luke Collingswood has graciously agreed to sing for us."

Corrie stood and handed Madeline to Bess, who looked at her shy sister in surprise. Corrie had a lovely singing voice, but she'd never had the courage to sing alone in front of anyone but family. It seemed she was blossoming in all sorts of ways since marrying Luke in February in a quiet ceremony at the ranch. His face was bright with pride as he watched her move to the piano.

Corrie's voice rang out sweet and true. The men were so still, they seemed to have stopped breathing. As Corrie began the third verse, Bess realized the wisdom of her choice of song. Certainly, these men would relate to the words.

"All beauty speaks of Thee:
the mountains and the rivers,
the line of lifted sea,
where spreading moonlight quivers—"

"What's going on here?" A woman's harsh voice called out, halting Corrie's song.

Shocked and angry at the interruption, Bess turned. A pretty, black-haired woman of about thirty stood in the open doorway, fists planted on the hips of a garish red dress. Bess gulped. She'd never seen the woman before, but she knew instantly the woman was Margaret Manning, who flaunted her dancing girls before Lickwind's men—and the dancing girls flanked Margaret Manning now.

Chapter 2

Anger and disbelief fought for supremacy in Bess's emotions. Had these. . .women. . .no sense of propriety? Back in Rhode Island, such women knew their place, and that place was not in a church service or in the presence of decent women like the Craig sisters.

She pushed aside the thought that in Rhode Island church services weren't held in saloons, which were the usual territory of dancing girls.

"Well, well, well." Margaret Manning walked between the tables, grinning at the self-conscious men as she made her way toward the piano. "What would your wife think if she knew you were in a saloon, Parson?"

The color drained from Parson Harris's face.

Bess glanced about the room. Bess was sure the circuit rider was glad his wife hadn't accompanied him on the circuit this time. Why didn't one of the men do something?

Margaret stopped beside Corrie. Up close, Bess saw that Margaret looked older than her years beneath her powder and rouge. Margaret ran her glance over Corrie, who appeared too shocked to move. Corrie—with her blond coronet and gray and mauve gown—looked like an angel beside the dance hall woman.

Luke and Jim bolted to their feet. They were beside Corrie in an instant, glaring at Margaret. "Maybe you should leave, Miss Manning," Luke suggested in a threatening tone.

The woman laughed. "Don't worry. I'm not the big, bad wolf. I'm not going to hurt the little lady."

Gideon Riker clasped Margaret's elbow. "Why don't you let me see you home?"

Margaret tugged her arm, but Gideon kept his hold. "When did you turn your saloon into a church, Gideon? You didn't act so religious when me and the girls were in here last night."

His mouth tightened into a thin line. He started walking, and Margaret had no choice but to join him. "Let's go," he said to the other girls at the door.

The red-haired boy whom Bess noticed earlier stood beside one of the dance hall girls, a redhead who appeared to be about Bertie's age. Her green dress wasn't as flamboyant as Margaret's. "I'd like to stay, Gideon," the girl said in a low voice. "I haven't been to a church service in ever so long."

Gideon appeared to hesitate. He glanced back at Parson Harris, who shrugged as if to say he didn't know what to answer.

"I won't be no trouble, Gideon," she urged. She rested her hand on the boy's shoulder. "Walter and I will stand back here by the door, quietlike."

Margaret reached for the girl. "Come on, Regina. These people don't want sinners like us here." Her harsh laugh showed her contempt for the "good" townspeople.

The truth of her words shamed Bess. How could they turn aside a young woman who wanted to listen to the service? How could they know her heart? Bess shot to her feet, Madeline still in her arms. "Anyone is welcome to stay if they truly wish to hear God's Word."

A murmur ran through the room, but no one protested Bess's declaration.

Gideon shrugged.

Margaret pointed her finger at Regina. "Don't you go turning religious on me." Laughing, Margaret walked through the batwing doors, followed by the two other dance hall girls.

Regina stayed, standing beside the door with Walter and looking young and frightened. Corrie, still trembling slightly from her experience, sat down beside Luke. Parson Harris cleared his throat and began his sermon. The crowd of men—most of whom Bess suspected would have enjoyed the dancing girls' presence under any other circumstances—breathed a collective sigh of relief.

When the final prayer was over, Bess looked for Regina. The young woman was slipping out between the batwing doors. "I'll be right back," Bess told Corrie, then started after the woman with the red hair and gentle expression.

Bess excused herself repeatedly as men tried to stop her to talk. If she didn't hurry, she'd lose sight of Regina.

The girl was in front of Amos Freeling's blacksmith shop when Bess reached the saloon's boardwalk. "Miss Regina, wait, please!"

The woman turned, a surprised expression on her pretty face. Men stared at Bess in shock. Bess's face heated, but she refused to allow her embarrassment to deter her. The rain had slowed to barely a drizzle and the wind had stopped, but Bess barely noticed as she left the protected saloon boardwalk and stepped onto the dirt road.

"I'm sorry, but I don't know your last name," Bess said when she reached Regina.

"Bently. Regina Bently. Thank you for speaking up for me back there, Miss Craig."

"You know who I am?"

Regina smiled. "Everyone around here knows who the Craig sisters are." Her smile died. "Same as everyone knows who I and the rest of Margaret's girls are. You shouldn't be talkin' with me, Miss."

"I hope you'll attend our services again, Miss Bently."

Regina dropped her green-eyed gaze to the ground. "Most people won't take kindly to my presence at the meetings."

"I doubt there's one of them so perfect before God that they can refuse you the right to hear God's Word and worship Him. Besides, my sister and I noticed your voice during the last hymn. The congregation can use another beautiful singing voice."

A shy smile lit Regina's eyes. "Thank you. I'll think on your invitation." She glanced over Bess's shoulder. "Good day." She started toward the back of the blacksmith shop to the building where Bess knew the dance hall girls stayed.

As Bess turned around, a frowning quartet comprised of Jim, Matty, Luke, and Corrie joined her.

"I don't think you should be talking with her, Bess," Jim warned, looking uncomfortable. "Maybe you don't realize, but—"

"I know how she earns her living, Jim, but something or Someone made her want to stay at the service this morning." Bess looked from Matty to Corrie. "Perhaps the Lord brought us here for reasons other than we believed."

Her sisters exchanged startled looks. Then they smiled. Corrie nodded. "Perhaps He did at that."

"Now, Corrie," Luke started.

Bess glanced at the street, which was filled with men from the service. "Where's Bertie?"

Chapter 3

Gideon stood outside the batwing doors, wondering whether he was dreaming the unusual morning occurrences. Men still milled in the street, casting longing gazes at Bess Craig. The unpredictable woman was, of all things, talking with Regina in plain sight of the entire town. He couldn't recall ever seeing a lady speak to a dance hall girl. The men who'd been hankering after Miss Craig's hand in marriage were probably reconsidering about now.

Like all the rest of the men in the area, Gideon had made a trip to the Rough Cs to meet the Craig sisters. Jim Collingswood had snatched up friendly Matty right off. Then Luke married that sweet Corrie. Bertie was too young to interest Gideon.

But, Bess...well, he still remembered the sight of her getting off the train. He'd considered getting in line to ask to court her but changed his mind right fast. A lady deserved better than a saloon owner for a husband. And it was as certain as sagebrush in Wyoming that pious, proper Bess would agree. Besides, her face looked too stern to entertain a smile. And the way she dressed—severe, dark clothes like that gray outfit she wore today, her dark brown hair pulled back tight in a bun. Dressed more like a widow in mourning than a lady looking for a husband. No, sir, he didn't cotton much to being hitched for life to a woman as sober and proper as Elizabeth Craig.

Gideon yawned. He wasn't accustomed to seeing the light of day at this time of morning. He rubbed the palm of his hand over his face, then grinned. He was the only man in town, besides Doc, who hadn't shaved this morning.

He heard a man clear his throat and realized Parson Harris stood beside him, Bible and hat in hand. "Thank you for allowing us to use your business establishment for the services, Mr. Riker. I hope we didn't cause you too much trouble."

"No trouble at all." Seemed more like entertainment to him, in fact. "Welcome to use it again any Sunday morning." He saw no harm in making the offer. It didn't rain often enough in Lickwind to expect Parson Harris to need the saloon again. Besides, once Bess and Bertie Craig married, church attendance would dwindle back to the normal handful of sincere faithful.

That was, assuming any man dared take Bess Craig on as a wife. Gideon chuckled, remembering the way she'd all but demanded the use of his saloon. He had to admit, he admired her gumption.

Gideon yawned again and pushed his way through the batwing doors. He should probably keep the saloon open with all those men in town. Some were sure to stop in for a drink. But all he wanted to do was get some shut-eye.

He stopped short. Bertie Craig stood behind the bar, her

back to him. Beside her, Harry proudly listed off the different types of alcohol available, pointing at the appropriate bottles.

"Harry, what are you. . . ?"

Harry and Bertie turned to stare at Gideon as he stormed across the room, boots thunking against the wooden floor. "Get out from behind that bar, the both of you."

Bertie hurried out, fear on her freckled, tomboyish face. "For true, I didn't hurt a thing, Sir. And I didn't even look at the picture."

"I should hope not." Gideon grabbed her arm just above the elbow. He started to escort her toward the door. She almost stumbled in her attempt to keep up with him. Her free hand pressed the brim of the hat to her strawberry blond hair to keep the hat from falling off.

A growl, accompanied by something yanking at his trousers, stopped him. The strangest-looking dog he'd ever seen glared up at him. He tried to shake it off.

"Don't hurt Ramon," the girl pleaded. "He's just being protective of me."

Gideon started toward the door again, his fingers still around the girl's arm and the dog dragging along.

Harry hurried alongside them. "Nothing happened, Gideon. I watched out for her."

"That's a comfort," Gideon said dryly.

"I know how to treat a lady." Harry's voice rose in indignation.

"Then you know a lady has no place in a saloon." He deserved this for being softhearted and taking Harry on as a barkeep. What he needed was someone with the brawn of

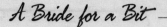

Amos the blacksmith, who could squelch fights in the saloon. But he'd felt sorry for Harry. He was only a kid with no family to look out for him.

Bertie's smile beamed. "Bess says I'm not a lady yet, but almost."

Gideon groaned. *Miss Bess Craig must have her hands full with this one.*

"Besides, all us Craig sisters were here for church," Bertie protested. "We were here for Ellis Stack's trial, too, but I couldn't see much then."

"Unless we have another rainstorm on a Sabbath morning before your sister is hitched, you'll not see the inside of this saloon again."

"For true, that's why I took advantage of the opportunity."

Gideon stopped, his hand still gripping her arm, and stared at her. "Opportunity?"

Her face shone bright with innocence. "Yes, Sir. The opportunity to see a den of iniquity up close." She squinted at him. "You don't look depraved."

He muttered under his breath and pushed open a batwing door, almost hitting Miss Bess Craig, who'd just stepped onto the saloon's boardwalk from the rain-soaked street. "There you are, Bertie. I was beginning to believe you'd headed back to the ranch on foot."

Gideon released his hold on Bertie.

"You can let go now, Ramon," the girl urged the dog.

To Gideon's amazement, the dog did as she said, though it continued growling. Gideon nodded toward Bertie. "You'd best keep a close watch on this one, Miss Craig. If ever there was a girl named Trouble, this one is it."

Anger flashed from Bess's brown eyes. She reached for Bertie, drawing the girl into her embrace. "I'll thank you not to insult my sister, Mr. Riker."

Gideon felt his face heat from her reproof. His embarrassment fueled his anger. He'd been fifteen the last time a woman used that tone with him. He bit back the reply dangling on the tip of his tongue. "Sorry, Miss."

Bess looked as though she'd like to refuse his apology, but she didn't. Instead she said in a hard voice, "The Collingswoods, Bertie and I, and Parson Harris are planning to picnic in the jailhouse. We'd be pleasured if you'd join us, since you allowed us. the use of your. . .premises for the service."

Pleasured? He'd bet his new house she wasn't a bit pleasured at the prospect of his company. "I'd be most honored, Miss Craig. Thank you kindly."

She nodded at him—a short, clipped sort of nod led by her pointed chin. "Come, Bertie."

He grinned, rubbing the palm of his hand across the stubble on his chin, as he watched them head next door to the jailhouse.

When Gideon started for the jailhouse twenty minutes later, he sported a clean-shaven face and smelled as good as the cheap aftershave from Jones's General Store allowed—just like all the other bachelors in the Lickwind vicinity. He even wore his best shirt. He chuckled as he walked along, amused that of all the bachelors at church that morning, he'd been the worst dressed and the only one not there voluntarily—but he was the one invited to picnic with Miss Bess Craig. Obviously not for romantic reasons, but that fact only added to the humor of the situation.

The sight that greeted him when he stepped inside the jailhouse knocked his pride down a peg. He evidently wasn't the only bachelor invited. He stood in the doorway and surveyed the men. If he'd prepared a list of the most eligible men in the area, these were the men whose names would be on that list: Jones, the owner of the general store; Squires, the feedstore owner; short and portly Oscar Hatch, the barber, with his cookie-duster mustache, and his lanky cousin Linus, the telegraph operator; Amos Freeling, the blacksmith; Mr. Llewellyn; the lawyer Donald Potter; and ranchers Josiah Temple and Clyde Kincaid.

Well, maybe Kincaid wouldn't make Gideon's list. Gideon hated to see the man enter the saloon. He cheated at cards as sure as wind whipped Wyoming.

"We're so glad you could join us, Mr. Riker." Mrs. Jim Collingswood smiled up at him. "The food is set out in the area that will be a cell once the bars arrive and are set in."

"Sure there's enough food, Ma'am? You've quite a crowd here."

"Yes, isn't it nice? They all just showed up. This is such a friendly town."

"Yes, Ma'am." *Friendly like a coyote after a chicken, and Bess Craig is the prey.* But Matty's comments restored his assurance that he was the only unmarried man here by invitation.

He made his way across the room, greeting people along the way, until he reached the barless cell. It was a mite crowded. Bess stood beside the mattressless wooden cot attached to the wall, where the food was set out. The banker,

Llewellyn, and the lawyer, Potter, flanked her. Others stood about with silly grins on their faces, hoping for a handout of Miss Craig's attention.

Gideon smirked. Nice of Jim's wife to let it slip that none of the other men were invited. This could be fun. Gideon softened his voice to courting tones. "So nice of you to invite me, Miss Craig."

Unpleasant surprise flickered across the banker's and lawyer's faces—just the reaction Gideon hoped to see. With a sense of reluctance, the lawyer stepped back to allow Gideon beside Bess. The faint floral scent she wore nudged away the scent of Gideon's aftershave and set his heart to quick-stepping.

Bess Craig lifted her chin and gave him a cool glance. "You made it, Mr. Riker. Would you like some fried chicken and dried apple pie?"

"I surely would, Miss."

She filled a plate and handed it to him.

"Thank you kindly." He winked at her.

She blinked, looking astonished, then blushed.

Llewellyn and Potter exchanged glances.

This is the most fun I've had since the Union Pacific gang moved on. Gideon took a bite of the drumstick.

Llewellyn hooked his thumbs on his vest pockets. "That house you're building is coming along well, Riker."

"That it is. Walls up, windows in, and roof on. Almost ready to move into." Gideon was right proud of that house. Doc Mitchel and Llewellyn owned the only other houses in town. Sleeping in the back room at the tavern was growing old. There was always someone coming around wanting to buy a drink when he was trying to get a little shut-eye. "I'm only waiting on the stove to arrive to move in."

Potter nudged Llewellyn. "Guess if we want to make a fortune, we should sell liquor."

Gideon thought the lawyer's grin held more spite-filled envy than amusement, but Gideon pretended not to notice and smiled amiably. "Business has been good for most in town since the Craig sisters arrived last June."

Oscar Hatch's cheeks jiggled as he chuckled. "That's the truth. Men in my place night and day wanting baths and their hair and whiskers trimmed."

"Can't keep shirts and Bay Rum Aftershave in stock at my place," Jones agreed.

"A businessman needs to take advantage of such things while he can," Gideon declared. "Once Miss Craig here and her little sister are married off, bachelors round here won't have any call to stay clean and smell passable good. Business will probably fall off so fierce you'll all be poor as church mice."

The men guffawed.

Gideon nudged Bess lightly and winked again, strangling his laugh at the lightning in her eyes.

"I'm so glad my and my sisters' presence has benefited you all." Her lips tightened into a thin line.

Gideon nodded. "Just like the parson said in the service this morning: 'It's good to be a blessing to others.' Right, Miss Craig?"

He almost choked on the furious look she darted his way.

Bess turned her back to him. "Mr. Llewellyn, who would I need to speak with concerning the possibility of renting this jailhouse?"

Llewellyn rocked back on the heels of his black boots—their shine showing even through the dust from Lickwind's only street. "Whatever would a little lady like you need with a jailhouse?"

"To live in it. There are no houses to rent in town. Not even a room."

"The Collingswood brothers aren't kicking you off the Rough Cs, are they?" Gideon asked. The Collingswood brothers weren't the kind of men to turn good women out on their own resources.

"Of course not. They haven't once intimated Bertie and I are an inconvenience, yet we most certainly are. Would any of you wish to support four women and two—or more—babies?"

Gideon followed her glance to Matty.

No one answered, but several of the men cringed. A few of them took a step back.

"I thought not," Bess continued. "In good weather, the ranch is still a long ride from Lickwind. How can Bertie and I support ourselves there? Even if we had goods to sell, the men haven't time to be driving us to town and back with any frequency. My brothers-in-law say they'll be starting roundup this week, so the men will have less time than ever to wait on us."

Llewellyn hooked his thumbs on his vest pockets again and gave Bess a downright fatherly look. "Even saying that's true, how would living in town make a difference?"

"We'd start a bakery."

Llewellyn rocked back on his heels again. "Tempting as that sounds, I doubt you'd make enough to support yourselves on it."

"You might at least give us a chance. At best, the town benefits from our rent and our services. If we don't make it, what has the town lost?"

"I don't see how we can allow you to live here, Miss Craig," Potter intervened. "What if we need to lock up some criminal?"

Bess cast a withering look his way. "Not one man has been arrested since my sisters and I stepped off the train. Besides, there aren't even bars on the cells or windows."

"There will be soon." Potter exchanged a scowling glance with Llewellyn. Both shook their heads.

"I'm afraid our answer must remain no," Llewellyn said. "It wouldn't be seemly, two unmarried women living in the town jail."

"What else would you have us do?" Bess's voice did nothing to disguise her disgust. "Trek to South Pass to search for gold? Or support ourselves in the manner of Lickwind's other women?"

Gideon noted with satisfaction that the men had the grace to look embarrassed at her suggestion. Bess Craig wasn't his idea of perfect femininity, but he admired her grit. The sudden desire to fight for her cause rose up within him. He squelched it. He didn't mind letting the men believe she'd invited him to this makeshift picnic, but he didn't want her thinking he was interested in her. Besides, if ever a female didn't need a man defending her, it was Bess Craig—which is why it made no sense at all when he heard himself say, "You're welcome to rent my new house, Miss Craig."

Chapter 4

Three days later, Bess stood in the doorway between the kitchen and parlor, surveying Gideon Riker's house. It was May 10, 1869, her twenty-fourth birthday, and the first day of her life absolutely on her own. Of course, she and Bertie would share the house, but the responsibility for supporting them fell on Bess's shoulders. She'd thought she'd feel frightened. Instead, an excitement for the challenge ahead surged through her. She breathed in the scent of new lumber and sawdust.

Bertie, wearing the ever-present brown felt hat, stopped beside Bess. Bess slid her arm around Bertie's shoulders and gave her a squeeze. "Isn't it amazing how the Lord provided for us, Bertie? A new house, with a kitchen, parlor, and two bedrooms, when all we asked Him for was that one-room jailhouse. Oh, God is good to us."

Behind them, Gideon grunted. Ramon growled. Bess jumped in surprise. Turning, she saw her hope chest balanced on Gideon's shoulder. His defiant gaze met hers. "I'd think I might get some credit. Didn't see God out here hammering and squaring up walls and laying down a floor."

"For true, Bess believes God can work through the worst sinner." Bertie's eyes shone with sincerity.

Bess resisted the impulse to put her hand over her sister's mouth.

The look Gideon shot Bess showed full well he believed she thought God had found His worst sinner in Gideon Riker. "Well," he drawled, "I expect God works through good folk, too, though He might find it takes longer, their pride getting in the way and all."

"You've been most kind." Bess refused to address the sinner question or acknowledge that he was the last man in Lickwind she'd expected to befriend her and Bertie.

"Where do you want this chest?"

"Beneath the parlor window." Bess pointed to the window, which looked out on the back of the saloon some thirty feet away. "It will double for a chair until we can afford furnishings."

Gideon placed the chest below the window, straightened, and looked about the empty parlor. "I'll bring over a table and some chairs from the saloon."

Bess started to say it wasn't necessary but stopped herself. She sent a silent thank-you to the Lord for meeting yet another need. "That would be a pure blessing, Mr. Riker."

Bertie walked to the center of the room and whirled in a circle, her arms out. "Are you going to paint or paper the walls, too, Mr. Riker? And get a rug for the floor? And curtains and—"

"Shush, Roberta Suzanne. He's exceeded the bounds of generosity already, allowing us to stay here." Even unfinished, this house was a palace in Lickwind. She nodded toward the kitchen. "I see your stove came in, Mr. Riker."

"Arrived on yesterday's train," Gideon acknowledged. "Put it in right off. Figured you'd need it for those baked goods you're planning to sell. It'll be a lot easier to use the stove for that than the parlor fireplace. I haven't set aside a separate pile of firewood. Take what you need from the cord behind the saloon."

"We'll keep track of what we use and pay for it," Bess said.

He crossed to the stairway leading to the second floor. "You'll find two bedrooms up there. I only had time to build one bed, though."

"A bed?" Surprise washed through Bess. She'd expected to sleep on the floor.

"Easy enough to do with leftover lumber. Sorry there's no mattress."

Same as sleeping on the floor. "Easy enough to buy a tick and fill it with straw." Bess matched his tone, mentally adding one more thing to her list of items to purchase at Jones's General Store: kerosene lamp, kerosene, candles, matches, broom, baking supplies, mattress tick.

They heard Jim Collingswood's boots cross the kitchen floor before he entered the parlor and set down two valises. "That's the last of it."

Not that there'd been much "it" to bring in from the ranch, Bess thought. Some kitchen items, her hope chest with its linens and blankets, her sewing basket, and the few clothes she and Bertie owned.

As though Jim's train of thought matched hers, he said, "Cow's tied to a porch post, and the crate with the chickens is on the back porch. Best keep a lookout against wolves until you get a shed and a chicken coop built."

Two more things Mr. Riker would need to supply, when he'd done so much for them already. Bess pushed down her guilt. He'd likely increase their rent for the outbuildings, but as Jim indicated, the buildings were necessary to protect their assets.

She raised her eyebrows in a look of question and expectation. "Mr. Riker?"

He scowled but acquiesced. "I think there's enough scraps of lumber left for something small. You can pay the rent for the outbuildings by sharing the milk and eggs with me."

Bess nodded briskly, relieved he'd agreed so quickly.

"If there's nothing more you need from me," Jim said, "I'll head over to the general store. Matty wants me to pick up some yarn for the baby clothes she's knitting. Meet you there, Bess."

"I'll only be a few minutes," she replied. He and Luke had agreed to arrange credit at the general store for the supplies she and Bertie needed. The women would repay them from their profits. Though a business arrangement, it implied the Collingswood brothers trusted her ability to make the bakery profitable, and that meant the world to her.

Bess, Bertie, and Gideon followed Jim through the kitchen and onto the porch. The tan cow mooed a greeting, and the confined chickens fussed. Bess looked out over the land and smiled. It faced north, and there were no buildings in view for miles. "One can see forever from here."

"That's why I put the porch on the back of the house," Gideon said. "Didn't make any sense looking at the rear of the saloon when a body could sit out here and look at all of

Wyoming. The purple sage makes a pretty sight later in the season."

Jim jabbed a finger in Gideon's direction. "I warned Bess this place is too close to the saloon for comfort, but she insisted on trying it. You let anything happen to these women, and I'm coming after you."

Gideon gave Jim a look Bess could only interpret as, "I'm their landlord, not their keeper," but he said, "I'll let my customers know the house is off limits. And there's a bar inside the door that'll keep out undesirables."

"See you use that bar," Jim ordered the women before taking off around the cow and the corner of the house.

Gideon pointed toward a narrow building. "Had this built for you, too. Didn't think you'd want to be sharing the town's public necessary."

Bess's face warmed. "You've thought of everything."

"The well's this way." He took the same path as Jim. Bess and Bertie followed. They'd just reached the well when gunfire rang out, followed by the sounds of galloping horses and a cowboy's "Whoopee!"

The noise startled Bess. Then fear roared through her, rooting her feet to the ground. She grabbed Bertie and pulled her close.

"What on earth—?" Gideon's head swiveled as he looked for the source of the gunfire. "Get down," he barked. He pushed Bess to the ground behind the well. She dragged Bertie with her. Gideon all but fell on top of them.

"Oof!" *Now I know what's meant by the term "eat dust."* Bess choked off a chuckle. She wondered if she was becoming hysterical.

The sounds grew closer. Bess tried to see the source, but she could barely move beneath Gideon's weight. All she saw was Bertie's old brown felt hat lying in the dust two feet away.

A moment later the hat jumped as though alive as a bullet struck the ground beside it.

Chapter 5

My hat!" Bertie wailed.

"Quit that fool shooting!" Gideon roared. Fury and fear for Bess and Bertie burned like fire inside him. For the life of him, he couldn't figure out what was going on. Men usually weren't drunk enough to start shooting up the town this early in the day. If someone was robbing the bank, why were they riding behind the saloon?

Gideon recognized the cowboy's face. He'd seen it often enough in his saloon but didn't know the man's name. Gideon leaped up and grabbed the halter of the shooter's horse. The horse pulled him off the ground as it rose on its hind legs, frightened by the gunshots. Gideon fell to the ground, and the horse and rider raced between the saloon and jailhouse back to Lickwind's only street, where more gunfire and horses' hooves sounded.

By the time Gideon picked himself up, the women were standing. Bess brushed dust from her skirt, her eyes spitting fire, while Bertie examined her hat. "He almost hit my hat!"

"Be glad it wasn't on your head at the time." Gideon looked from one to the other. "You two okay?"

They nodded.

"Good. Get back in the house," he ordered. "You end up shot and the Collingswood brothers will have my hide. I'm going to find out what's going on."

He stayed close to the saloon wall as he headed toward the street, his heart pounding faster than train wheels chugging at full speed. Never knew where a stray bullet might land. He peered onto the street. Half a dozen men charged up and down the road on near-crazed steeds, raising a dust cloud like a thick, gritty fog and shooting off pistols—mostly into the air. Cautiously, he stepped onto the boardwalk in front of his saloon.

Jim was running toward him but looking beyond him. Gideon swung around, expecting trouble. He found it. "Bess!"

Jim halted beside them. "You all right, Bess?"

"Yes, but—"

Gideon pushed her against the wall, shielding her from possible stray bullets. "Where's Bertie?"

"In the house."

Gideon grabbed her arm and pulled her into the saloon. Jim followed on their heels. "You haven't the sense God gave grass," Gideon stormed. "You could have gotten yourself killed."

Bess jerked from his grasp and smoothed the dark blue calico of her dress's arm. "What's happening?"

"It's the Union Pacific," Jim answered. "Linus Hatch just received the telegraph. One word—'Done.' The railroad has reached the Pacific."

"They made it!" Gideon whooped. Grasping Bess around the waist, he swung her around in circles. "They did it!"

Her laughter rang in his ears. Even in the midst of his celebration, he was aware that her laughter was softer and sweeter than he'd expected. It warmed him right through to his bones.

That scared the daylights out of him. Scared him more than the shooting outside. He set her down and steadied her with his hands on her waist while she regained her balance.

Jim watched them with a strange expression.

Bess's eyes, which Gideon saw so often flash in anger or cynicism, danced with laughter. "Sorry, Miss Craig. Afraid I got carried away."

Bess dropped her gaze to the floor and smoothed back the strands of dark hair that had come loose from her bun. "No harm done, Mr. Riker. A little excitement is understandable under the circumstances."

He grinned. "Hard to believe the railroad reached here only eighteen months ago. Never truly believed it would make it all the way to the Pacific Ocean." If the railroad had run across the entire country five years ago, his life would be completely different today. He wouldn't live in Lickwind or own a saloon, and Stan. . . He pushed away the memories.

A loud clopping sounded against the floorboards. Bess looked over his shoulder toward the door, her mouth agape. He followed her gaze. A black horse stood between the batwing doors, half-in and half-out of the saloon. The cowboy who'd almost shot Bertie's hat sat astride the horse.

"Hey, get your horse out of my saloon." Gideon started toward him.

Bess moved quicker. She grasped the horse's halter and glared up at the man. "You could hurt someone, shooting up the town. Haven't you any sense?"

The man's face registered shock, then amusement. "Let go of my horse, Lady."

"I will not." She looked at Gideon. "Arrest him."

Gideon stared at her. "Arrest him? Me? I'm not a lawman." She looked at her brother-in-law.

He shook his head. "Sorry, Bess. We could throw him in the jailhouse, but we couldn't keep him there."

"What is the matter with you two?" Bess demanded. "He's endangered people's lives. Get the sheriff."

Gideon snorted. "There is no sheriff. Besides, the men hereabouts have their own ideas of what is and isn't law-abiding behavior. You won't find twelve men in Wyoming who think a cowpoke celebrating the railroad's final spike is a crime."

" 'Fraid he's right," Jim agreed.

"Will you two get this woman off my horse?" the cowboy whined.

Gideon peeled Bess's fingerhold from the halter. "Back that horse up and keep it out of my saloon."

The cowboy gave a jaunty salute, smiled, and did as commanded.

Bess wheeled on Gideon. "No wonder the jail's stood empty all this time. Bertie and I could just as well be renting it."

"Couldn't agree with you more, but the banker and lawyer don't, and they've more say in the matter than I do. Now if you'll excuse me, men are wantin' to celebrate, and I intend to make some money off their plans."

❧

Bess glanced about the saloon. Gideon was right. Men were

entering, wanting to celebrate. She doubted their manner of celebrating was safer than that of the shooters in the streets. Likely gunfire would increase after the drink flowed freely.

And after everyone was done drinking and sobered up, they'd be hungry. She and Bertie could capitalize on that.

Jim squeezed her elbow. "We'll go out the back door. Safer that way."

"Wait a minute." She explained her plan to feed the celebrators. "Bertie and I will need supplies."

He frowned. "You can't be going to the general store in this fracas. Let's get you home safe. Then you can give me a list of what you need. I'll get it for you."

They headed toward the back door. Men watched her with curious expressions, but none made lewd remarks with Jim at her side.

She grabbed some firewood from the back of the saloon, much to Jim's exasperation. "The longer we're outside, the longer you're in danger."

"The hooligans are all on the main street right now. We need firewood to bake. It would be nice if we had a variety of wood to choose from, but it all heats, and I prefer it to buffalo chips. Here, you take some, too." She handed him a log.

"Women," he muttered, but he took the log and grabbed a couple more.

A few minutes later, Bess's list in hand, he stood in the doorway ready to leave for the general store. "You and Bertie stay inside and away from the windows. And use that bar to keep the lice away."

"Lice?" Bertie directed the question toward the door closing behind Jim.

"Unsavory men," Bess explained, lowering the bar. "Get a fire started in the stove. I'll write up a menu. We'll post copies at the saloon and telegraph office. Need to let men know we've got food to offer them."

Bess named their bakery the Back Porch and put the name in capital letters at the top of the menu. She allowed five hours before opening—time for Jim to return with supplies and for her and Bertie to mix and knead bread, heat the stove, mix eggless cookie dough, and bake.

"We'll put a rice pudding on the stove," she told Bertie while she wrote. "And a kettle of dried applesauce. The more we have to offer, the better."

Jim posted the menus and brought more firewood after he returned to the house with their supplies and before he headed back to the ranch. "I'll bring back some beef. Men are sure to gobble it up along with your baked goods. Round here men mostly eat what they hunt—buffalo, antelope, venison, rabbit. They'll appreciate a good beefsteak."

Bess welcomed his offer. They both knew there'd still be plenty of men looking for a meal when he returned. And later. "It's a sure bet the celebrating will go on all night," Jim said. "Men will pour into town as the news spreads. They'll be looking for meals tonight and tomorrow when they dry out from the liquor."

"I hope they've got money left after celebrating." Bess turned to Bertie while tying the sashes of an oversized apron. "Make sure you see their money up front before you take their orders."

Excitement, purpose, and hope bubbled up in Bess as she and Bertie baked. Their new enterprise was about to receive its first test. "It feels like Christmas," she confided to Bertie as she pulled the first brown, fragrant loaves of bread from the shiny cast-iron oven hours later.

"For true. Smells like it, too, from the baking."

"These loaves look good. I was a little worried. It's wise to season the stove by heating it a few times before baking in it the first time."

"Good thing you brought so much sourdough starter."

Bertie was right. Bess sent up a silent thank-you that she'd had the foresight to set the starter aside. She'd planned to begin baking the day after they arrived. God had known they would need it sooner. They also had the bread Corrie sent with them that morning, should they need something to sell before their own baking was ready.

All the while Bess worked in the kitchen, Gideon Riker slipped into her thoughts and had to be forcefully thrust from them. In the midst of kneading bread—her arms tired, her hands sticky with flour and dough, and her nostrils filled with the scents of sourdough and woodsmoke—she remembered the feel of his arms strong around her waist and his chest hard against her. Brushing at a stray lock of her hair, she remembered the feel of his long blond hair brushing her cheek as he spun her around. As the applesauce sputtered on the back of the stove, sending cinnamon scent into the air, she recalled the sound of his laughter, his breath brushing her ear. And she recalled how feminine she felt, held in his arms that way, sharing his joy and wonder at the world-changing event of the transcontinental railroad.

With each memory, it became more difficult to push the thoughts of Gideon Riker aside. *A saloon owner. Honestly,*

Elizabeth Craig. Have you no standards? Why did I ever agree to come to Lickwind as a mail-order bride? I haven't met a single man I'd trust past Tuesday, excepting the Collingswood brothers. At least Matty and Corrie married well.

She was grateful her work helped to force her attentions from her daydreams. She put the dough into loaf pans to rise. Next, she filled a kettle with water and set it on the stove, then set out the new tin wash pan and scraped soap chips into it. They hadn't many plates or tableware. They'd need to wash dishes between customers.

The first customers trickled in before Jim returned—cowboys Jim had met on the way home who were hungry after their ride to town. The coins they exchanged gave a cheerful ring when dropped into the tin button box Bess and Bertie used to collect money.

Gideon slid back into Bess's thoughts, his laughter tickling her ear, as she set a huge galvanized coffeepot on the stove.

"Why isn't this door barred?"

Gideon's voice jarred her from the too-sweet memory. She spun around, as embarrassed as though he'd heard her thoughts. Her glance darted to the kitchen door through which he'd entered. "I guess we forgot it after the last customers."

"Don't forget again."

His obey-or-else tone angered her, but she knew the wisdom in his advice. "We won't."

Ramon stood beside her, growling at Gideon and the redheaded boy with him. "Shush, Ramon." The dog lay down but continued a low growl.

Bess's gaze fell on the rifle Gideon carried. "What's that for?"

"You." He held it toward her.

She put her hands behind her, shook her head, and stepped back until she bumped against the counter. "Oh, no."

"You might need it to protect yourself."

"I won't have a gun in this house. Besides, I don't know how to shoot one."

"I don't have time to teach you now. If someone threatens you or Bertie, just point it in their direction. If that doesn't stop them, cock the hammer and pull the trigger."

"I will not. Get it out of here."

He glanced at her sister. "Bertie?"

Bess reached her arm between him and Bertie, glaring at him. "Don't even consider asking it of her."

"If you won't use it to protect yourselves, at least promise you'll shoot it off if you have trouble. I'll hear it and come running."

"How will you distinguish the sound from the other gunfire in town?" Sporadic celebratory gunfire had sounded all day.

Gideon frowned without replying.

"That's what I thought. Are you and the boy hungry?" Bess recognized him as the boy who'd stood with Regina Bently during the church service.

"Yes, Ma'am," the boy replied hastily.

Gideon rested a hand on the boy's shoulder. "This is Walter."

Bess nodded toward the boy. "Hello, Walter. I'm Miss Craig."

Gideon set the rifle stock gently against the floor. "Thought he might be a help to you. I'd appreciate it if you'd let him stay the night. Be safer here than at the saloon."

Bess refrained from asking in front of the lad why the boy should stay at the saloon at all. "Of course he may stay. Bertie, give him a bowl of rice pudding and a slice of bread."

"I'll be right back." Gideon left by the kitchen door; then he opened it and peered inside. "Don't forget the bar." Then he was gone again.

Five minutes later, he returned with a metal triangle and a small metal bar. Bess recognized it as the same kind of implement used to call the hands out on the Rough Cs. "Since you won't use the rifle, sound this if there's trouble. You can be sure I'll know its clang from any cowpoke's gunfire."

Bess accepted it solemnly. "Thank you."

"I best be going. There's a full house at the saloon."

"Then I doubly thank you for looking out for our welfare instead of your own business."

Bertie handed him a slice of bread spread thick with butter. "Don't worry, Mr. Riker. Ramon will protect us."

Gideon sidled past the still-growling dog. "Don't forget the bar."

❦

Gideon swallowed the desire to growl back at the gray excuse for a dog that lay in his path to the door. He usually liked dogs, but this one had hated him since he ushered Bertie out of the saloon last Sunday. He warily passed the dog, opened the door, and slid through it. "Don't forget the bar."

He almost collided with Linus and Oscar Hatch. He nodded at them and kept walking. The women wouldn't have time to bar the door, but he didn't fear for them with the Hatch cousins.

What had come over him that he'd offered his home to the Craig sisters? Someone must've slipped locoweed into the apple pie at the jailhouse Sunday. He'd spent most of the time between then and this morning finishing up the house and putting in the outhouse, with the help of grumbling Harry. Now he'd committed to putting up a chicken coop and a cow shed for the sisters, neither of which he needed for himself.

Worse, ever since that first gunshot earlier today, he'd spent his time worrying over those women. Twice he'd thrown himself between Bess and bullets. Never had he done a thing like that before in his life! The woman was downright dangerous. Wouldn't even take a gun to protect herself and her kid sister. Instead, he'd offered to answer that clanging call whenever they felt they needed protection. Pure foolishness, that's what it was.

He took a bite of the bread as he reached the saloon's back door. Mm. He hadn't had homemade sourdough bread in years. Mostly he just cooked up some biscuits on the little stove beside the bed in the back room.

The feel of Bess's soft cheek against his as he twirled her around that afternoon whispered into his memory along with the soft floral scent she wore. *Forget it. You don't need or want a woman like Bess Craig, even if she'd have anything to do with a saloonkeeper.*

But the picture of her brown eyes dancing with laughter as she stood in his arms persisted as he entered the bar with its yeasty smell of hops and the laughter of celebrating cowboys and dance hall girls.

Chapter 6

At five the next morning, Bess sat on her hope chest in the otherwise empty parlor and slumped back against the window. On the floor beside the chest, her only lantern shed a flickering light. Laughter, piano music, and singing sounded loudly from the saloon. Harry wasn't playing hymns this morning.

Bess ran the palm of her hand lightly over Rhubarb's back. She lay curled on her lap, giving welcome added warmth. Bess and Bertie had brought Ramon to town with them to give Rhubarb a respite from Ramon, but the cat had other ideas. When Jim Collingswood arrived with the goods from the farm earlier that evening, the cat had jumped out of the wagon, surprising the rancher and the sisters. The cat made straight for Bertie and twined about the girl's booted legs with a purr that almost drowned out the noise of the celebrating cowboys.

Bess stretched, and her movement wakened the cat. Rhubarb jumped down and made his way across the floor and up the stairs. *Likely looking for Bertie*, Bess thought.

Was Bertie asleep? Bess had sent her to bed—with quilts

since they had no mattress tick yet—three hours ago. Walter slept in the spare bedroom. She didn't know how anyone could sleep with this noise, but neither Bertie nor Walter had come back downstairs.

A knock on the door caused her to rise with a sigh. Another customer. She wasn't about to turn down the money. Perhaps she'd catch her second wind soon.

She set the lantern on the counter, lifted the bar, and opened the door. The redheaded dance hall girl stood on the porch, shivering beneath her shawl. "Miss Bently, this is a surprise. Won't you come in?"

"Miss Bently," Regina repeated with a touch of wonder in her voice. "Sounds nice. Ladylike." She stepped inside, and Bess closed the door behind her. "I'll only stay a minute. Gideon said my brother is staying with you. I just wanted to make sure he isn't a bother."

"Your brother?" Bess stared at her, startled.

"Yes, Walter."

"Of course. I don't know where my mind's gone. I guess I'm more tired than I thought." Bess wasn't about to admit she'd thought Walter was Gideon's son and maybe Regina's, too. A sense of relief slid through her. "Walter's no trouble at all. He's sleeping upstairs. Matter of fact, he was a help to us. Bertie and I had a hard time keeping up with all those hungry men."

"I hear your food is mighty good."

"Are you hungry?"

Regina hesitated, glancing at the kettle of oatmeal on the back of the stove. "I guess not."

"Why don't I slice you some bread? You can take it with

you in case you get hungry later."

Regina hesitated again. "How much would it cost?"

"Consider it a thank-you for Walter's help."

"That's mighty kind. I was wonderin'. . ."

"Yes?" Bess encouraged as she pulled a flour-sack towel off a loaf of bread.

"Would you consider boardin' Walter? Gideon's been good about letting Walt sleep at his place, but—"

Bess turned around, bread knife in one hand. "At the saloon?"

"Yes. I know it's not the best place for a boy, but it's better than Margaret's place, where I live. And Gideon doesn't let the boy in the saloon durin' business hours."

Bess concentrated on cutting the bread, trying to hide her horror at a young child's only choices being a dance hall girls' home or a saloon. She swallowed hard. "Of course he can stay with us. There are two bedrooms upstairs. He can sleep in one."

Regina heaved a sigh of relief. "I'll find a way to pay you, I promise."

"If Walter is willing to help with chores, that'll be payment enough."

"You sure?"

"I'm sure." Bess handed Regina two slices of bread. She and Regina met each other's gazes for a long moment before Regina said softly, "You're a good woman, Miss Craig, and not just because you're a Sunday-go-to-meetin' kind of lady."

Bess couldn't remember when she'd felt so complimented and so humbled at the same time. What must life be like for Regina Bently that she thought it extraordinary another woman would treat her brother, a ten-year-old child, with kindness?

Regina played with the black fringe on her shawl. "Miss Craig, do you know how to read?"

"Yes."

"Might you consider teachin' Walter readin' and writin'? There ain't no teacher in Lickwind."

"Of course." She'd find time somehow. "I'm still working with Bertie on her schooling. One more student won't be a problem."

"Thank you kindly."

"Don't you know how to read?"

Regina looked at the floor. "No. My pappy didn't think it necessary for a girl."

"Would you like to learn?"

Regina raised her gaze. "Somethin' fierce."

"I'd gladly teach you."

"You'd do that?"

"Surely. We can start later this week."

Regina beamed. "Thank you kindly. I'd best get along. Margaret will be wonderin' where I am. She's a spitfire when she's mad."

When she opened the door, Gideon was walking up the porch steps. "Regina." He nodded to her as they passed on the porch. "May I come in, Miss Craig?" He didn't wait for Bess to answer. He slipped inside along with the raw Wyoming air, closed the door behind him, and cast a wary look around. "Where's the dog?"

"Ramon's upstairs with Bertie."

"I saw the light in the parlor window and thought I'd

best check on you. Everything all right here?"

"Yes, wonderful. There's been a steady stream of men all night until the last twenty minutes or so. We've already made enough money to pay for the supplies we purchased at the general store and pay you our first week's rent. Bertie hates baking, but she pitched in with barely a murmur. We're so grateful the Lord brought us to town yesterday. I doubt there'll be many days we make this much money."

"You're right. News of your good cooking is traveling fast. Men at the saloon are talking your place up. Expect you'll see more of them soon as the sun's up. The ones who are still able to stand."

"From the music, I'd guess there are a few of those left. Time to think about breakfast soon. I'm keeping a fire going in the stove, as you can tell, so I won't need to build it up again. It's more comfortable in the parlor—not so hot." Bess led the way to the other room and set the lantern on the windowsill. When she turned around, Gideon looked distressed.

"I forgot all about bringing a table and chairs over."

Bess smiled. "You had a bit on your mind."

"Men at the saloon said you're selling beefsteak along with bread and baked goods."

"Jim brought the steak in from the Rough Cs, along with more bread and cake from Corrie and some extra eggs. Can hardly believe the way food flew out of this place."

"Hope young Walt didn't get in the way."

"No, he was a help." She grinned. "He even milked the cow for us."

"I didn't know he knew how."

"He didn't. Bertie taught him."

Gideon chuckled. "Well, Grandmother's bloomers."

Bess laughed at his imitation of one of Bertie's favorite sayings. "Miss Bently asked if Walter might stay with us. I said yes. I'm afraid I forgot it's your house and your decision."

He tilted his head and looked at her with a curious expression. "You'd be willing to take him in?"

"Yes. Weren't you?"

"That's different."

"Why?"

He appeared at a loss for an answer.

"You'll let him stay here?" she persisted.

"Yes. I'll bring his bed over tomorrow. It'll be much better for him staying here than at the saloon."

She wanted to ask why he ran a saloon since he thought it was a bad place for a boy. More than that, she wanted to ask if there was a reason he befriended Regina Bently in particular, taking her brother under his wing. Was Miss Bently special to him? Bess pushed away the questions. A part of her didn't want to know the answers.

"I will be needing that table and chairs," Bess said. "I'll be teaching Walter and Regina to read."

He gaped. "Here? In my. . .your. . .this house?"

"Yes. Where else?"

"I forbid it!"

Chapter 7

B ess stared at him. "You forbid it?"

"Yes. This is still my house. You and your sister may live in it, but I make the rules."

"You befriended Miss Bently. You took in her brother."

"I don't raise him. I just let him sleep in my back room and spend time there when. . .when he can't be with his sister."

"Why would you forbid my teaching them to read?"

"I'm not. I'm only saying that you can't teach her here."

Bess lifted her hands, perplexed. "Why?"

Gideon looked at the ceiling and back to her. "Have you thought what it will do to your reputation, having that woman in your home? What it will do to Bertie's reputation?"

She hadn't. It's true that back in Rhode Island, she wouldn't have considered inviting Regina into her home. But then, she'd never met a soiled dove in Rhode Island. She couldn't turn her back on Regina when she wanted to improve herself. "If not here, where? I certainly can't go to. . .to her home to teach her, and there's no school building."

"That's your problem. Find another place or tell her you rescind your offer."

Bess planted her fists on her hips. "You allow the woman to work in your saloon. Isn't it hypocritical to forbid her in your house, especially when her brother is staying here?"

"I won't change my mind."

And I won't rescind my offer. She'd find some way to keep her promise. For the moment, the best tactic appeared to be to divert his focus. "How did Miss Bently and Walter end up in Lickwind?"

"Same way a lot of us did. They were traveling to Oregon with their folks. Wagon broke down crossing a river. Their folks died. Lost everything. Not that there was much to lose, from the way Regina tells it. She and Walter made it as far as Lickwind before what little money she had ran out. They had no way to continue on to Oregon and no way to go back East. Some of Margaret's girls joined up with a traveling. . ." He cast Bess a sharp glance. "A service that trailed the Union Pacific crew back in '68. Regina thought that would be worse for Walter than living here, so—" He shrugged.

"But why did she choose. . .what she does. . .instead of something else?"

"What else?"

Bess lifted her hands again as she searched for possibilities. "Baking, like me and Bertie. Or sewing or doing laundry."

"Regina wasn't as fortunate as you and Bertie. She didn't have the Collingswood brothers or anyone else backing her credit while she laid in supplies and rented a place to live."

"Oh. I guess I didn't think it through."

"Seems decent folk usually don't when it comes to ladies like Regina."

"That's not fair."

"No?" He sighed. "Maybe not. I'd better head back to the saloon. I'll get that table and chairs over here. Don't forget what I said about Regina."

"How could I?" Bess retorted.

Gideon didn't answer. He just left saying, "Bar the door."

Bess swung the bar into place, venting her fury on the piece of wood. "Men. They're all impossible."

❧

Three days later Gideon awoke from his first good night's sleep since the arrival of the telegraph announcing the driving of the final railroad spike. His saloon hadn't been that busy since the Union Pacific crew laying the track came through Lickwind. Those were good moneymaking days. . .or rather, nights. The railroad expected the crews to work during daylight hours.

He washed up, shaved, brushed his hair, and picked up the least-worn shirt he owned, trying to ignore the fact he attended to such things more regular now that Bess Craig lived thirty feet away. He wrinkled his nose as he buttoned the shirt. Time to wash clothes or buy new ones.

Gideon looked into his battered coffeepot. Some coffee still remained from yesterday. He stirred the coals in his stove and set the pot to heat. His stomach growled, and an image of hotcakes, fresh from the Craig sisters' stove, appeared large as life. That and fresh coffee sounded like heaven. Or temptation. He wasn't about to wind up outside their door every day like every other male in town.

He could hear chairs scraping in the saloon. Harry must be up and cleaning the place. Gideon never could make himself clean up the saloon before morning.

When he walked into the bar with a tin cup of thick coffee, he discovered Harry wasn't the only person there. At the sight of Bess and Regina sitting side by side at the table nearest the door, he stopped so fast the coffee sloshed over the edge of the cup. "Ow!" He winced and shook his hand.

The women looked at him.

He walked toward them, wanting to scold Bess Craig as if she were a child. He hoped Harry had wiped the table off for the women. "Morning, Miss Craig. Regina. What brings you two in here this time of day?" As if he couldn't tell from the slate between them with A-E-I-O-U printed on it in capital letters.

Regina's face positively glowed, in spite of the late night he knew she'd spent working. "Miss Craig is teaching me my letters. Ain't that something?"

Gideon forced a smile. "It surely is, Regina." He'd be glad for her if it weren't happening in his saloon. Or his house.

Miss Craig looked the part of the schoolmarm, dressed in gray as usual, with a prim black bow at her throat, a wool shawl wrapped about her against the cool May morning, and her dark brown hair prudishly pulled back in a bun. She contrasted sharply with Regina, whose red hair curled past her shoulders and whose green plaid dress, though more modest than most of Margaret's girls' clothes, was low cut and trimmed with lace.

He lifted his coffee cup and met Bess's defiant gaze over the cup's rim. "Not baking today, Miss Craig?"

"Fed breakfast to most of the men in town. Most don't sleep in as late as you do. There's more bread rising. Bertie's watching the oven to allow Miss Bently and me a little time together."

He ignored the jibe at his sleeping habits. "I've something on my own stove I'd like to ask you about. Would you mind?" He waved toward the back room.

Bess frowned. "Now?"

"Hate to interrupt the lesson, but the pot is on the stove right this minute."

As the door to the back room closed behind them, Bess looked around the area where Gideon stored inventory. "I don't see a stove."

"It's behind the curtain."

Bess took a step toward it.

"Where Harry and I sleep," Gideon expanded.

She stopped, her expression a mixture of curiosity and outrage.

"Don't bother going in," Gideon continued. "The only pot on my stove is filled with this awful stuff I call coffee." He took a drink. Grimaced. "I asked you back here—"

"It sounded more like a demand." Bess crossed her arms over her chest and stared at him, one toe bouncing against the floorboards in an irritated rhythm.

What right had she to be angry when she'd invaded his saloon? He pointed toward the door separating them from the bar and leaned forward, dropping his voice to a stage whisper. "What are you thinking, coming in here with that woman?"

"Do you normally object to that woman's presence here?"

He took a deep breath and counted to ten. It wasn't high enough, but he spoke anyway. "Didn't you understand a word I said the other night?"

"Yes. You forbade me to teach Regina in your house."

"So—"

"This isn't your house. It's your place of business. She's in here every night. How can you object to her presence here in the morning?"

He closed the space between them with two steps and brought his face close to hers. "You aren't in here every night. That's the point."

"You'll see me here every day from now on. I should think you'd be pleased."

"Pleased?"

She shrugged. "You claim it will hurt my reputation if I allow Miss Bently into your home. If I teach her here, everyone will know our relationship is that of teacher and student. You'll no longer need concern yourself for my reputation."

"You're determined to misunderstand me."

"I don't think I misunderstand at all. Now if you'll excuse me, Miss Bently and I only have an hour for the lesson, and you're using up precious minutes."

She brushed past him, entered the saloon, and closed the door firmly behind her.

Gideon stalked through the curtains to the stove and added more thick coffee to his cup. For a moment, he considered partaking of something stronger, but he'd given up drinking almost a year ago. An ornery woman like Bess Craig wasn't going to drive him back to it. He liked to keep his head about him, even if he did make a living helping others lose theirs.

It didn't do his temper a bit of good to find four doughnuts on the bar when he returned to the saloon. "Miss Craig brought them," Harry said, "for the use of the table. I said it wasn't necessary, but she insisted. I ate two already. They're mighty good."

Gideon grunted and walked to the other end of the bar, pretending to check the stock. He wouldn't be bribed by Bess Craig's baking. "Sweep the floor, Harry."

He kept his resolve for all of ten minutes before grabbing one of the doughnuts. Just one, he told himself. But that doughnut was the best thing he'd eaten since he went to Cheyenne almost a year ago to celebrate the Fourth of July, so he helped himself to another and almost considered it a blessing the day the Craig sisters moved into town.

Twenty minutes later Doc Mitchel strolled in.

"First customer of the day, just like normal," Harry whispered as he passed Gideon.

Only a few men came in before late afternoon, as a rule. "Least he didn't sleep here last night," Gideon whispered back.

Doc Mitchel didn't walk directly to the bar as usual. He swerved to the table where Bess and Regina sat. Standing across from them, he tipped his hat. "Morning, ladies. Miss Craig, what a delightful surprise."

Bess's neck and cheeks colored, but she met the doctor's gaze and nodded. "Doctor."

Gideon froze, watching the encounter, listening for every word and nuance. He didn't like the way Doc looked at Bess. A nasty expression had slipped over Doc's face. Some might call it a smile, but Gideon knew better. He could see Regina did, too, from the way she cringed.

"Is the good Miss Craig teaching you letters, Regina?" Exaggerated innocence turned Doc's tone syrupy.

Regina straightened her backbone but stared at her slate. "Yes, Sir."

"And what would you be teaching the good Miss Craig?" Doc raised his eyebrows suggestively.

Gideon set the bottle he was holding down harder than necessary, walked around the bar, and headed for the table. He'd known something like this would happen sooner or later. Now he knew how Ramon felt protecting Bertie. Gideon felt like growling himself. Instead, he groaned as three more men walked in, all of them stopping to stare at Bess, Regina, and Doc.

Doc leaned on the table and grinned. "Why don't you show me, Regina? Or perhaps you'll show me yourself, Miss Craig? Or do you go by Bessie now?"

Bess surged to her feet. "Mr. Mitchel, I demand an apology. For myself and Miss Bently."

"Apology?" Doc laughed. It turned into a guffaw by the time Gideon reached him.

Gideon grabbed Doc's jacket at the back of the neck.

Doc's laugh choked off. "What—? Gideon?"

" 'Fraid you're leaving here for the day, Doc."

"But—"

"Before you leave, how about that apology?"

The three male spectators snickered. Gideon glared at them. The snickers stopped.

"But, Gideon—" Doc wailed.

"You apologize, and I'll consider letting you come back tomorrow."

"Course I'll apologize. Meant to all along. Just teasing the ladies a mite."

"Uh-huh. Let's hear it."

Doc wiggled. "If you'd just loosen your hold a bit—"

Gideon let go.

Doc ran his fingers between his collar and his throat.

Gideon pulled Doc's felt hat from his head and slapped it against Doc's stomach. "The apology."

Doc clutched the hat with both hands. "Uh, ladies—"

"They have names," Gideon reminded.

"Uh, yes, Miss Craig. Regina."

"Miss Bently," Gideon suggested firmly.

"Uh, yes. Miss Bently. I'm sure you realize I was joking when I said. . .suggested. . .I realize my remarks were, um, tasteless. I'm sure two such fine ladies as yourselves will forgive me for my, um, breach of manners."

"Apology acceptable?" Gideon looked from Bess to Regina.

Bess glared at Doc. Regina stared, openmouthed, but nodded.

Gideon ushered Doc toward the door past the again-snickering cowboys. "Don't come back until tomorrow, Doc."

"Can't you send home a bottle with me? One little old bottle?"

"Try Cheyenne's saloons." He pushed Doc through the batwing doors and turned back to the saloon. He stopped, hands on his hips, in front of the three grinning cowboys. "You here for drinks, or will you be following Doc?"

"Drinks, just drinks." One of the men held up his hands as though Gideon was robbing him. All three back-stepped toward the bar, watching Gideon the entire way.

Gideon walked back to the table, his heart still pumping wildly from his anger.

"Thank you," Bess said, looking relieved.

Regina stood. "I'm sorry I caused trouble, Gideon."

Bess gave her a shocked look. "Dr. Mitchel caused trouble, not you."

Gideon exchanged glances with Regina. They understood each other. The saloon was their world, not Bess's. "It's all right, Reg. . .Miss Bently."

Her smile lit up the room.

All that for calling her Miss Bently? He never thought Margaret's girls cared that they were called by their given names. He hadn't even known Regina's last name until he heard Bess use it.

Bess rested her hand on Regina's sleeve. "Perhaps we should end the lesson for today. The hour's almost up anyway."

Regina nodded. "Thank you kindly, Miss Craig."

Bess handed her the slate. "We'll meet here tomorrow at the same time."

Regina glanced at Gideon.

Gideon clamped his lips together and looked away. Bess Craig would never forgive him if he told Regina not to come back tomorrow morning. But he couldn't clamp down his frustration at Bess Craig's foolishness.

"All right, Miss Craig," Regina agreed.

The doors swung behind her as she left. Gideon allowed himself to meet Bess's gaze.

She was smiling. "You were quite wonderful, Mr. Riker."

He snorted. "I told you this wasn't a good idea."

"But—"

"If you think this won't happen again with some other customer, you're wrong."

Her smile died. Her face tightened into that rigid look he found so off-putting.

Gideon sighed. "All right, I apologize for insulting you. But the warning stands."

She glared at him and left.

He marched back to the bar where Harry was serving the three men in time to overhear, "Imagine one of Margaret's girls thinkin' she can learn to read."

Gideon glared at the cowboy. "You jealous 'cause you can't read?"

"Uh, no." The cowboy finished off his drink in one gulp and wiped the back of his hand across his mouth. "Let's go, boys."

Gideon watched them leave. Those women were costing him business. This wasn't good. This wasn't good at all.

Chapter 8

The day hasn't improved one iota, Gideon thought, listening to a retelling of the morning's events by one of the men at the bar. Almost midnight and men were still laughing at Doc. Just so they didn't laugh at Bess.

A clatter broke through the laughter, music, and bottles clinking against glasses. It didn't register for a moment, but it went on and on and, suddenly, Gideon recognized the sound. The lunch triangle at the house! Fear shot through him.

He took off running. A crash resounded as the bottle he dropped hit the floor. He grabbed his rifle from behind the counter as he passed it and ran through the back room and out the back door. His chest ached with fright as he rounded the back porch of the house.

A lantern cast swinging shadows across the porch and yard. The cow stood on the porch, bawling. Bess was yelling and ringing the triangle.

Gideon heard a growl and slid to a stop so fast he fell down. He was up in a flash. His gaze searched for Ramon. He spotted the dog on the porch near the cow, growling, straining to get away from Bertie. "What's going on?"

Another growl, low and fierce and way too near, sent him onto the porch pronto. "What—?"

"It's wolves," Bess yelled over the clanging. "After the cow."

Something bumped into him from behind. He jumped and felt like his heart jumped higher than he did.

"What's going on, Gideon?" a voice behind him asked.

"Harry, what're you doing here? Never mind. Stay put. Bess, stop that banging."

She didn't. "I thought the sound might frighten them away."

Gideon grabbed the metal bar from her. "It's going to frighten me away." He shot off the rifle. There were soft thudding sounds out in the night and then silence.

"They're gone." Bertie sounded surprised.

"They'll be back." Gideon motioned toward the open back door where Walter stood, wide-eyed. "Get that dog inside. He's no match for a pack of wolves. And bring me some lit kindling."

Bertie, Walter, and Harry together dragged Ramon inside.

In the lantern light, Gideon could see Bess's hair tumbling over her shoulders to her waist. He caught his breath at the sight.

"What are you going to do with the kindling?"

Her question brought him back to the present. "Wolves don't like fire. But they like cows staked out like a dinner invitation."

"We haven't a cow shed."

Business had kept him so busy, he'd forgotten his promise to build the shed. "We'll take her to the jailhouse."

"What will Mr. Llewellyn and Mr. Potter say to that?"

"I'm not planning to ask them. Where are the chickens? Did the wolves get them?"

"No. We put the chicken crate on the roof at night to keep them from the wolves."

"Good idea."

Bess insisted on going with him to the jailhouse. She led the terrified cow while he carried the torch and rifle. They stopped at the well for a pail of water for the cow.

"Are you sure the w—wolves will come back?" Bess asked on their way back to the house.

"I'm sure. Once they find the cow gone, they'll leave you alone. If it'll make you more comfortable, I'll stay at the house awhile."

"Don't be silly. You need to get back to your business." Her voice trembled in spite of her bravado.

The tremble gentled his own tone. "Harry can handle things."

"If you're sure—"

The relief in her voice made him very sure.

When they arrived back, Gideon sent Harry to the saloon, and Bess sent Walter and Bertie to bed. Then Bess and Gideon settled down in the parlor: Bess on the hope chest, Gideon leaning against the wall where he could see out the window, his rifle near at hand.

His gaze drifted to Bess's hair, where the lamplight played on it. "If you'd like to go to bed, I'll keep watch."

Bess shook her head and drew her wool shawl more closely about her. "I'll keep you company. How did you end up in Lickwind, Mr. Riker?"

Only the Craig sisters called him Mr. Riker. It sounded

strange but nice, too. Like the respectful way people addressed each other back East where he'd grown up. "Came out after the war."

"Is that how your eye was injured? In the war?"

"Yes. After the war, my brother Stanley and I returned home to find our parents dead. Nothing to keep us in Virginia after that, so we headed to Oregon country." He paused, remembering the journey, the excitement with which he and Stan set out, the trials along the trail, the way it ended.

"Why did you stop here?"

He took a deep breath and let it out slowly. "Stan took sick. He's buried along the Platte River Trail, along with thousands of others."

"I'm sorry." Her fingers, soft and gentle like her voice, touched the back of his hand. He fought the desire to lift her fingers to his cheek, to bury his face in her neck, and comfort himself in her arms.

"When I lost Stan, I lost the last person who mattered in my life. I 'bout went loco. I turned away from the wagon trail with my prairie schooner, not caring where I was going, not caring it was still Indian territory, not caring about anything. Came across Lickwind. It was just a spit-in-the-wind place then. I took up residence at a table in the saloon and tried to drink myself out of this life." He gave a sharp laugh. "As you can see, I didn't succeed."

"I'm glad."

He shot her a curious glance but didn't pursue her statement. "As time passed, I pulled myself out of the bottle occasionally, but I never had a good reason to continue on to

Oregon. People pretty much leave a man alone here, and that's the way I like it. In '67, someone discovered gold at South Pass. The saloon owner here traded the saloon to me for my prairie schooner and a note. I was mighty mad at God for takin' away my family. Sellin' liquor seemed a good way to pay Him back. Then the Union Pacific came through. They had their own traveling saloon to keep the crew happy, but the men liked seeing a different place for a change. Made enough money off the crew to pay off the note on the saloon and buy lumber for my house." He shrugged. "So that's my story. War and the trek west—those things are hard on families."

"Yes," Bess murmured.

"You lose anyone in the war?"

"No relatives. Friends." She smiled a little sadly.

"I'm sorry. Is that why you and your sisters didn't marry back East?" The war had killed off a lot of young men and made it difficult for those who returned home to establish themselves enough to support a wife and family.

"Perhaps to some extent." Bess sighed deeply; then she sat up straighter and squared her shoulders. "Are you still angry at God?"

He hadn't asked himself that question for a long time. He considered it for a minute. "Not so much anymore. Now it's more like I don't care."

"But you still run the saloon."

He shrugged. "It's the way I make my living. Man has to support himself. Besides, there's lots of men hurting inside out here. They need a way to forget that hurt for awhile. It's the only way they can keep going. I listen to men's troubles and provide them something to take the pain away for awhile."

"Wouldn't it be better to give them something to help them get through their troubles, so they can stand up again after life's knocked them down?"

"Be glad to offer something like that, but if such a thing exists, I don't know what it is."

Bess stood up, her hair cascading down her back. Her gaze met his squarely. "God's love, Mr. Riker. God's unconditional love. Good night."

He watched her cross the parlor and climb the stairs. He wasn't sure he believed God loved anyone. He sure didn't know how God's love could help a person get through losing everyone they cared about. Bess Craig might believe in God's love, but to him, God's love was nothing but words.

❦

Bess didn't fall asleep immediately upon slipping into bed beside Bertie. Her thoughts remained on her discussion with Gideon and on God's unconditional love. She recalled her conversation with Matty and Corrie after the church service in the saloon. She'd thought then God had brought them here to help change the hearts of Regina and the other women who worked for Margaret Manning. She still believed that. But she was beginning to believe God brought her to Lickwind to stretch her own soul as well.

She'd thought women like Regina crude and ungodly, not as wounded people who didn't know how to find God's love.

And Gideon Riker. She pictured his strong, lined face with a patch over one eye. She'd thought him rough and evil, tempting others with drink. Before tonight, she'd never considered he might be hurting and that, like Regina, he might not know how to reach out to God. But there was a tender spot in his heart. He'd taken in Walter; he looked out for her and Bertie; he had stood up for her and Regina against Doc Mitchel; and he wanted to help the men who came to his saloon to stop hurting inside.

Maybe God brought her here to see people as souls He loves, as hearts that need healing.

"Help Gideon and Regina, Lord," she whispered into the night. "Help them find You, that Your love might heal their wounds, and they might in turn be available to heal others. Amen."

❦

When Gideon slid into bed hours later, after checking on the cow at the jailhouse one last time, he relived his conversation with Bess. He hadn't thought about God or His love for a long time. Now he was surprised to realize he'd told Bess the truth. He wasn't sure how he felt about God, but he wasn't mad at Him anymore.

He mentally kicked himself for getting involved with the Craig sisters. He'd rented them his house, protected them from bullets, attempted to protect Bess's reputation, even forced Doc to apologize to one of Margaret's girls, and now he was protecting a cow. Tomorrow—rather, later today— he'd build a shed he didn't need. Something had to change.

But later in his dreams, Bess Craig smiled up at him from the circle of his arms, her dark hair smelling sweetly of violets and framing her face in beauty; and before he woke, he promised to protect her forever.

❦

Bess glanced up from polishing the stove as Bertie came

inside. Walter and Bertie had spent most of the day outside helping Gideon with the shed. Keeping Bertie in a kitchen was impossible when there was such work as building to help with. Bess had noticed Gideon waited until after her morning lesson with Regina was over before beginning the building.

Bess shook her head in despair. Bertie's scuffed boots were dustier than ever, her skirt covered with sawdust, and the sleeves of her blouse snagged. "I declare, Roberta Suzanne. Mama would think me a failure indeed in the raising of you were she to see you now."

Bertie looked down at herself. "For true, I don't know why. They're only clothes. Besides, Harry says men here would marry anything that got off the railroad."

"Bertie!"

"Well, that's what he said. He doesn't understand why you haven't married up already. Harry says—"

Bess's backbone stiffened. "My marriage preferences are none of his business. Nor yours."

"Grandmother's bloomers, Bess, I'm only trying to be helpful."

"I've no intention of marrying at the moment."

"Then why did you come to Lickwind?"

"To watch over you and your sisters. I'll not marry until you're safely and well a wife, so you can quit contemplating possible suitors for me."

"Harry says you shouldn't be so off-putting. He says the men in town call you 'Bossy Bess.' "

Bess's mouth sagged open. She snapped it shut. "Do they indeed? I should think, in that case, they'd be glad I'm not interested in them as suitors."

"Harry says once you're married up, that's bound to change. The bossy part, I mean."

Bess raised her eyebrows and crossed her arms over her apron. "Indeed?"

Bertie nodded. "He says the right man will know how to tame you."

"Tame me?"

"I told him no man could do that."

"Well, thank you."

"Only love can do that, the love of a woman for a man."

Bess's anger turned to surprise. Perhaps little Bertie was becoming a woman after all beneath that unfeminine attire.

Bertie glanced over Bess's shoulder. The girl's face brightened in a smile. "Hello, Mr. Riker."

Bess wanted to sink through the floorboards. How long had Gideon been standing in the doorway? Had he heard the entire disgusting, embarrassing conversation? She bit back a groan. Likely, he'd already heard the town's feelings about her from liquor-loosened tongues in his establishment. Attempting to gather her shredded dignity, she pasted on a smile and turned to face him. "What can we do for you?"

"Just wanted to let you know the shed and chicken coop are finished."

"Already? My, that was quick." *If he heard our conversation, he's pretending he didn't.* Relief relaxed the muscles about her smile a bit.

"Had good help."

Bess walked outside with him to see the outbuildings and complimented him on them. He gathered up his tools while she stepped into the shed. He was ready to leave when she came out. "Let me know if there's anything else I can do for you," he said. He'd taken six steps before he turned around. "By the way, I agree."

"Agree?"

"No man will ever tame you, Elizabeth Craig." He winked, turned on his heel, and left the yard.

"O-o-o-oh!" Bess stamped her foot. It made only an unsatisfying soft thud. "It's time someone tamed you, Gideon Riker, and all of Lickwind."

❧

Knowing the townsmen ridiculed Bess behind her back made it especially sweet when, within two weeks, two more of Margaret's girls joined Bess and Regina for lessons. All three ladies paid for the teaching—only a pittance, but Bess began the work without expectation of pay, so she accepted it as a gift from God.

Two more boys, Leonard and Jethro Smit, had joined Walter and Bertie in lessons at the house. Bess wasn't about to expose the children to the saloon. Besides, Mr. Smit understandably didn't want his boys near Margaret's girls. Mr. Smit also paid Bess a small fee. Every little bit helped. But it was exhausting trying to keep up with all the schooling, the housework, and the Back Porch.

Gideon kept close watch over the table where the women took their lessons. News had spread that he wouldn't tolerate harassment of the group. Men gave the table a wide berth, though Bess was well aware they watched from a distance.

Mr. Llewellyn, the banker, took up where Gideon left off, trying to convince Bess to give up teaching Margaret's girls.

"Be reasonable, Miss Craig. How will it look for the wife of an upstanding citizen of Lickwind to associate with. . .women of their character?"

"I'm not the wife of any upstanding citizen."

"I'm hoping that will change." He gave her a you-know-what-I-mean smile.

Bess couldn't honestly say his statement surprised her. He came around the Back Porch three times a day and over-stayed his welcome each time, but this was the closest he'd come to openly stating his intentions. "You think that should entice me to give up teaching Miss Bently and the others?"

"I should hope so." He folded his hands over his stomach and rocked back on his heels. "And after all, what good will learning to read and write do any of them?"

"What harm will it do them?"

"Now, Miss Craig—"

"Miss Bently wants to learn to read for a number of reasons—primarily so she can read the Bible one day. Does that sound like foolishness to you?"

He spread his hands. "I'm sure that's laudable, but—"

"But not laudable enough for a wife of yours to continue associating with her? Are you afraid she'll lead me into temptation?"

He looked shocked she would say such a thing. "Of course not. But your reputation, my dear—"

"I've not given you leave to address me by such an endearment. Do not do so again. Now, if you'll excuse me, I've baking to do."

She'd all but shoved him out of the house, her temper

hotter than the perking coffee on the stove.

But when he'd left, she stood looking out the parlor window at the back of the saloon. Was she right in continuing her work and so quickly dismissing Mr. Llewellyn and his offer? She didn't like his attitude, but he was better able than most men to provide a home for her and Bertie. Was it unfair to Bertie to refuse the proposal at which he'd hinted, though she didn't care a smidgen for the man? "Guide me, Lord," she whispered.

Chapter 9

Gideon looked up from behind the bar on a hot June afternoon to see a contingent of surly-looking men enter the saloon. The group included most of the businesspeople in town plus a couple of ranchers: Llewellyn the banker, Potter the attorney, Amos the blacksmith, Jones from the general store, Squires the feedstore owner, the Hatch cousins, Josiah Temple, and weasely Clyde Kincaid. The only people not represented were Doc Mitchel, Margaret Manning, and Bess Craig.

This didn't bode well.

Might as well face it head-on—whatever it was. "Any of you gentlemen want a drink?"

They all did. He poured their drinks, then said, "Now that you've drunk your courage, what're you here for?"

Llewellyn cleared his throat. "It's about the schooling going on in here."

More trouble for Bess. Gideon's blood began to boil. Whatever these men wanted, he wasn't going to make it easy for them. "You men want to join the class?"

Llewellyn uttered an oath. "We want you to put a stop to it."

Gideon nodded slowly. "You find women learning to read and write offensive to your morals, do you?"

Potter glared. "Women like that don't need to know how to read and write."

"Do they need a reason to want to learn?" Gideon put a dirty glass in the tin pan beneath the bar.

Oscar hitched at his trousers. "It don't seem proper, women like that knowing more than a man."

Gideon crossed his arms over his chest. "If that's what's bothering you, I expect Miss Craig would let you join her class."

"Aw, Gideon." Linus pushed his fingers through his hair. "We can't even come in here for a drink anymore for fear of running into Miss Craig. Decent men don't drink in front of God-fearin' women."

Come to think of it, Gideon hadn't seen much of this bunch in his saloon the last month. "She's only in here an hour or so each morning."

Llewellyn slammed his fancy gray hat down on the bar. "Tell the women they can't be holding their lesson here; that's all we're asking."

"You expect me to throw the women out forcibly? Any of you willing to do that?" Gideon looked from one face to another. "I thought not." He rested his elbows on the bar. "But there is a solution."

Every face on the other side of the bar brightened.

Gideon nodded. "Yup. We just need to build Lickwind a school."

"Build a school for Margaret's girls?" Llewellyn roared.

Potter glowered. "With our money?"

Gideon shook his head. "Not just for Margaret's girls. Miss Craig is teaching four of the town's youngsters at her house. You men considering marrying one of the Craig sisters might do well to remember—after marriage come babies. There'll be more youngsters needing schooling, and they might be yours."

He saw right off that was the wrong argument. These men obviously hadn't thought far enough to get to the cradle part of a marriage.

"Second," he continued before they had a chance to think on the first reason too long, "the building could be used for a church and a town meeting hall."

Potter snorted. "We don't need a church or meeting hall."

"I didn't see the parson holding any meetings in your office during the rainstorm last month," Gideon reminded.

Llewellyn carefully settled his hat back on his head. "I'm not aiming to pay for a school for nobody else's kids. If I wanted to spend my money on that sort of thing, I'd have stayed back East." He turned on his heel and headed for the door.

The rest of the men followed—all except Amos. When the others had left the building, Amos leaned against the bar. He smelled of metal and smoke, as always. His skin was almost as gray as his shirt from his work. He reached between his leather apron and shirt and pulled out a crumpled magazine. He smoothed the magazine out on the bar, refusing to meet Gideon's gaze. "I was wonderin' if you'd read somethin' for me."

"Sure, Amos." Gideon glanced down at the magazine

and almost bit his tongue to keep from embarrassing the blacksmith. It was a mail-order bride magazine.

Amos opened it and pointed to a sketch. "Would you read 'bout her?"

Gideon read the glowing terms describing the prospective bride. He hadn't the heart to remind Amos the woman may not be as desirable as described.

"Would you write to her for me, Gideon? See if she'd consider comin' to Lickwind?"

"Why you looking to send for a wife, Amos? Don't you find Bess or Bertie Craig attractive?"

"Aw, Miss Bertie, she's not lookin' for a husband. And Miss Bess, she's too smart for a guy like me. Besides, it's plain as sand in Wyoming that you two are stuck on each other."

Gideon jerked up straight. "I'm not even in line to court her."

"I might not be able to read or write, but I know what it means when a man looks out for a woman the way you look out for her and when a woman looks at a man the way she looks at you."

"She doesn't look at me any particular way."

"If you say so." Amos tugged at his handlebar mustache. "Do you think Miss Craig would teach me to read and write?"

"Don't know why not." Sure seemed to Gideon this was one Lickwind man thinking about a wife, babies, and schooling. Gideon snapped his fingers. "Say, I just came up with a plan to get us a schoolhouse and church." He leaned closer to Amos and explained his plan in a rush. "You with me?"

Amos reached out one of his huge hands and shook with Gideon. "Count me in."

When Amos left, Gideon pulled out a chair, hiked his feet up on a table, and joined his fingers behind his head. Yep, a schoolhouse and church building would solve all his problems. He'd have his saloon back again. One of the men in town would marry Bess Craig then. After all, no one could expect a man to propose to a woman when she spent her days in a saloon with soiled doves, no matter how honorable her intentions. Once Bess Craig was married, he'd have his house back.

He allowed himself to daydream about life in his own house. His new house. No women to protect from drunken men or cows to protect from wolves. No men coming and going all hours of the day for meals or baked goods or to court women. No cats or dogs. Just him and his new house. That's all he wanted.

So why did the thought of it put him in such a foul mood?

❧

The hay-filled mattress ticking scrunched beneath the blanket when Bess sat on the edge of the bed. She pulled the pins from her hair, undid her bun, and started to brush her hair. The Wyoming wind filled it with sand, no matter how she wore it.

Bertie flopped down beside her. "Are you going to marry Mr. Riker?"

"What? Ouch!" The brush bristles caught on Bess's ear. "Why would you ask such a thing? You know I'm not courting him."

"Harry says anyone can see you and Mr. Riker are sweet on each other."

Bess's heart seemed to leap in her chest, but she only said,

"Harry is as good as a newspaper—one that spreads nonsense."

"I like him."

"Harry?"

"No, Mr. Riker. Don't you think he'd make you a good husband? Better than that two-faced banker or too-good-looking lawyer."

"Mr. Riker owns a saloon," Bess reminded. "If the Lord has a husband in mind for me, I'm certain he'll be a God-fearing man."

"Harry says he's seen you making calf eyes at Mr. Riker."

"I have not!" Bess swallowed hard. "Calf eyes, indeed. You must quit spending time with that young man. His language is frightful."

"He likes me. He wants to ask your permission to let him court me, but I said no."

Surprise washed through Bess. "He wants to court you?"

"For true."

Bess lowered the hairbrush and studied Bertie's face. The girl looked extremely pleased with herself, but she didn't look like a girl who'd lost her heart to a man. Bess breathed a sigh of relief. "Apparently, the young man has more sense than I believed."

Bertie sat up. "You think so? For true? Even if I don't dress like a lady?"

"You've a beautiful heart, Bertie. You'll be a blessing to a husband one day."

Bertie beamed. "I don't want to marry Harry, though. I don't want to marry anyone."

"Then the Lord must not think it's time for you to marry yet."

Bertie chewed her lower lip, a sure sign that she had more to say. Bess continued brushing her hair and waited.

"If I married Harry, you could get married, too. You wouldn't need to worry any more about ending up an old maid."

Bess dropped her brush. "An old. . ." She leaned forward to pick up the brush from the floor and hide her face.

"I'll stay with you always, Bess. I won't leave you to grow old alone."

Bess swallowed twice before she trusted her voice. "It's sweet you're willing to make such a sacrifice for me, but let's see what the next couple of years bring before we decide whether it's necessary."

Bertie flopped back, hands behind her head. "Do you think God truly cares about us?"

"Of course He does." But Bess's heart caught at the thought of the future spreading out before the two of them. She loved Bertie dearly and would never abandon her to live on her own, but she did want marriage for each of them. Corrie had Luke and the twins. Matty had Jim and their new son, Matthew.

Each day it grew more difficult to deny her attraction to Gideon Riker. Even if Gideon didn't own a saloon, Bess couldn't expect him or any man to take on the responsibility of Bertie along with a wife.

Sadness settled over Bess's spirit as she put out the lamp and laid down. She'd told Bertie the truth. She did want a God-fearing man for a husband. So why was Gideon Riker, saloon owner, the only man in the vicinity of Lickwind—or anywhere else in the country—who lit a candle in her heart?

Chapter 10

When Bess arrived at the saloon the next day, Gideon stood on the saloon's boardwalk. He grinned at her. "Morning. See my new shingle?" He pointed overhead.

She looked up at the sign that creaked in the wind that swept down the street. Large white letters advertised "Riker's Saloon" as they had since the day she stepped off the train, but this morning a large red X was painted through "Saloon." Below it in red letters, someone had added "Skool."

She burst into laughter.

Gideon joined her.

When they finally caught their breath, Gideon said, "It's intended as an insult, but the spelling shows how desperately the painter could use your lessons."

The mistake provided a fun example in her spelling lesson for Margaret's girls and brought many townspeople into the saloon to tease Gideon.

Bess noticed most of the men's humor changed to anger when they spoke to Gideon. The anger seemed to center on a large tin can on the bar. Curious, she approached Gideon when the lesson was over. "What is the can for?"

"It's the school and church fund."

"What?" Surely she hadn't heard right.

"Town needs a school and a church. No one wants to fund them, so Amos and I decided to do something about it."

She eyed him warily. "How?"

"Amos doesn't provide service to anyone unless they contribute money or labor to the school and church. We figure one building will suffice for both."

Bess shook the can. It rattled. She peeked inside. A handful of coins lay on the bottom. She raised her eyebrows and gave Gideon a skeptical look. "And Amos's customers come here to make their contribution?"

Gideon grinned. "Nope. That's my customers' contributions. I have the same rules as Amos. I serve no one who doesn't contribute."

Bess wondered whether God would want money raised from selling liquor to be used for a house of worship.

"Maybe the money from here will go for the school part of the building," Gideon suggested.

Obviously, he'd guessed her thoughts. "At this rate, it's going to be a long time to afford even a small building."

Bess's doubts were soon banished. The other businessmen, furious that they had to pay above and beyond the normal price for Amos's and Gideon's goods and services, began to demand the same of their customers. Soon all the businesspeople required donations as a prerequisite to providing services. As the fund grew, everyone stopped being mad and grew excited.

❦

One evening as dusk fell, Gideon slipped into a stiff new

shirt, shaved for the second time that day, left the saloon in Harry's care, and headed over to the Back Porch. "Mighty nice sunset, Miss Craig. Could I convince you to go walking with me?"

Was it wishful thinking, or did she look pleased at the invitation? He knew it pleased him when she said yes.

He wasn't brave enough to jump right into his purpose in seeing her. "The school and church committee think we've enough money to begin plans," he told her. The banker, lawyer, and Linus Hatch made up the committee. Gideon had thought Bess should be on it, but the other men didn't agree. Bess suggested Gideon, but the other men didn't agree to him, either. Both Bess and Gideon were grateful the rest of the town was finally behind the project, regardless of who staffed the committee.

"I'm so glad. Have they decided where to build it?"

"At the end of the street, by Doc Mitchel and Llewellyn's houses."

They walked on in silence a few minutes, Gideon working up his courage. "I'm making some changes in my life, Miss Craig. I wanted to tell you about them before you heard about them from someone else."

She stopped walking and turned to him, a question in her eyes and something that looked like fear in her face.

"Nothing awful," he hurried to reassure her. "I'm quitting the saloon."

"Quitting? Selling?"

He shook his head and laughed. "Can't sell. My conscience won't let me." He risked reaching for her hand. Hope flickered when she gently returned the pressure of his fingers.

"My life changed the day you walked into my saloon, Bess Craig. I watched you and saw that unconditional love of God you talked about lived out in your life."

"Mine?" She looked stunned.

"Yours. You reached out to Walter and Regina and Margaret's other girls—people others thought beneath them. You've changed their lives. You changed my life. I couldn't deny God's love when I saw you living it."

Bess looked down at the ground. "You exaggerate my importance in God's work."

"I don't agree. I don't want to keep selling liquor. God's opened my eyes. I can't pretend anymore that liquor's going to help men who are cut up inside. I was angry with God for a long time. I'm not angry at Him anymore."

A beautiful smile brightened her face. "That's the best news you could give me, Gideon."

She didn't seem to realize she'd used his given name. The sound of it on her lips stepped up his heartbeat. Did her heart beat faster, too?

"What will you do with the saloon?"

"I have an idea about that, but it depends on you."

"Me?"

"Your Back Porch business has about outgrown the house. Do you think you'd like to expand it into a restaurant? We could build a kitchen in the saloon's back room. There are already tables and chairs and lots of glasses."

"It sounds perfect, but I'll need to go over the figures and see whether we can afford to rent it from you. And, oh, where will you live? Do you want your house back?"

"I have an idea about that, too."

He hesitated, rubbing his thumb across the back of her hand.

"Yes?" she encouraged.

"I thought if you're willing. . ." He swallowed hard. "We might court a bit. Until the church is built." He reached for her other hand. "Then, if you find me passable, we might start that church out right with a wedding."

Bess gasped.

He trembled. "Is that a no, Miss Craig?"

"No, but I can't be accepting unless you're willing to take in Bertie."

He swept her into his arms, laughing, and twirled her about, the way he'd done back in May. "Never crossed my mind not to, Bess. I love you. I'm plumb loco with love for you."

Her arms tightened about his neck, the sweet violet scent she wore filled his senses, and her soft laughter filled his ears. And then he heard the most beautiful words in the world. "I love you, too, Gideon Riker."

❧

Gideon stood before the simple altar at the front of the church completed only days earlier in a town church-raising. He held out his fist toward his best man. "Here," he whispered.

Jim Collingswood frowned. "What is it?" he whispered back.

"Reimbursement for the money paid Ellis Stack for Bess. A buck-fifty. Figure it's only fair I pay for it, seeing she's my bride."

Jim grinned. "Welcome to the family."

❧

Bess stood in the front of the new white church in Matty's

wedding dress as Harry played the first strains of "The Wedding March." After one last hug from each of her sisters, Bess watched Matty start up the aisle, followed by Corrie. Bertie whispered, "I always knew you were sweet on Gideon." She grinned and followed her sisters.

Bess stepped inside the church. Her gaze sought out Gideon. He met it, smiling, and the warmth in it wrapped around her heart. Imagine this strong, compassionate man loving her!

She'd never expected anything as wonderful as Gideon's love to come from Ellis Stack's mistake. She should have known—God doesn't let mistakes happen. Ellis Stack's mistake was a miracle of love in disguise.

BESS'S EGGLESS COOKIES

Two cups sugar
One cup milk
One cup butter
Raisins or currants
Half-teaspoon nutmeg
Half-teaspoon baking soda
Flour to make thick enough to roll

Mix nutmeg and baking soda with one cup of flour and set aside. Cream together sugar and butter. Mix in milk. Add flour mixture. Add more flour as needed to make the mixture thick enough to roll out.

Sprinkle with granulated sugar and roll over lightly with the rolling pin. Then cut out and press a whole raisin in the center of each; or when done very light brown, brush over while still hot with a soft bit of rag dipped in a thick syrup of sugar and water, sprinkle with currants, and return them to the oven for a moment. These require a quick oven, if using a woodstove. For modern stoves, bake at 375 degrees for 6–8 minutes.

Recipe based on eggless cookie recipe from *Buckeye Cookery*, 1880.

JOANN A. GROTE

JoAnn lives in Minnesota where she grew up. She uses the state for most of her story settings, and like her characters, JoAnn seeks to serve Christ in her work. She believes that readers of novels can receive a message of salvation and encouragement from well-crafted fiction. An award-winning author, she has had over 35 books published, including several novels published with Barbour Publishing in the **Heartsong Presents** line as well as in the American Adventure series for kids.

From Alarming to Charming

by Pamela Kaye Tracy

Dedication

In a book about sisters,
it only seems right to honor my own sisters.
To Roxanne Gould, the sister I recently found:
I look forward to creating memories that concrete a family.
I wish we'd met sooner.
To Patti Osback, my very first sister-in-law:
You were the perfect matchmaker.
I thank God every day for you.
To Cathy McDavid and Alison Hentges,
the sisters of my heart:
Words cannot express the meaning of our friendship.

Chapter 1

July 1869

The town of Lickwind greeted Thomas Hardin the younger much as it had bid him farewell all those years ago. Fistfuls of fine Wyoming dirt pelted his cheeks, this time flung by nature instead of from the hands of cowboys so angry at Thomas Hardin the elder they didn't care about the feelings of his impressionable fifteen-year-old son. Of course, in the last eight years, Thomas had seen more than his share of cowboy justice and knew sometimes it was called for, but just as often it wasn't.

Dust coated his throat, and he coughed as he turned sideways. He'd forgotten about the wicked western wind and how alive it often seemed. Today it whispered angrily as it swirled around him, pressing him to leave.

Leave? Not a chance. As soon as he cleared the grit from his throat, he wanted to meet the town head-on, let it know he'd returned and intended to stay.

Behind him, the pride of the Union Pacific hissed and growled like an angry tomcat, poised for flight but statue still. Heat from the iron horse blistered the air. Thomas blinked a few times, getting his bearings. Train travel might save time and energy, but he'd take a horse any day.

Horses meant freedom. When he'd turned sixteen, he'd jumped on the back of his father's best gelding and galloped away from his father and a memory that threatened to suck the very breath from his chest.

Horses also meant money.

Thomas took a coin from his pocket and danced it between his fingers. Spotting a young man lounging uselessly against what might be called an excuse for a depot, he called, "Hey, Boy." Time to unload five prime mares, and Thomas could use some help. If bloodlines and spirit could be turned into a profit, he intended to make yet another fortune here in the mire of his childhood nightmares.

Horses also took a lot of time.

"Boy," Thomas called again, raising an eyebrow. Either times had changed, or the young man sitting on the rickety depot step had a hearing problem. Money in Lickwind had never been so plentiful—except for the landowners—that a boy didn't keep an eye out for a way to make a little extra.

"Bo—"

"I ain't a boy."

No, she wasn't. Thomas could see that now that she glanced up. Freckles spotted high cheekbones. A hint of strawberry blond hair framed a face protected from the sun by an old, ugly, brown hat. A giant gray-and-black-striped cat indignantly climbed off the girl's lap; and belatedly, Thomas noted the brown skirt that graced the top of scuffed, brown leather boots.

"Roberta Suzanne Craig!" A brunette hurried across a dirt street. This one, from the tips of her high-top laced boots to the lacy bonnet covering her head, was not of the type to be mistaken for a boy.

Before he could move, the boy impersonator jumped up and hid behind him. Peeking over his shoulder, she asked, "How can I earn that money?"

Surprised, he answered, "I wanted help moving my horses."

"Sure, I can help, but you need to convince my sister."

He stepped aside as the pretty one skidded to a stop. She looked like a schoolmistress ready to dress down a truant pupil. He didn't want to get in her way. On the other hand, the tomboy one, Roberta, bobbed up and down like a cork in water. Truthfully, he didn't know which sister posed the bigger threat. He had the feeling that to side with the pretty one would earn him the ire of the other one.

Women.

He preferred horses.

"Bertie, you come around him now!"

To her credit, the girl—she looked like a Bertie—stepped to the side and met her sister's gaze head-on. Her lips pursed together, and Thomas decided that he'd like to see these two take on his two top hands, Rex and Mikey. Rex could shoot a mosquito at twenty paces. Mikey used a bullwhip to slice bread.

The pretty girl's words came out in a rush. "I've been looking for you all morning. You were supposed to make Butter Buds this morning. You know train days are always busy. Also, I checked your sewing basket, and there's enough dust on it to plant a garden. And, you left dirty clothes on the floor again."

Before Thomas had an inkling what she was about to do, Bertie grabbed his arm and yanked him closer to the scolding sister.

"I'm helping with his horses. He's paying me. He's new to town. You always tell me we have to be neighborly."

Two pairs of eyes focused all their attention on him. He stammered, "Wh–wh–whoa, now. I j–ju–just. . ."

"Just what?" Hands went to her hips as Mrs. Bossy frowned at him.

"I th–thought she w–was a boy," Thomas admitted. He wished his tongue would return to normal size and that he'd never noticed the urchin sitting on the stoop.

Masculine laughter rang out behind him. At the sound, Thomas felt his teeth clamp together viselike. Mrs. Bossy smiled a half-hearted greeting. It was Bertie who caught Thomas's attention, and his opinion of her increased. She looked like a foul smell accosted her, and Thomas easily identified the source. Unless he was mistaken, Josiah Temple stood behind him.

This was not how Thomas wanted to face Temple.

Thomas wanted his wealth and power to counter Temple's local prestige. Instead, Temple not only heard Thomas stutter, but also witnessed him mistake a girl for a boy.

Lickwind may have grown, what with the railroad and all—and where had all these women come from?—but in other ways, it stayed small or at least small-minded. No one escaped the scrutiny of Josiah Temple. Thomas likened the man to a burr of a cholla cactus. He'd discovered the stubborn pricklies in the Arizona Territory. About the time he cleared a squatter from his right pant leg, three more settled on his left boot. They seemed to know when he wasn't looking, and here they came, clinging and pestering. Rex said he'd seen one jump more than a mile, just to annoy a man.

"Mrs. Riker." Josiah took off his hat. "Good afternoon."

With a smile that didn't reach his eyes, he turned to Bertie and said, "Boy."

Bertie stuck her tongue out.

Although it annoyed him to ape Temple, Thomas swept the hat from his head. He plain wasn't expecting womenfolk in Lickwind. Mrs. Riker didn't seem to notice, but the homely girl grinned and did the same. Thomas shook his head. Nothing about this day was turning out as he wanted. At least Bertie kept her tongue in her mouth as she smirked at him.

Mrs. Riker grasped Bertie by the arm. "Roberta Suzanne—"

"Bertie!" the urchin insisted.

"Roberta Suzanne, you are too old to be sticking out your tongue. Now march right—"

Bertie dug in her heels. "I'm helping him with the horses."

"That might mean you're assisting a horse thief." Temple's mustache barely moved, yet the words sounded as loud as thunder.

Thomas's fingers itched. Just one minute, no, two—that's all it would take to toss this depraved fool to the ground and pound his face to pulp.

But he couldn't. It looked like Lickwind had turned respectable. It had ladies, one who might swoon and another who might join the fight. Neither circumstance appealed to him. A lifetime of hate wouldn't let him walk away from Temple, but common sense warned that Thomas not act so rash as to find himself facing the end of a rope during his first day in town.

"You look just like your father," Temple said.

At age fifteen, Thomas had looked up to all the cowboys and few landowners. Not any longer. Now, he pretty much expected them to look up to him. "And you look like a man who'd pound a nail into the casket before the doctor filled out the death certificate."

"Tommy," Temple advised, "the best thing for you to do is hop back on that train and leave."

Thomas grinned. "Not a chance."

Temple said nothing.

"You got a problem with me?" Thomas didn't stutter now.

"That a threat?" Temple noted the gun and stepped in front of the ladies.

No doubt they—or at least the pretty one—thought he was being a gentleman.

Yellow-livered. Just the thought made Thomas smile. "You're not worth my time." Thomas put his hat on and winked at Bertie before walking away.

❧

Bertie felt the hair at the back of her neck prickle. Usually Josiah Temple couldn't round a corner without her knowing. He'd snuck up on her today. She'd thought Rhubarb took off because of the man on the train, but now Bertie blamed Josiah for the cat's desertion. Cats were great judges of character, and Rhubarb never erred. The cat adored James, Luke, and Gideon. As for Josiah, Rhubarb wouldn't stay in the same room.

The man on the train obviously felt the same way. Bertie could almost forgive him for mistaking her for a boy.

"Nothing good ever came from a Hardin." Josiah looked bright, but Bertie didn't think it ran deep. Not if he didn't recognize the expression on Bess's face. Of course, Josiah wasn't even looking at Bess; he watched the man he called Hardin walk toward Donald Potter's law office.

Hardin. Bertie liked the sound of it. If Rhubarb had kittens again, Bertie would name the biggest, toughest one Hardin.

Bess's nose twitched, just a bit. A true sign she'd been offended. "You know the man enough to judge?" she asked Josiah.

When Bess used her "teacher" voice, grown men cowered. Even Corrie's little girls, Brianne and Madeline, quieted. Bertie practiced the tone, but she never got it right. Matty said it had something to do with maturing.

Yup, Josiah was for true a fool. He rambled on, still watching Hardin. "I knew his father well enough to judge. We ran Tommy and his old man out of town when it barely rated as a town. Weren't but four or five settling families hereabouts. The Smits, when the boys were younger and before Rachel died." His voice dropped; and if Bertie hadn't known better, she'd think he was being reverent. "Then, the Webbers moved on; they didn't squat but a few months and claimed it got too crowded. As I recall, I think the missus died right before they left. The Collingswoods, but I don't need to tell you about them." Josiah was too much the politician to leer, but Bertie wished she were a man so she could wipe that look off his face.

Josiah was a talker, always, but seldom did he concentrate on anything but himself. Tommy Hardin's arrival really must have shaken him. He barely took a breath before continuing, "The Kincaid brothers were among the first settlers. They beat me here. Cyrus, he was a smart one, not like his brother. Then, there was me. The cowboys were a lot rougher back then—'twasn't anything like it is today. Tommy Hardin's pa was the worst of them. Worked at the Kincaid spread."

Josiah finally turned to face Bess, and Bertie thought he took a step back. But he still wasn't smart enough to stop talking. "Caught Tommy Hardin's daddy rustling my cattle.

I wanted to string him up."

Bertie waited to hear more, but Josiah stopped talking as the land office door closed behind Hardin.

Was Tommy Hardin a cowboy? He didn't dress like one or smell like one. Or was he a rustler like his father?

"It was just a surprise, seeing Tommy." Josiah had the good grace to look sheepish. "Excuse me, ladies, I said too much. Fact is, Scotty stuck up for the Hardins and so most of the men were willing to go easy on his dad."

It was a good thing Bess was just as mesmerized with today's events as Josiah, because it not only saved Josiah from the tongue-lashing he deserved, but it allowed Bertie to slink away unnoticed. Standing behind the railroad depot, she waited until Bess was safely inside their restaurant, The Back Porch, before hurrying in the opposite direction.

Oh, Grandmother's bloomers! Bertie couldn't remember anything so exciting as Thomas Hardin, unless you counted her sisters' weddings. And watching Josiah Temple puff up and then deflate just made Bertie's day.

Bertie peeked around the corner of the train. Any minute now Bess would realize she had neglected to retrieve her student. Escape now meant retribution later, but it would be worth it. Who could she get to accompany her to Matty's and Corrie's place so she could find Scotty? He'd saved Tommy Hardin's father from death. Scotty was a master storyteller. Bertie couldn't imagine why he hadn't already divulged this exciting tale.

Bertie pivoted but didn't manage even one step. In front of her stood the smallest man she'd ever seen. He smiled as Rhubarb wove between his ankles. The cat's tail stood straight up, a true sign of feline contentment. After a moment, Rhubarb deserted her bandy-legged quarry and investigated a cart so loaded with trunks that Bertie couldn't imagine this man pulling it. Bertie got the distinct impression he approved of her. Not a notion she gleaned from most of the adult population in Lickwind.

"Hello," Bertie said.

The man bowed, easily maneuvered the cart, and headed for the middle of the street. Not even the thought of Bess could keep Bertie from following.

Bertie figured that this day packed about as much excitement—at least for her—as had the day the sisters arrived in Lickwind.

The Chinaman positioned his cart out of the way in front of Donald Potter's office. He stood as still as Bertie had ever seen a man be and waited. A handful of people made it to town on Thursdays, but those who did were just as fascinated as Bertie. The Chinaman ignored the stares, and his stoic face didn't acknowledge the few rude words that were thrown his way.

Bertie grew uncomfortable. If Bess found out Bertie had spent an hour standing in the middle of town just staring at a stranger, there'd be a price. Most likely an essay on China's history!

A low whistle saved Bertie. Ramon barked and ran for Jones's store.

Scotty!

Bertie skidded to a stop before the cowboy had time to tie his horse to the post. "There's a man from China, and he's standing on the stoop in from of the land office. I think he came with a man named Tommy Hardin."

Ramon's head nudged Scotty's hand until the old cowboy chuckled. "If that dog herded cattle the way he herds you, he'd be worth something."

Bertie gave her favorite cowboy a quick hug.

Scotty's eyes lit up. "Little Tommy Hardin. Now there's a name I ain't heard in awhile. I taught him to read from the Bible. Not sure it did him any good." Scotty grinned, his mouth cracking open in a toothless display of glee. "Spit and vinegar on two legs and some to spare."

"I'm taller than the Chinaman," Bertie announced.

"They do be skimpy fellas. The railroad employs scores of them."

"I followed him. He's definitely with Tommy Hardin, not the railroad."

Scotty cackled. "That boy could find trouble blindfolded."

"Mr. Temple said he was a thief."

"Well, now, there's some that think that and others who don't."

"What do you think, Scotty?"

Scotty frowned. "I think Tommy's father made some unfortunate choices, but that doesn't mean—"

"They call me Thomas now, and I see you're still sticking up for me." Thomas Hardin took the horse's reins from Scotty's hand and secured them to the post.

Bertie couldn't remember ever seeing a man so handsome.

"Hello, Miss Bertie, and good-bye, Miss Bertie." Thomas Hardin quickly dismissed her presence and slapped Scotty on the back.

Even as Scotty shooed her away, Bertie was wishing, for the first time, that she looked and acted like a woman.

Chapter 2

Bess Riker's kitchen floor shone like the bald spot on Amos Freeling's head. Bertie carried the water bucket out to the garden and emptied it. Her fingers were red and rough from the lye soap Bess favored. Scotty said the Indians lived on dirt floors; and when the floors got dirty, the Indians covered their trash with more dirt, thus creating a new, slightly higher floor.

For true, she loved July in Wyoming. Green as far as you could see and trees so tall they looked like climbing posts to heaven. The bucket banged against her leg as she headed back home, whistling for Rhubarb. The cat always managed to disappear. Today, Bertie didn't have a hope for escape. Any minute now it would be time to head to school, and Bess remained thin-lipped from last week's spectacle.

Apparently the whole town had watched Roberta Suzanne Craig follow a Chinaman from one end of the street to the other. Albert Smit had even come to town special to warn Gideon and Bess that Chinamen were not to be trusted. Albert admitted he personally hadn't dealt with any, but he'd heard and thought that both Hardin and his friends should be run out of town.

Four hours later, with chores and schoolwork behind her, Bertie stood and headed for the door. Her first chance at escape in five days.

She'd barely made two steps before Bess asked, "Bertie, can you recite the nine rules for the use of capital letters?"

Bertie recited, and Regina Bently echoed the rules in a whisper.

"Bertie, you haven't done any piecework all week, and—"

"I need to look for Rhubarb. She hasn't been around all morning."

Bess looked up from the spelling words on Leonard Smit's slate. Her eyes surveyed the room where she held school five days a week. Usually the cat curled up on the floor near where Bertie sat.

Leonard always sat closest to Bess, not only because he needed the most help, but because he was smitten with her. His younger brother Jethro used to sit by the door, escape as much on his mind as Bertie's, but then Harry—Gideon's former barkeep—halfheartedly started attending, and Jethro lost his favorite perch. Walter, more family than student, liked to sit on the floor in front of the piano bench. His sister Regina usually sat next to him.

"Did you look in the shed?" Bess handed Leonard his slate to correct.

"During recess and before spelling."

"He wasn't at our house this morning," Walter offered.

"It's not our house," Regina reminded. They were staying in Frank Llewellyn's house while the banker was out of town.

"Do you want some help?" asked Bess.

A wave of longing washed over Bertie, and she almost said yes. The soft tone of her sister's voice reminded her of their mother—a memory fading faster than Bertie thought possible. Her sisters tried to make up for the loss. She went from having one mother to having four. Even Adele, for a brief time, tried to assume the role. In some ways, their smothering had obliterated any recollection she had of the sweet-voiced woman who called her Baby.

Baby.

The sisters had tried calling Bertie "Baby," but she'd put a stop to that. A neighbor boy back in Rhode Island taught her how to hold her breath until she turned blue. Matty scolded, Corrie cried, and Bess pounded her on the back until she hiccupped, but the sisters got the idea. For true, she hated being the baby of the family. It meant doing everything last, and it meant that the others could always do things better. Bertie didn't even want to try if it meant an older sister was going to judge. She learned to be a baby who didn't cry and who didn't come when called, except sometimes for Bess.

Bess, who sometimes had a soft voice so like Mama's.

Bertie closed her eyes. She intended to disobey her big sister, and the urge to follow the rules suddenly stalled her. "No, I'll find her."

As the door closed behind her, Bertie whistled for Ramon and pretended not to hear Bess's plea to stay out of trouble and not venture far. It wasn't that Bertie went looking for trouble; it was just that trouble always managed to find her.

The town of Lickwind didn't harbor a stray cat in its midst, neither near the smithy where Rhubarb liked to bat small discarded pieces of whatever Amos threw away nor behind the general store where Mr. Jones sometimes tossed the cat tidbits.

Mr. Jones saved the day. He might have been too busy loading up his wagon to entertain Rhubarb, but he wasn't too busy to close up shop and make some deliveries. The mention of Matty's and Corrie's names as a destination sent Bertie scampering back to Bess for permission to keep the grizzled storekeeper company.

Ramon jumped in back of the wagon and fell asleep. The sun beat down steadily as they traveled the hour it took to get to the Collingswood's ranch. Bertie suspected Mr. Jones wanted some advice from Jim about what supplies needed to be stocked now that the train was bringing more business.

At Matty's and Corrie's ranch, neither sister claimed a visit from the cat but both enjoyed their enthusiastic greeting from Ramon. Bertie tickled the twins for a few minutes just to get them laughing. Baby Matthew slept; he was really too little to do much with. Ramon visited all his old haunts and pestered Scotty.

The sun dipped a bit closer to the west than Bertie wanted it to while Jones and Jim jawed about rising prices and populations. After good-byes were said, Mr. Jones headed the wagon in the direction of the Two Horse, the Kincaid spread. Bertie held onto the seat and tried not to bounce. Jones wouldn't like it. The only reason he allowed Bertie to tag along was, as he said, she "didn't act like most fool females." It was unlikely that Rhubarb had strayed so far as the Kincaid spread, but maybe the cat was as curious as the whole town of Lickwind.

Thomas Hardin had dominated the conversation at church last Sunday. Bertie listened to Parson Harris's sermon and tried to remember what the preacher looked like back in Rhode Island. He'd been shorter and talked louder. Bertie liked Harris better. He told more stories. Bertie wished he'd tell about Thomas Hardin.

Later, at the Riker home, Bess and Gideon tried to separate fact from fiction; but by all accounts no one considered it good news that the Hardin boy had returned to town. Even the news of a Chinaman took second place to a returning cattle rustler. Gideon had only raised a speculative eyebrow to Bertie's insistent "son of a cattle rustler" interjection.

In an ironic twist, Thomas—who once fled town with nothing more than the clothes on his back—rode into town followed by rumors of a healthy bank account and more cattle than even Josiah Temple owned. That Hardin had purchased Clyde Kincaid's ranch kept Bess and Gideon whispering well into the night. Bertie almost crawled out of her bed to lean against their door, so strong was the urge to eavesdrop.

The Kincaid ranch needed loving, tender care, Bertie thought, as she sat beside Mr. Jones and watched the world's ugliest ranch loom into sight. It looked exactly like what Clyde Kincaid deserved. The main house was a drab structure. Even from a distance, Bertie could see gaps between the chinks in the wood. There were two other buildings. One might be an outhouse. Who knew what the other was—maybe a hen house?

Walking beside one of the smaller buildings was the Chinaman. Rhubarb meowed at his feet.

Rhubarb had the run of the town and its perimeters. She loved everyone, and everyone loved her; but she only "talked" to Bertie.

Until today.

Bertie jumped from the wagon in time to watch Tommy Hardin exit the house. He joined the Chinaman and her cat.

The man crouched in front of Rhubarb and looked to be offering the cat something.

Bertie sidled closer.

An egg? Yup, for true, Tommy was a cowboy. All the cowboys fed Rhubarb eggs. Someday, Bertie half-expected Rhubarb to cluck.

❧

He'd purchased the Kincaid place almost sight unseen. Donald Potter, the attorney, tried to warn him, but Thomas had been waiting more than five years for prime property in Lickwind to become available. Maybe it was providence that Kincaid sold out.

Looking around, Thomas tried to associate Kincaid's spread today to the spread of yesteryear. When the Hardins worked here, Clyde's brother had run the show. Cyrus had been a tightfisted yet fair man, who worked his cowboys hard but provided for them. Thomas had no idea what had happened to the bunkhouse. If it had burned, surely there'd be charred remains. Instead, dying grass in varying shades of brown and yellow grew over his final remnants of a childhood memory. Clyde probably sold the lumber, anything for a buck. The barn was missing, too.

Donald Potter didn't recall the Kincaid place having many cattle; but when Thomas Hardin the elder put in his time, the spread had enough to make a young boy's eyes burn when the wind blew. Cyrus turned a profit, kept the money, left the ranch to Clyde, and headed for California and fool's gold.

Cyrus had been a fool to leave a working ranch to his younger brother.

Thomas often profited from the foolishness of others. What did it say in the Bible about fools? Something about

282

being hotheaded and reckless.

"Look." Tien-Lu, the Chinaman, pointed.

Thomas glanced over his shoulder and almost moaned. Bertie Craig slid off the front seat of a wagon before the wheels ceased to turn. Any other girl might have inspired him to hurry over and assist, but not this one. She looked like she belonged to the land.

Donald said the Craig girls had a reputation for setting their sight on a man and turning his life upside-down until he married her. Seemed the town, up until a few months ago, had a thriving saloon and a well-visited bordello. Then the saloon manager faced off with one Bess Craig, and now there was a restaurant and church services instead of rowdy Saturday nights and hung-over Sunday mornings. The bordello remained, but business no longer boomed.

The other two sisters took the Collingswood brothers, perfectly good ranchers and horsemen, and turned them into homebodies. Thomas had neither known the touch of a mother nor the caress of a woman who loved only him, but he did know shrewd businessmen who sometimes put a gentle woman before a good business deal.

Thomas made more money than they did.

According to Donald, there remained one single filly in the Craig stable.

Thomas wanted her off his land before bad luck got a fingerhold.

"Hello, Jones. Glad to see you."

Jones jerked a thumb at Bertie. "I picked up a stray in town."

"You need something, Roberta Suzanne Craig?" Thomas ambled over.

She took off her hat and pointed toward Tien-Lu. "That's my cat."

Glancing behind him, this time Thomas did moan. The cat from the train depot, the one who'd lain on Bertie's lap so he'd thought she wore pants. It was partly the cat's fault he'd met up with Josiah in such a comical manner.

"Your cat's trespassing." Thomas frowned. The cat was as unpredictable as her owner. How had the feline gotten this far from town? To think he'd welcomed the critter to his spread and practically laid out the red carpet for a visit from this female.

He'd been amiss yesterday when he'd assessed the other sister as being the comely one. Bertie Craig had the prettiest hair he'd ever seen and more of it, too. It had been all bunched up under that hat yesterday. Today it reminded him of a horse's mane—shiny and blowing in the wind, long enough to stream behind her if the wind picked up. Or maybe if a man's fingers went exploring.

He shook his head, clearing it, then opened his mouth to suggest she take her cat and wait in the wagon for Jones's departure; but Bertie had somehow managed to cross the yard to the shed and was interfering with Tien-Lu as the man struggled to pull down a piece of lumber that far exceeded his reach. The silliest looking dog jumped from the back of Jones's wagon and joined Rhubarb at Tien-Lu's feet, almost tripping the man. Thomas really should have pitched in and helped Jones unload the supplies; instead he followed Bertie. He wanted to see what this slip of a female was up to.

"What are you doing?" Bertie asked.

"Making it into a house."

Thomas figured it was safe to assume that Tien-Lu

answered in English because Bertie surprised him. Most white people, women especially, went out of their way to ignore Tien-Lu's existence. They certainly didn't talk to him. Tien-Lu had perfected the art of pretending he didn't speak or understand English.

Bertie made a face. "A house? It's too small."

"We don't need room."

"We?"

As if knowing they were being talked about, from inside the shed came Tien-Lu's wife and daughter, Trieu and Anna. Anna hid behind her mother, as always. The cat went straight for the little girl, arching her back to an impossible curve until her fur touched the tip of Anna's fingers, and the child had no choice but to reach down and pet the mewling feline.

Bertie's face transformed again. Thomas blinked. Yesterday, she'd been a boy. Ten minutes ago, he'd recognized the hint of a woman. Now, he saw the future and almost lost his breath at the possibility.

Bertie went to Anna and dropped to her knees.

"Her name is Rhubarb. She loves to be scratched right here." Bertie rubbed the cat's back until it collapsed, limp with contentment.

Anna hunched down and stroked Rhubarb's back.

"Rhubarb? Pretty cat." Anna spoke softly, in better English than her father. Her mother spoke no English; and no matter how Thomas prodded, Trieu refused to make an effort to learn.

"Rhubarb, what kind of name is that?" Thomas asked.

"My sister hates rhubarb," Bertie announced.

"Your sister hates this cat?"

"No, Matty loves the cat; she just hates the taste of rhubarb."

"What's that got to do with the cat's name?" Thomas wanted to get back to work, and he wanted this woman off his land.

"I named the cat Rhubarb to annoy my sister Matty."

It was the first time he'd laughed—at least a deep belly type of laugh—in months, maybe years. It felt good, and that scared him. He needed to get her off his ranch. He needed to stop conversing with her as if he enjoyed it. He needed to get back to work. Instead, he asked, "Don't you like your sister?"

"Oh, I love her, but I also like to annoy her." Bertie stood and brushed the grass off her knees. She looked at Trieu and said, "I'm Bertie Craig."

Trieu nodded but didn't speak. Bertie turned to Anna. "You really gonna live in this shed?"

Anna pointed at the dog. "What's its name?"

"Ramon."

"A nice, normal name," Thomas mused.

"I didn't name him," Bertie admitted.

"I want a dog," Anna announced.

The adults laughed. Then Bertie asked Anna again, "Are you going to live there?"

"For a little while," Anna said.

Bertie shot Thomas a dirty look. He raised his hands in helplessness. He'd offered the main house to Tien-Lu, but the man refused.

Tien-Lu wasn't great at taking orders and neither was Bertie. Which is why instead of taking her cat and waiting in the wagon, like Thomas suggested, Bertie started offering advice not only about Anna attending school in town but about rebuilding the shed. Soon, she had Anna and

Trieu slopping in the mud, making chinking.

Thomas frowned as he went to help Jones. Bertie Craig, quite frankly, was as much a nuisance as that cat.

Chapter 3

Thomas opened his eyes in protest. Squinting, he tried to figure out what had awakened him.

The walls were flickering, an orange and yellow inconsistent dance.

Grabbing his trousers, he jerked them on and stumbled from the house to face a small fire. For a moment, he stared in disbelief at the proof of a town that did not welcome him. Obviously the desire had been to frighten and not to harm. There'd be no saving the shed; and so it wouldn't spread to the dry grasses and weeds, Thomas headed for the well and shouted for Tien-Lu.

It took a moment as the small tent almost took on personality as Tien-Lu struggled from his bed. A lump to the left, a poke to the right, and one peg came loose before a pale face poked from the opening.

Thomas barked, "Get out here and help!"

Tien-Lu joined his boss and nodded. Anna and her mother soon crawled from the tent.

"I hear no noise," Tien-Lu muttered, stomping on burning embers. Together they put out the fire as Trieu put a fist in her mouth, biting back tears.

That didn't surprise Thomas. For the past week, Tien-Lu, Trieu, and Anna had worked tirelessly on the shed, turning it into what looked like a miniature cottage. Just that afternoon, Scotty and Bertie had shown up. They'd dismantled the old roof and started work on an arched contraption that Bertie insisted would prevent not only rain deposits but also allow better light. They were a team, that old cowboy and the young girl. Thomas had put off important work just to enjoy listening to Scotty fill Bertie, Anna, and Tien-Lu in on Lickwind's history. The man knew everybody and everything. He could find something good to say about just about everybody, including Josiah Temple.

The concept of five or six families founding Lickwind seemed to fascinate Bertie. Actually, there had been fewer. The Collingswoods were brothers. Amos Smit and Josiah were brothers-in-law. That left only the Webbers and Kincaids as stand-alone settlers.

Lickwind had certainly grown, and every day brought something new to be grateful for. Lost in thought, it took Thomas a moment to realize that a mass of snorting cattle stretched across the landscape.

"Impeccable timing," Thomas said.

"Thanks for the beacon." Mikey didn't dismount. The cattle, spooked by the fire, swerved in a direction opposite from the intentions of the cowboys.

Thomas, grateful to be diverted from the smoking remains of Tien-Lu's home, moved forward to offer guidance. "Rex on point?"

"Yup."

"Who's riding drag?"

"New guy called Jack."

For the next hour, while Tien-Lu diligently patrolled the area for errant sparks, Thomas, Mikey, Rex, and four new hands put the cattle to bed.

"Lose many?" Thomas asked.

Mikey bounced a coiled rope against his leg, exhaustion so tangible, it roiled off him like dust. "We lost some two-year-old heifers. They got spooked when the buffalo came too close."

Thomas nodded. "Any other trouble?"

"Buffalo made the grass a bit scarce. We sure were glad when we came close to Lickwind and saw the grazing land."

❧

Anna started school the next week. For the first time, Bertie looked forward to lessons. Anna, who'd never been to school before, was too excited to sit still. Bertie so enjoyed helping Anna that she forgot to pretend she didn't understand her own lessons. It took four days for Bess to catch on.

"I'm giving you the eighth-grade final examination next week," Bess declared.

Bertie had been playing at school way too long anyway. Ellis had kept her from attending; Bess had been determined Bertie that would finish; and Bertie had been content to drift along.

Bertie finished her math problems, hurried through her duties at the restaurant, neglected her household chores, and finally escaped out the front door. She was more than ready to move, and she knew exactly how she wanted to spend her afternoon. Not in the restaurant, either. She wanted to be at the Two Horse and just maybe Jones would be making a delivery. After all, Bess always said, "We're supposed to be neighborly."

But Jones only chuckled when Bertie skidded to a stop

in front of his store. Pointing toward something behind her, he resumed sweeping the dirt from his front door. In front of The Back Porch, Gideon finished loading one of the restaurant's tables in the back of his wagon.

"You going somewhere?" Bertie asked, already guessing their destination.

"Thought we'd go visit Thomas Hardin and see what you and Scotty find so enticing." Gideon didn't look at her as he said the words.

Guilt painted red splotches across Bertie's cheeks. She'd never been able to keep things from Bess.

Gideon helped Bertie into the wagon and gave Bess one of those married looks that Bertie never could read.

"Gee up!" he shouted after settling in beside his wife.

Bess hugged Bertie; and because it felt right, Bertie didn't shrug away.

They were working on the main house now. Tien-Lu, Trieu, Anna, Bertie, and Scotty. Poor Thomas, Bertie thought. For a man who didn't want women on his ranch, every time he turned around, a new one appeared. Susan, the young wife of Jack, one of Thomas's newly hired cowboys, arrived by train just yesterday. She and Jack had taken a meal at the Back Porch. She was just Bertie's age, and she wore the contentment and awe of the newly married like a shawl around her shoulders. She never took it off, and it was a stunning example of joy, commitment, and love.

And now even more women would gather on the Two Horse soil. Bertie had no doubt but the Collingswoods were en route to this surprise picnic.

"I didn't realize Clyde left such a small house," Bess observed.

Bertie nodded, glad to leave her confusing thoughts for another time. "I'll bet Thomas lets Jack and Susan live in it."

"Bertie, you need to call him Mr. Hardin," Bess advised.

"I'll try to remember," Bertie promised.

Matty and Corrie were already pulling baskets and blankets and such from their wagons while their husbands carried chairs. Tien-Lu and Anna were busy spreading blankets on the ground. Thomas scowled from the doorway of the house.

Matty, jiggling baby Matthew, called, "Come help, Bertie. We've brought a feast."

Bertie had no choice but to pitch in. After a few moments, she asked softly, "Everyone knew that Scotty and I were coming out here?"

"Scotty's had Jim's permission since the beginning. At first, I was a bit concerned; but Scotty said this Thomas Hardin is a good man. Bertie, I've really been looking forward to today. I've been wanting to see this man that you've taken such a shine to. I've never seen you take such pains with your appearance." Matty reached over to push a stray piece of hair away from Bertie's eyes. "Except for Papa's hat." Matty's eyes softened as she gazed at the worn, brown, felt hat on her sister's head. Matty said, "It might be time to put it away, Bertie."

Looking down, Bertie tried to figure how her sister noticed any difference. She mentally kicked herself. Certainly, she wanted Thomas to notice. How could she have been so dense as to not realize others—especially her sisters—might notice first!

"Oh, Grandmother's bloomers," Bertie muttered. Her sisters were joining forces. Any one of the sisters could have put a stop to Bertie's visits to the Two Horse, but all the sisters had had a hand in Bertie's upbringing. They wanted to see just what Bertie was up to. They wanted to see this Thomas Hardin who so had Bertie's head a-spinning.

Fried chicken, potatoes, corn bread, greens, and lemonade were soon unloaded; and the rumor of a meal brought forth the ranch hands hours before their usual suppertime.

Within minutes, a banquet was spread out and the prayer said. Bertie watched as Tien-Lu wrinkled his nose at the American fare. Anna hid behind her mother in a game of hide-and-seek with Bess. Susan and Matty discussed an upcoming baby.

Susan was in the family way? Bertie swallowed. Susan was two months younger than Bertie, yet years more mature in actions and appearance. Unconsciously, Bertie touched the brim of her hat. Lately, she'd been thinking more about her family and the loss of their dairy farm back in Rhode Island. All her girlish dreams, her memories of happiness, centered around dairy farms. Ever since arriving in Lickwind, she'd wanted one of the sisters to start a dairy farm. Her only hope had been Bess. But maybe instead of happiness being a place, maybe it was a person?

Where was Thomas anyway? She knew he hated a crowd, but he'd lost his scowl earlier after accepting a piece of Corrie's apple pie. Bertie headed for the remnants of the burnt shed. No doubt, Thomas was explaining his theory of the fire to some willing ear.

The ear turned out to be Corrie's husband, who deftly changed the subject from heat lightning to. . . "We hope Bertie's not bothering you."

"No, not a bit. She's been quite a help. I never figured I'd let loose a female architect on my land, but she's doing a great job. She and Scotty make quite a team."

Can a smile spread so big as to reach the ears? Bertie wondered. Thomas liked having her around!

"She's good with her hands, " Luke agreed. "We, the family, are a bit concerned with her coming out here—"

"—with someone of my reputation," Thomas finished.

"There is that," Luke agreed.

"Well, she never leaves Scotty's side. Trieu loves her. And little Anna's favorite saying is 'Grandmother's bloomers!' " Thomas laughed. "She's good for Anna."

The feeling of pleasure disappeared as the men laughed at her expense. Bertie almost backed away, torn by the guilt of eavesdropping and the pall of what she was hearing.

I'm good for Anna?

The baby, always treated like the baby.

"Sorry to hear you had a fire," Luke said. "Albert Smit was talking about it over at Jones's store. Guess you were lucky to only lose a shed."

"More than lucky," Thomas agreed.

"You think that fire started by accident?" Luke asked.

"Not sure."

The men were silent for a few moments; then Thomas spoke. "We do appreciate the chance of education for Anna. You sure your sister-in-law is ready for the backlash taking a Chinese into the schoolroom will bring?"

"You don't know Bess very well," Luke observed.

"Ah, but I know Bertie; and I guess if Bess is anything like Bertie, I'll be more than pleased with the outcome. That right, Bertie?"

It took a moment for Bertie to realize he was addressing her. Crouched behind the house, she'd been sure the men were unaware of her.

"Yes," she squeaked.

Luke had the audacity to pat her shoulder as he walked by in search of his wife.

Thomas ambled by next. "Need something, Bertie?"

"Not exactly."

"What do you mean, 'Not exactly'?"

Bertie shook her head. "You think I come here because of Anna?"

"Mostly."

"I come here because it's where I feel at home."

"Where you feel at home?" Thomas echoed. "Here?"

"Yes, here."

He didn't know about dairy farms and security. He didn't know what she was trying to tell him because she wasn't exactly sure herself.

"How do you equate here with home?"

Bertie shrugged. She didn't quite understand her motives for wanting to spend so much time here at the Two Horse Ranch. For true, she felt needed, included; she felt as if these people somehow belonged to her. But even more, every time she caught a glimpse of Thomas, her whole body grew warm, and she suddenly had trouble breathing.

"Well, Squirt, we like having you around." With a careless sweep of his hand, Thomas nudged her hat so it covered her eyes.

He walked away not noticing the scowl on Bertie's face. He liked having her around. She took off her hat and banged it against her leg.

Squirt?

She didn't want to be his squirt.

Chapter 4

Thomas knew that women had no place on his ranch; but now, watching his cowboys make a fuss over baby Matthew and Corrie's twins, he realized that children didn't belong, either—at least not on his ranch. Maybe on some other ranch where fairy tales had happily-ever-after endings and the word "family" actually meant something. Family took too much time—time that could be spent growing the herd, making money.

One of the twins took a few steps, tumbled to the ground, and instead of crying—as Thomas thought most children would do—laughed.

Thomas figured Bertie must have been a child something like this.

"I see you cotton to my youngest daughter." Luke took the plate full of chicken bones out of Thomas's hand and passed it to Bertie. Before Thomas could step back, run, or grunt an "I don't think so," little Brianne nestled in his arms.

He immediately wanted to hand the child back to the proud father, but a quick glance around showed that he was the center of attention. At the Two Horse Ranch, he was supposed to be the center of attention. It suited him fine when giving orders about branding calves and split hooves. It didn't suit so well when, as the person in charge, he wanted nothing more than to admit he was scared to death of a little child. Brianne, who made a half-intrigued and half-irritated face.

Too close. Thomas gathered the girl under her armpits and held her away. Feet dangled in the air in way too trusting an attitude.

And that's when the little flirt smiled at him.

Bertie expertly adjusted Brianne's dress, reminding him that although Bertie often acted like a boy, he'd best remember her womanly side. And along with remembering that, he needed to remind himself that babies and women went hand and hand. When and if he decided it was time to take a wife, he'd go back East for one. He wanted a proper lady who would know her place, and that would be in the kitchen, not designing and rebuilding sheds into cottages, dividing houses, or riding astride horses.

He should have told Scotty to leave Bertie behind from the beginning, before he—and everybody else—started looking forward to the sunshine she brought.

Thomas started to pull the little girl closer, but she puckered up her lips, and her little hands fisted, twirling wildly in the air. Brianne turned a splotchy shade of red.

"You'd best give her to m—" Bertie started.

Brianne didn't exactly throw up. It was more a lumpy, white spit, and the aim was true. The stuff headed straight for Thomas's shirt.

Gut reaction transferred the child to Bertie's arms faster than Thomas thought possible.

"Something wrong, Boss?" Rex asked.

"You step in worse than that all the time," Jack added, laughing.

Untucking his shirt, Thomas used the tail to dab at the wet spot. "Just surprised me, that's all."

Glancing at Bertie, he saw suppressed laughter in her eyes; but worse, she still held Brianne, who no longer wore a pained expression. Instead, with the same wide smile—one looking surprisingly similar to Bertie's—the baby held out her arms, clearly wanting him. He wouldn't have taken her, really, except she whimpered.

Hours later, Bertie's family gathered up the remnants of the feast, along with their children, and prepared to leave.

Thomas relinquished Brianne. He opened his mouth, every instinct urging him to say, "Come again, anytime." Instead he said, "Thanks for the meal."

Luke said the words Thomas couldn't. "You're welcome to visit our spread anytime. It's been, what—a good seven years since you've been around?"

Thomas nodded. He'd spent a bit of time at the Collingswood's spread, probably unbeknownst to them. Scotty had been the pull. Thomas learned to read under the cowboy's direction. The Bible had been the only book Scotty owned. Thomas still carried it. Scotty and a few others saw past the rowdy father to the boy. But that all changed once the words "cattle rustler" became a well-versed whisper.

❧

Fourteen hour days did much in the way of helping Thomas push the thought of family to the back of his mind. He'd never had much luck with family—as any son of a cattle rustler could claim. He barely remembered his mother, and he didn't want to remember his father. It was best to acknowledge that the equation of Thomas Hardin plus family equaled heartache.

Still, it bothered him that Bertie no longer accompanied Scotty to the Two Horse. Scotty dropped by often, Bible in hand and preaching forgiveness on his agenda. He seemed convinced that Thomas should forgive his father. Forgive? Thomas had a hard time swallowing that notion, and Scotty offering up an address for Thomas the elder didn't make things easier. Still, Thomas put up with the visits because sometimes the old cowboy mentioned Bertie. Thomas also discreetly drew school-related Bertie tales from Anna. He was careful not to mention Bertie in front of Tien-Lu. It would only take the merest hint of interest, and Tien-Lu and Trieu would start sewing wedding garments.

Thomas spit out a nail and hammered it into a log. He should be glad Bertie had other things to occupy her time. No doubt, if she were here, she'd be organizing the rebuilding of the shed and stealing his precious nails.

He had plans for his nails.

Now that he had more cowboys to help with the cattle, he was putting his attention to his horses. He loved the cows because they helped line his pockets, but he loved his horses more. He loved being responsible for training them. He could take a wobbly colt and turn it into an outstanding piece of horseflesh. He loved bonding with the animal. And he loved the feeling of trust that he sometimes felt with his mount. It was a kind of trust he felt with few humans, and it bothered him that Lickwind—the place that had ostracized both him and his father—seemed to be filled with people who deserved trust. With that thought, he squinted at the sun and figured it was more than time to head for town.

He didn't trust banks, and Lickwind had a bank and a banker.

According to Donald Potter, Frank Llewellyn stuck out like a sore thumb. The banker wore bright colors and Eastern styles in a place where mud was the favorite color.

Frank had been East for more than a month due to some family emergency, but he'd returned to Lickwind on yesterday's train and would be opening the bank today. Thomas figured the dutiful ranchers—or any man with two pennies to rub together—would check their accounts first thing, so Thomas waited until well past noon before heading to town.

When Thomas finally took a seat in the banker's office, he saw judgment pass over the man's expression. Since the bank didn't rate a clerk, no one had announced Thomas. Frank figured he had an illiterate cowpoke in front of him. It worked in Thomas's favor. He often used a young, unkempt appearance to place his adversaries at a disadvantage. Today he used the cowboy persona through and through.

"Can I help you?" Frank, a chubby man shaped like a water barrel, rested his hands on his stomach and took on the look of a man used to giving advice.

Thomas took a wad of national bank notes from his pocket. "I'd like to make a deposit."

"You new around here? Maybe working on the Kincaid spread?"

"It's the Hardin spread now."

"Takes awhile for change to take root in Lickwind." Frank smiled condescendingly. "You get your first payday? It's a smart thing to start an account."

"I have an account."

Frank blinked, unable to mask his surprise. "You do?"

"Donald Potter opened it more than six months ago."

"Mr. Potter opened an account for Thomas Hard. . ." The banker's words tapered off as understanding dawned. "You're Thomas Hardin."

"In the flesh." Thomas couldn't—and didn't want to—hide the grin.

Frank sat up straight, took the notes from Thomas's hand, and opened the ledger on his desk. Dipping the pen in ink, he quickly made some notations, then fixed Thomas a receipt.

"This isn't correct," Thomas said after glancing at his balance.

"I assure you, I never err in my figures."

"Well, although it occurs to me to let the mistake remain, as it is in my favor, common courtesy demands otherwise."

Frank turned a bit red in the face. "I assure you, there is no error."

And there wasn't, at least not in addition and subtraction.

Thomas's finger didn't have far to trace. There should have only been three transactions listed: his original deposit, his withdrawal for the Kincaid ranch, and the deposit he'd just made. Instead there were four. "When was this twenty-dollar deposit made?"

"This morning. About noon I found a double eagle on top of a note asking me to credit it to your account. It was left on the front table. I assumed you were too busy to wait. I did wonder why you were so trusting."

"Let me see the note."

Frank pulled open the bottom drawer of his desk. Clamped together was a stack of paperwork that Thomas figured represented today's dealings. August twenty-second had been a busy day, it looked like. The note—written on the back of what looked to be a handbill from some long-gone patent medicine man—about the twenty-dollar deposit was at the bottom.

Chicken scratch might be easier to read. Thomas's name and the amount were barely distinguishable scrawls.

❧

"What do you mean, call you Roberta?" Bess's hands, buried deep in a mass of sourdough, stilled. "I'm not sure I can do that."

"Why not?" Bertie said, picking up a glass to dry. "It's my name." And while Bertie might be a name for a squirt, Roberta was a name for a woman.

At first Bertie had loved helping in the restaurant. Just standing on the wooden floors, looking at the gold trim, and admiring the sparkling chandelier made her feel like she was getting away with something decadent. After all, this used to be a place where spirits were sold. Somehow Bertie figured the ground should open up and swallow her whole just for being inside.

It was hard to believe that Gideon once ran a saloon. She gave the glass one last swipe. Drying dishes ruined the shady atmosphere somewhat. Her staid, one-eyed brother-in-law rated as the most serious of the three Craig girls' husbands. And God must still be smiling at the idea of a former saloon hosting Sunday morning sermons. Or at least it did before the new church was built and Gideon moved the piano over. Now that Luke took to preaching on Parson Harris's off-weeks, besides housing the school, the new church got plenty of use.

Bess took the glass from Bertie's hand. "Dry them

smoothly, then set them upside-down. Why do you want to be called Roberta? Yes, it is your name, but you've always refused to answer when we use it."

"I was. . . ," Bertie thought fast, ". . .being unreasonable."

Bess started kneading again. "Anything else you want us to do differently?"

"I'm done with school. I passed the test, right?"

"Yes, you did."

"Can I work here at the restaurant for pay, maybe as a waitress?"

Bess bit the inside of her lip so severely that Bertie could see the indent. "I'll talk with Gideon. We are getting busier, and Regina could use some help. But. . ."

"But what?"

"What you can do," Bess said quietly, "is teach school."

Bertie made a lemonade face.

Bess laughed. "It's not that bad."

⚜

But it was that bad, Bertie thought a few weeks later. The Smit boys weren't that impressed with the change, especially Leonard, who moaned every day for a week about the loss of his beloved Mrs. Riker. Just when Bertie thought she'd reached her limit and might need to knock the two boys' heads together, Jethro decided he'd reached the age to notice girls. Anna was too young to be a contender; the former soiled dove, Regina, was too old and, well, too worldly; and that left Bertie, who was only five years Jethro's senior.

Unfortunately, Bertie would rather find frogs in her lunchbox than have Jethro's puppy-dog eyes follow her every movement. Some days it was all she could do not to stomp her feet and throw a tantrum in front of her students. Instead she imitated Matty's patient voice and tried to stay calm. Still, she always felt relief when three o'clock rolled around.

Today was no exception. She waved good-bye to her pupils from the church's door. Jethro and Leonard disappeared down the street. For them, school meant freedom from the never-ending chores of a ranch. Mr. Smit did without them because he thought schooling might make them better ranchers in the long haul. He didn't even complain about sending them to school during the peak months of July and August. He claimed concern that they'd missed so much schooling. Bertie did admire that he wanted what was best for his boys. Gossip in Lickwind had Mr. Smit pegged as a wealthy man.

Anna rode behind her father on a horse so broad it could have carried Tien-Lu and five more men his size. Neither mentioned Bertie's absence from the Two Horse. Either they thought she was too busy to drop by or they didn't miss her. Tien-Lu just bowed and nodded his approval all the while appraising her with his shiny, black eyes as if she were supposed to say something, know something, do something.

To be honest, both the restaurant and school paled in comparison to the excitement of helping at the Two Horse. Helping at a place where she obviously wasn't missed. Thomas Hardin never even came to town. She'd never even had time to let him know that she wasn't his squirt.

Bertie stopped waving once Regina and Walter entered the restaurant. Besides Bess, Regina was the Back Porch's only waitress. She did a great job and many of the patrons requested her. Bertie shook her head as she thought of the fancy banker, Frank Llewellyn, who often left the comfort of his home to eat at The Back Porch. And since Regina hired on as his housekeeper, the banker was almost bearable, although when Regina had time to clean was anybody's guess.

Still Regina's little brother Walter claimed Lewellyn was tolerable to live with. Though for a boy, living in Llewellyn's house was like living in a mansion, not that Walter had ever seen a mansion.

Watching Regina and Walter enter the restaurant made Bertie think about Harry, Gideon's old barkeep. She missed him. He'd been offered Regina's job, but he claimed it didn't pay enough. Odd jobs didn't suit him; schooling didn't inspire him; and Lickwind no longer seemed to have anything to offer him. One morning he'd not shown up for class, and that afternoon Bertie watched him board the Union Pacific for parts unknown.

The wind kicked up, sending Bertie's dress whipping around her legs. Maybe a storm was brewing. She closed the door and went to her desk. Actually, sometimes she liked the quiet of the church after all the students were gone. Growing up as the youngest Craig girl, she'd never spent much quiet, private time indoors. Seemed there was always a sister hanging around wanting to know what she was doing or wanting to tell her what to do. She'd escaped outdoors for solitude.

A few hours later, after she'd graded all the papers and outlined the next day's lesson, she blew out the lantern and headed down the steps.

Mr. Smit rode his horse straight for the church. Funny, it was much too early for a rancher to cease work. He took off his hat before he slid off his horse.

"Mr. Smit." Bertie hoped the man—who always looked like he had a stomachache—wasn't here to court. Since

Bertie took on the role of schoolmarm, half the cowboys in Lickwind decided she was on the market.

"I need to be talking to you about my boys."

Oh, good. He was here to discuss Jethro's crush. She could deal with that. "Jethro will outgrow this, Mr. Smit, I'm sure."

"I'm disturbed that my boys have to be in a classroom with a dirty Chinese child."

"Dirty? The child is quite clean."

Mr. Smit's face reddened. "I shoulda came back when yer sister was a-teaching. She being older and all. But the truth is, I didn't have time. And now I'm here to tell ya that if the little Chinese girl continues in this school, my boys will stay home."

"Your boys are doing great. They've gone from being illiterate to reading from the second primer. That's extraordinary. You'd deny them an education because of your fear of a five-year-old girl?"

If anything, Mr. Smit's face reddened even more. "Not sure I want them in a classroom with a female got a tongue like yours."

"I'm not removing Anna from my classroom. Good day, Mr. Smit."

Mr. Smit got back on his horse, shaking his head. "You're young. I'll be talking to that brother-in-law of yours. He'll set things right. My boys have a right to an education. They're Americans."

Bertie closed the door behind her. Bess had already experienced outrage from Mr. Smit about Regina. Looked like it was Bertie's turn to deal with the man's prejudice. This time, however, Mr. Smit was picking on a defenseless child. Regina had been no stranger to the callousness of men.

If Bertie had her way, Anna would never witness it.

Chapter 5

Josiah Temple entered the restaurant as dusk spread out over the town. He strode purposely for his favorite table by the front window. Bertie grimaced. Her table. She'd already had a rotten day and now to wait on the man who made her skin crawl. He reminded her of Ellis.

"Coffee?" she asked.

"Yes, and I need to talk to Gideon."

"I'll tell him."

The men went through four cups of coffee before Josiah pushed away from the table and left. Gideon looked ready to smash a window. Bertie and Bess peered from the kitchen door and slowly came out. Gideon changed the front sign to CLOSED; and brushing a hand across his eyes, he walked toward them.

"Bertie, something happen at school today that you want to share with me?"

"Mr. Smit came to visit."

"Mr. Smit!" Bess exclaimed. "Is Leonard sweet on you?"

"No, Jethro is, but that's not why Mr. Smit paid me a visit."

"Seems the school board's against the idea of a Chinese child attending public school." Gideon leaned against the counter and shook his head. "According to them, you either have to prohibit her from attending or stop using the church."

"What?" Bess gasped.

"Who makes up the school board?" Bertie asked.

"Llewellyn, Potter, Linus Hatch."

"Then why is Temple delivering the news?"

"Because he somehow swayed their opinions," Bess said grimly.

"I refuse to stop Anna from attending school," Bertie said.

"Fact is," Gideon said, "you can't refuse."

Bess's eyes sparked with challenge. "She can, and she w—"

"Josiah says he's already met with the school board members, and they're in agreement."

"Those men attend church!" Bess exclaimed. "How could they? I expect this type of prejudice from Temple but not from the others. I'll go talk to them."

"We'll both talk to them," Gideon said. "But for now, school's suspended for the rest of the week. He's already spread the word. Bertie, he wants us to ride out and tell Anna's family tomorrow."

"I won't. And I quit. I never wanted to be a schoolteacher anyhow."

Bess shook her head. "If you quit, then you're giving up. And we Craig girls are not quitters."

Gideon added, "Besides, you'll be punishing the innocent. I've no doubt the Smit boys wish they'd kept their mouths shut. Seems they were smart enough to keep her attendance a secret. Mr. Smit overheard them after school today. That's how he found out. You stop teaching school, and you'll be heaping a whole lot of guilt on those boys' consciences along with their losing out on schooling.

"And, fact is, if we don't ride out and tell Anna's family, Josiah says he will. Don't you think it would be kinder coming from you?"

"I'll do it," Bess offered. "But, then we're going to fight it."

"No," Bertie said. "I'll do it."

❧

Bertie woke early—not that she'd gotten much sleep, knowing that Gideon wanted to get this done early so he could return to the restaurant. Bess was staying behind to handle the few who might show up to order breakfast.

Bertie wasn't sure what words she'd use to crumble Anna's world. Bertie had been the first to suggest Anna attend school, and it just might have been Bertie's approach to teaching—so different from Bess's—that had the Smit boys so talkative. If Gideon and Bess came along, they'd take over. Bertie was the schoolteacher now. Not a baby; not a squirt. Sitting down, she tried to think of the words to say. In a way, she was like a student passing an invisible test. She just hated that she had to visit the Two Horse to expel Anna. Bertie wanted to return to the ranch because Thomas missed her.

Crawling from bed, she quietly opened her bureau and, instead of taking the old brown homespun she favored because it blended in, she took the blue-and-white-striped calico skirt that Matty had given her. She'd not worn it yet. Tucking in a white blouse, she briefly considered taking the time to iron out the wrinkles; but her stomach roiled, protesting against what she had to do today. Shoes were the easiest. No choice there. She wore boots, brown and made of leather, just like her father had. They looked funny and big, peeking out from under her skirt.

Ramon barked. Bertie took a breath. Any minute they'd be leaving for Thomas's farm. This morning she had to tell Anna not to come to school for awhile. It almost seemed wrong to be wearing good clothes and doing something so ordinary as brushing her strawberry blond hair.

Her boots made loud *clop, clop* noises as she headed for the restaurant's kitchen. Funny, she'd never noticed before.

Bess stirred eggs into a big bowl. "You hungry, Bertie?"

"No."

For once, Bess didn't insist. "I did it again. Called you Bertie when you want to be called Roberta. Guess I can't get used to you growing up."

"You ready?" Gideon called from the front.

Bess offered a quick hug and ordered Ramon to stay behind. Before Bertie was really ready, it was time to go.

They weren't taking the wagon. Bertie half thought this was Gideon's way of trying to do something to please her. It had been awhile since she'd ridden. Funny, she hadn't really missed it, although at one time riding had been her favorite pastime.

She tossed saddlebags over one of Gideon's horses and plopped her father's hat on her head before climbing on the horse's back. Then, she artistically arranged her new skirt and galloped after her brother-in-law toward the Two Horse.

A few miles out, she told Gideon, "I want to do the talking."

"You need any advice?" he offered.

"I'll look to you if I do."

"Fair enough." He left it at that, and she was grateful.

An hour later, Gideon was off his horse.

"What's wrong?" Bertie asked.

"He's taken a stone. It will just take me a minute to deal

with it. You ride on ahead."

Freedom. She remembered it from when Papa and Mama were alive, and she experienced it now as she lived with Bess and Gideon.

Things were changing so quickly in her life that she almost felt like she was trying to catch a butterfly that always managed to fly just outside her grasp. She didn't like being a schoolteacher, but she could be good at it. She didn't enjoy being a waitress although it was more fun than teaching, and she made money almost immediately. Why, a man from last Thursday's train left her a quarter. A quarter! He also proposed marriage.

She brought her horse to a walk, trying to give Gideon time to catch up. Lost in her thoughts, she saw the men before she heard them. At first she thought she'd stumbled across Thomas. She reined the horse and slid from his back. No, it was not Thomas, and there were two men. One sat on a fallen tree and laughed at something the other man said.

What was Josiah Temple doing on Thomas's land?

And who was the other man?

Josiah scared Bertie enough, and the other man looked meaner than a snake. She felt her legs start to wobble. She needed to get out of there before the horse snorted or before something else happened to alert the men of her proximity.

She quietly led the horse in the opposite direction and took off. She couldn't say which bothered her more: thinking about telling Tien-Lu and his family about Anna not being allowed to attend school or thinking about Josiah meeting up with what looked like an outlaw on Thomas's land.

❧

Thomas slowed his horse and squinted at a landmark. He

wanted to mark his land's boundaries. He had an old map Cyrus had drawn and every reason to believe it was reliable, but it didn't look like he'd get much done today. A female—wearing a blue-and-white-striped skirt and an old, ugly hat—galloped toward him followed by Gideon Riker. Thomas couldn't help but smile. He'd have to be blind to miss the woman Bertie'd become.

The smile soon faded. As they neared him, he saw that something was wrong. He saw that not only was Bertie out of breath, but Gideon looked a bit concerned. His observations were confirmed as they slowed. Instead of a cheerful greeting, Bertie stammered, "Did you see the men?"

"What men?"

Gideon answered, "Bertie saw Josiah and some cowboy a few miles back. It spooked her."

"It wasn't a cowboy. He was an outlaw, and they were up to no good," she urged, wheeling her horse around. "I just know it. We need to find where they've gone."

Exchanging a quizzical look with Gideon, Thomas rode beside her as she galloped toward the east. He had to admire the way she handled a horse. Gideon followed a few paces behind. Finally she stopped near a clump of fallen trees he'd been meaning to convert to firewood. Sweat glistened on her forehead, and her cheeks flushed a bright pink. "They were right here."

"Who was with Josiah?" asked Thomas.

"Some outlaw."

He almost laughed, but she didn't look in the mood for pranks. "An outlaw?"

"Yes, talking to Josiah."

"What were they talking about?"

"I didn't get close enough to hear."

"How do you know it was an outlaw?" Gideon asked.

"I've seen pictures of outlaws on the posters in Jones's store."

Bertie Craig was scared, and she looked up at Thomas with the same trust her niece had just a few weeks ago.

"Josiah is as free to roam it as you are. And, just because a man looks like an outlaw doesn't mean he is one."

Gideon added, "Bertie, I'm sure everything's all right."

She made a face and looked like she wanted to say more.

"Don't worry about us out here at the Two Horse. We'll be just fine. We can take care of ourselves. Besides, Josiah's a mosquito I'd just love to squash." Thomas rode next to her. "What brings you out to the Two Horse?"

"I'm here on school business."

He grinned. "Anna tells me you're her favorite teacher, never mind that you're her only teacher. She's pretending to read from the Bible each night. I think she mimics the stories you tell during the day. Most interesting. I've always thought Eve handed Adam an apple. Anna insists that the type of fruit is unknown. Is that your doing?"

To his surprise, Bertie didn't pick up on his teasing. If she'd been a different girl, maybe he'd think the glistening in her eyes was the beginning of tears.

"Bertie, what is it? Are you still afraid because you think you saw an outlaw?"

"I did see an outlaw."

"Phew, you are in a mood today. Why are you so grumpy?"

"Life isn't fair."

He wondered what brought this on. Life wasn't fair; she was right. He'd been dealt some bad luck early in life, but he'd dealt with it alone. According to Donald, the Craig girls had been dealt an equal amount of bad luck, only they'd had each other. He noticed the way the girls watched over each other, and the way they hovered over Bertie made him understand why she acted as outrageously as she did.

They rode toward the Two Horse. Bertie was silent, seemingly lost in thought. Gideon just shook his head. Thomas figured she'd open up soon enough. Something certainly had her vexed today.

But she didn't speak again. And when they got to his land and Anna's head peeked from a window, he heard Bertie take a deep breath.

Oh no. No wonder Josiah and the outlaw had Bertie so spooked. If Thomas had been any other rancher, he'd have blamed the calamities his ranch seemed to attract on the townspeople warning the Chinese away. But in Lickwind, it was the Hardin name that most people wanted to forget. It maybe just took the town a bit longer to target Tien-Lu.

"Teacher! You look so pretty." Anna burst from the house, a small tornado of energy with a smile that split her face.

And Bertie did look beautiful. Her hair, even topped by that ridiculous hat, cascaded down an elegant, curved back. She sat the saddle poised and confident. The kind of woman any rancher would be proud to have by his side.

Whoa, those were thoughts Thomas didn't deserve to consider, especially not about this female who changed from a boy to a child to woman back to child on a whim.

"Anna, go get your father. I need to speak with him." Bertie's face looked pale under the freckles.

Thomas watched Anna turn around and fly toward the back of the house where Tien-Lu prepared the noon meal.

"You don't have the guts to tell that child she's not welcome in your school so you'll tell her father and let him do the deed?"

"Slow down, Thomas," Gideon advised.

"I've got guts and plenty extra," said Bertie, pulling her horse to a halt in front of the house, dismounting, and tying Nugget to a post. "But if I didn't come out here, your friend Josiah volunteered. I figured I was the lesser of the two evils."

"Missy Bertie." Tien-Lu rounded the house, grinning and bowing. He handed her a pastry wrapped in a towel.

"Josiah's no friend of mine." Thomas felt like he was losing control of the conversation.

Anna held on to her father's knee. "I helpt to make that, Miss Craig." She cast a look Gideon's way. "Oh, I shoulda brought you one, too."

"That's all right, Sweetie," Gideon said.

Bertie took a bite and closed her eyes in contentment. If only she were here to visit and sample Tien-Lu's cooking. Handing Gideon the pastry to finish, she knelt down so she was eye level with Anna. "What do you think, Anna, about me coming here to teach you on Saturdays so you won't have to travel all the way to town?"

"I like town. It's exciting. And Mama says I can't have a brown hat like yours, but I'm gonna keep asking."

"Town is exciting, but your papa has lots of chores, and town is a long way. Can we try it for awhile and see how it works?"

Gideon cleared his throat, and Bertie looked at him, expecting some sort of rebuttal. "I'll bring the ladies out here; I'm sure Bess will want to pitch in. You think you can see them home, Thomas?"

Anna looked up at Tien-Lu.

He nodded, his eyes meeting Bertie's head-on.

It isn't fair, Thomas mentally agreed with Bertie's earlier statement.

"Okay," Anna whispered, looking unhappy.

"Great." Bertie took off her hat. "Oh, and Anna, this hat always helped me when I did my homework. Why don't you see if it helps you?"

Thomas swallowed, watching as a too-big hat enveloped Anna's face.

Chapter 6

Thomas frowned but didn't lose his temper. He'd arrived in town a few minutes ago to pick up the fringe-top surrey he'd ordered almost a month ago. Instead of parading through town with a first-class surrey, he surveyed the damage done by what must have been a madman wielding an axe.

Funny, he was more disappointed than mad. When he'd ordered the contraption, he'd been thinking about an Eastern bride, which Bertie Craig wasn't. Now he realized that when he pictured himself in the vehicle, Bertie's image was planted firmly by his side. No wonder her sister and brother-in-law worried. He'd been aware of Bertie's crush since she'd first tagged along with Scotty to pitch in with fixing up the Two Horse. What he hadn't been aware of was how much he really enjoyed having her around—the squirt.

Townspeople, gathered round as if viewing a social event, took it as a bad omen. With the exception of Saturday night fights involving cowboys letting off steam, this type of crime left Lickwind alone—at least since the rustling problem some years back. In Thomas's presence, no one mentioned that the Hardin name seemed synonymous with disaster. Since his arrival, the Kincaid place suffered a fire plus the theft of two saddles. Thomas and his men worked daily trying to build a barn, and often either work was destroyed or supplies went missing overnight. Thomas wasn't inclined to blame acts of nature for any of the calamities befalling him.

"Boss, what do you need me to do?" Rex asked. Along with the surrey, Thomas had arranged for the delivery of a stallion. Rex held Zeus steady. If anything, it was Rex who needed calming. He was not the sort of cowboy to stand around. All Thomas needed to do was point, and Rex would attack.

"Nothing," Thomas said, a strange sense of calm subduing him. He'd expected Lickwind to be unwelcoming—but he'd expected a frontal attack: bitter looks, refusal of services, and a sense of exile. Instead, looks were impassive or welcoming—thanks to the Craig sisters, especially that spitfire Bertie. His money guaranteed services even from those thoroughly committed to Josiah's camp. Instead of exile, his ranch was turning into a regular social community—complete with women and children.

And yet someone, stealthy as a shadow, struck when no one was looking. The surrey had been taken from the train and left beside the depot. It couldn't have been left alone more than an hour, but that was probably about how long it took. Surprising to think that no one had heard anything. Thomas turned and marched down the street.

"You got an idea?" Rex asked, keeping up.

"A destination."

The bank was empty. Any customer it might have had now stood in the audience just outside the door. Thomas, more a main attraction than he ever wanted to be, headed for the bank's office.

Frank Llewellyn was not at his desk; when Thomas turned around to face the door, he met the guarded eyes of the banker. Sweat, courtesy of the August sun, dotted his forehead. Thomas knew in that instant that Frank had been in the crowd by the wrecked wagon—which meant he'd left the bank unmanned.

Their eyes met, the banker and the rancher, and almost in one accord they slowly turned and surveyed the lobby—both sensing what they would find.

Money, with a scrap of paper specifying Thomas's account.

"How much did you pay for the wagon?" Frank picked up the offering from the little table where customers often sat waiting their turn.

"Seventy-five dollars."

"Give me a minute, I'll count."

It didn't even take a minute. Frank might consider himself a contemporary of Josiah, but the continuous deposits made to Thomas's account by a person or persons unknown made Frank and Thomas partners of a sort.

"Seventy-five dollars," Frank verified. Neither man was surprised that the amount of the deposit matched what Thomas had paid for the wagon. In the past month, a deposit had been made each and every time something belonging to Thomas was stolen or destroyed. Two saddles meant another double eagle in Thomas's account. The bantam hen fetched a gold dollar.

Whoever made the deposits used quite a bit of patent medicine, because the scraps of paper were the only clues as to the benefactor. The store didn't sell this particular brand of medicine, which halted Thomas's momentary foray into detective work.

No one, save Rex, chanced entering the bank. It was as if the town thought an invisible line should keep them from getting too close to Thomas. Stepping out into the sunshine, Thomas looked across the town. Most of the townspeople had the dignity to pretend conversation. Albert Smit and Amos Freeling shook their heads in disgust. Thomas couldn't tell if their feelings were about him or about the situation. Even Doc Mitchel found the day's events more interesting than a bottle. Thomas didn't really care.

Across the street, he could see Bertie's look of sympathy. Rex tossed Walter a nickel, said a few words, and the boy headed toward Amos Freeling's blacksmith shop. Surely, something could be salvaged.

Thomas followed his heart to the restaurant. He hadn't taken the time to dine at the restaurant partly because he was too busy getting the ranch together and partly because he wanted to choose the time to rub his existence into the face of Lickwind.

He might need to rethink his strategy.

The kitchen was a lot smaller than he'd imagined. It had probably, at one time, housed liquor. An iron stove took up one whole wall. Hand-tooled tables were covered with an assortment of dishes and a row of still-steaming desserts. No one could bake like the Craig women. Bertie stood next to a small window. She was just finishing up the final twist of a very long braid.

"Bertie."

She took an apron from a drawer and turned to face him. He'd seen that face—in the flesh or in his thoughts—almost daily since coming to Lickwind. And always her eyes were snapping, eager, happy to see him. He'd never appreciated that particular "Bertie" trait.

He felt as if he were noticing her face for the first time.

Her eyes stared at him as impassive as the crowd outside. "That wasn't aimed at Tien-Lu; that was aimed at you."

A month ago, a week ago, maybe even yesterday, he'd have let anger roil over him like a rattlesnake ready to strike. But something he saw in Bertie's eyes warned him to take care with his words. "Not all men are good, Bertie."

"You think Josiah did that? You think that's why he was on your place with that outlaw?"

"Josiah's not in the crowd outside. I don't know who to blame."

"Were you going to take me riding in that surrey?"

"You would have been first."

They stood there, not touching, but both aware that something was changing. It would take more than a destroyed surrey and protective sisters to stop whatever it was.

❧

One week later, Bertie hung clothes on the line and took a deep breath of the flowers that dotted the fringe of Bess's garden. She loved Saturday; but since the dismissal of school, Saturday didn't feel quite so special.

In church last Sunday, Parson Harris spoke about laying your burdens at God's feet. It was past time for Bertie to hear that sermon. She'd been afraid to put anything at God's feet since her parents had died. None of her prayers about their safety had been answered. Later, while living with Adele and Ellis, Bertie had tried prayer again.

She'd always kind of thought God had forgotten about her, and that's when she'd stopped talking to Him. No wonder her sisters wanted to called her Baby. Bertie deserved it.

She acted childish; she always had. But maybe bringing her to Lickwind had been the slow-coming answer to her prayer. Corrie always urged Bertie to not expect answer so fast. Corrie advised that Bertie should think of Abraham, who, after so patiently waiting, received what was promised.

Matty always claimed Bertie to be stubborn. Matty was right. It was time to pray again, and Bertie had something to pray about. Thomas had yet to step into church, although Scotty faithfully reminded him about services.

Scotty wasn't the only one, either. Last Saturday morning Gideon drove Bess and Bertie out to the Two Horse for their first tutoring session. Thomas drove them back, and Bess issued a standing invitation not only to church but to a meal afterwards. Thomas didn't say yes, but he also didn't say no.

Bertie knew Bess was impressed with Thomas Hardin. As a team, the two women taught both Anna, Trieu, and even Susan lessons. Susan was an apt student and practically beamed at the thought that she might someday be able to read to the child she now carried. Maybe by that time the Lickwind school would be reopened. For the last week and a half, Walter and Regina took their lessons between meals at the restaurant. The Smit boys hadn't been allowed near Bertie and the family since school disbanded.

It was past time to make some changes. Her first one started weeks ago, when she'd ordered a hat from Mr. Jones. Serving food at the Back Porch gave her a little personal money. Ordering that hat had made giving her father's hat to Anna seem the right thing to do. And, last Monday morning, she became the perfect sister. It did Bertie's heart good to watch Bess looking so mystified as Bertie willingly picked up not only her piecework but her clothes from the bedroom floor.

Whistling for Ramon, Bertie started back for the house. Two sharp barks greeted her. The dog burst from the back door of Bess's house and zoomed to Bertie's side. Rhubarb hissed, arched, and headed for a nearby tree.

"Why are you inside on such a beautiful day?" Bertie asked as she managed not to tumble over the excited poodle.

Inside Bess's kitchen, all the sisters gathered around the kitchen table. Matthew gurgled happily in an empty wash tub on the floor at Matty's feet. The twins played with sock dolls and engaged in a nonsense conversation.

"We're finally bringing Parson Harris here full-time," Matty announced the moment Bertie came through the door.

"And since we already have a church," Corrie continued, finishing Matty's sentence, "all we need is a parsonage."

"So," Bess added, "we're trying to think of some kind of fund-raiser. Do you have any ideas?"

The sisters, pink-cheeked and excited, all looked at Bertie. She took a step back. It had to be a conspiracy. They wanted something, but advice about a fund-raiser probably wasn't it. They never came to Bertie for advice, although they went to each other for advice about Bertie. She narrowed her eyes and waited.

Bess grinned. "I'd love to do a box social; but with Bertie being the only respectable single female besides Regina, it might be terrifying."

The train's whistle saved Bertie from making the ulti-mate sacrifice. She'd been about to enter the kitchen and sit down with her sisters as an equal. Once she took that step, there'd be no turning back. She'd be expected to always sit in a buggy instead of astride a horse. She'd be expected to cook and sew willingly!

"Train's here," Bertie said by way of explanation as she bolted out the door. Only four hours overdue, the Union Pacific roared into a town no longer anticipating its arrival. It could not have chosen a better time to arrive.

"You expecting a package?" Linus Hatch winked.

Bertie smiled uncomfortably, although she knew it was too soon for the new hat's arrival.

Hmmm, Linus never used to wink.

She tugged her dress down so it covered the tips of her brown leather boots and pushed a strand of hair behind her ear before taking a deep breath of coal dust and heat. It was a warm September. Just over a year ago she had disembarked from this very train. Her sisters had clutched clothes and determination and responsibility. Bertie had clutched a hatbox containing Rhubarb and the hope that she could recover what was left of her childhood. Her sisters had somehow known that Lickwind represented security and roots. Bertie knew nothing of the sort. All she wanted was a return to a way of life she barely remembered and to figure out why she never felt like she belonged.

Almost against her will, she thought of the Two Horse Ranch. Thomas's place—where she truly felt she belonged.

But why?

It wasn't like Thomas greeted her with open arms every time she showed up. No, he treated her much the same way he treated his new cowboys: half suspicion that she'd do something to muck things up and half boss telling her what to do.

Lately, he'd acted all stiff and uncomfortable. He almost tripped over himself before driving them back from Anna's tutoring to make sure Bess sat in front beside him.

Bertie grinned. Come to think of it, he was stuttering again; and she sure didn't think it had anything to do with Josiah. She liked to think it had something to do with her. "Yes, I'm expecting a package," she told Linus. "Did it arrive?"

"They've not unloaded the mail yet."

Bertie's first inclination was to take a seat on the step, but she didn't want to get her new pink-striped dress dirty. Matty had only finished sewing it last week. Bess said Bertie should save it for good, but lately every day felt good—just in case Thomas Hardin came to town.

Only one passenger disembarked—an older man with brown, rugged skin and the walk of one who was more at home in a saddle. He wore a hat pressed down over his eyes, as if he didn't want to be recognized.

"Can I help you, Sir?" Linus asked.

The cowboy looked at Linus, then noticed Bertie. He wearily removed his hat. He had startling blue eyes, familiar eyes; and Bertie thought she'd never seen anybody looking so lost.

Chapter 7

The preacher stood in the front of the room. He spoke the words to the sermon, but his eyes were not as bright as usual. Bertie liked and listened to Parson Harris. She knew him well because he was a friend of Scotty's. Bertie wondered what the man was thinking now that he stood before a crossroad in life. He'd been offered a church of his own, complete with a parsonage: roots, permanence.

It wouldn't be an easy decision. He was a circuit preacher through and through, and Bertie had spoken with him often enough to know how much he relished his time on the trail. Harris formulated his sermons on the back of his horse. He scratched down the words using his saddle as a desk. He rehearsed his sermons using the stars as his trial first audience. And now Lickwind offered him—and his family— refuge. His wife accompanied him for the first time. Mrs. Harris wanted her man beside her every night. She worried when he roamed the open range for days on end. She wanted roots. She wanted their two sons to know their papa.

Harris really didn't have a choice, Bertie realized in that moment. The pull of family was a powerful magnet.

Bertie did not turn around to look, although she knew

Thomas Hardin sat somewhere behind her. She wasn't surprised. Scotty had told her it would happen and to just wait. She hadn't seen Thomas arrive; but with the way everyone around her craned their necks at the commotion a short time ago, nothing else could have rated such rapt attention. Bertie didn't dare adjust her new hat, or Matty would notice and elbow her. The sisters were already atwitter at the idea of Bertie buying a bonnet at a store!

"Don't tell me what you paid." Matty had blanched.

"All you needed to do was ask," Corrie said, "and Matty would have made whatever you wanted."

Bess shook her head.

But Bertie didn't want a bonnet made out of everyday, already-been-seen material. She wanted one that was hers alone, and half the fun had been anticipating its arrival. It had taken three weeks and two trains for the color she wanted to arrive.

Lately, Thomas was spending more time in town than on his ranch. Nightly, he took his meals at the restaurant, always at one of Bertie's tables.

His stutter had finally stopped, but she'd welcome it back if it meant he said the words she wanted to hear. He didn't ask Gideon for permission to court. He didn't say I think I love you.

Think? Was there really any thinking involved? Bertie had considered it something of a lark when the men of Lickwind had flocked around her and her sisters. She'd retreated behind her papa's hat and old, leather boots and been a spectator in a game that now held her firmly in its clutch.

The game of love. Her sisters had all been winners, and for once Bertie intended to follow their example.

She wanted to smile. She wanted the world to know that Thomas Hardin thought enough of her to come to the restaurant most every night and now, finally, to church.

The sermon looked to be nearing summation. Bertie had listened with one ear and agreed with Parson Harris's premise. It was easier to forgive a stranger than someone you loved. She'd always had trouble forgiving those she loved. She'd not forgiven her parents for dying. She'd not forgiven Adele for marrying a weak-kneed poor excuse for a man. She'd not forgiven herself.

Harris called for a prayer, and all around her heads bowed. Down the pew from her, Bertie noticed the man who'd arrived by train just two days ago. His head was bowed, and Bertie wondered if he knew etiquette called for the removal of his hat.

Bertie bowed her head.

After the amen, Harris called for any sinners to come forward and repent.

The church was a bit stuffy, but nobody was leaving. Even Corrie's babies and Matty's little one seemed to sense that now was not a good time to whimper. Parson Harris came from behind the podium and walked to meet the cowboy from the train, the one with the familiar blue eyes. He walked down the center aisle, reached the front of the church, shook the parson's hand, and turned to face the audience.

"Take off your hat," Bertie silently mouthed; and as if he'd heard her, the old man slowly removed his hat.

Even before she heard his name whispered, she figured out who the man was. This time Bertie did turn around and then stood up, pushing past Bess and Gideon, stepping over the twins and on Corrie in her hurry to get to Thomas.

To say that Thomas looked surprised to see his father at church was an understatement. Such a mixture of shock, denial, and anger crossed his features that Bertie momentarily paused and lost the opportunity to reach him. When she reached the church's exit, Thomas was already on his horse and galloping down the street.

A gentle hand rested on Bertie's shoulder and Bess whispered, "Give him time."

❦

Thomas Harding the elder was no longer a typical cowboy. He sat at Bertie's table and passed his sheriff's badge around. Bertie poured him another cup of coffee and tried to imagine him stealing cattle.

The restaurant had no more room, and customers were eating while leaning against the wall. Josiah Temple was conspicuously absent. Even Albert Smit, looking pained, came to hear what Hardin had to say. Bertie didn't think Smit had ever put out money for a meal, not even for baked goods.

Jim and Luke frowned at the badge but listened to Hardin's story while Thomas's cowboys, Rex and Davey, flanked the sheriff as if worried he'd bolt.

Sheriff Hardin had no trouble talking. "I found the Lord or should I say, He found me. I need to make sure my boy knows the truth. I didn't steal them cattle. I admit, I'm not proud of my behavior in those days. I was young and had more responsibility than I felt I could handle. I took to the liquor a bit more than I needed to. I did make mistakes, and I've laid my guilt at the foot of the cross. But I didn't steal them cattle. I had me a good job and good wages back then."

Jim spoke up, "Then why didn't you protest? Why didn't you say you weren't guilty? I remember the day you were run out of town. You acted guilty."

The sheriff had the grace to look at his feet. "Somebody paid me off. Just a few minutes before the posse arrived, I found a note in my saddlebag along with enough money to give me and my boy a new life—if we left and didn't say anything. I'm ashamed now to say I took it. That money meant the kind of life my late wife had always dreamed of for our son."

"Is that how Tommy got enough money to buy the Kincaid spread?" Amos Freeling asked.

Both Sheriff Hardin and Donald Potter shook their heads.

Rex said, "Tommy hasn't taken a cent from his old man. Not that it's anybody's business, but he's made his money from the railroad and more recently right here in southwest Wyoming, investing money in a very lucrative mine."

"That's right," Sheriff Hardin said. "It didn't take me but a few weeks to realize that in accepting that bribe, I'd paid the ultimate price—my son. He had no reason to not believe I'd become a rustler; and before I realized the importance of telling him the truth, he'd run away. If it weren't for Scotty tracking me down, I'd not know Thomas's whereabouts today. Looks like, in spite of me, my son has made something of himself."

"How many cattle were you accused of rustling, Mr. Hardin?" Frank Llewellyn stood up. He'd just finished a bowl of jackrabbit stew and clutched a spoon in his fist, swinging it like a judge's mallet.

Sheriff Hardin shrugged. "About twenty."

"And," Frank continued, "that was roughly eight years ago. Does anybody know about how much cattle would have been worth back then?"

Jim and Luke looked at each other.

"Depends on the weight of the animals," Jim said.

"And where they were sold," Luke added.

Frank gripped the spoon tightly, deep in thought. "Mr. Hardin, just how much money were you given?"

Sheriff Hardin took a piece of faded leather pouch from his belt. He unfolded it so that a small pile of bills spread across the table. "It's right here. Once Tommy left, I didn't spend no more, and I replaced what I had spent. It's a hundred and fifteen dollars."

"Cattle were fetching good prices back then," Luke remembered.

"Then we can figure you were given the cost of the cattle," Frank said.

"Makes sense now, but that sure didn't occur to me then."

"So, you were paid for stealing the cattle?" Luke asked.

"But I didn't steal the cattle."

"Whose cattle were stolen?" Linus Hatch wanted to know.

"A few head, here and there," Luke said.

"Josiah Temple's," Jim remembered.

❧

Zeus had arrived with the broken surrey; and as of yet, none of the cowboys had been willing to climb on the beast's back. Over fifteen hands and high-strung, the stallion was purchased for breeding purposes; but every animal on the Two Horse needed to pull its load, and it was time for Zeus to be broken. The horse snorted and threw his head in a catch-me-if-you-dare attitude.

The horse's rebellion reminded Thomas of his father. Just how long had the man been in the area? Thomas shook his head. He wanted to blame his father for the mishaps on the ranch. But why? His father had nothing to gain by sabotaging his son. Why come back now?

Thomas stood, one foot perched on the bottom rung of the gate and the other planted firmly in the dirt. He'd been standing thus for over an hour trying to clear his mind, all the while debating the foolishness of breaking Zeus without the help of his men.

It was his fault. He had saddled up this morning bound for church. Rex, blinking away sleep and surprise, had followed, which inspired some of the other cowboys to see just what was going on. Susan and Jack always attended.

His cowboys were still in town with the church crowd. A crowd that hadn't blinked twice when he entered the door. Thomas actually felt welcomed as he took his place on a bench. At the moment, he couldn't figure what inspired him to saddle up this morning carrying the Bible Scotty had given him so many years ago. A Bible that hadn't entered a church since Scotty owned it.

Nothing had gone as planned from the moment Thomas stepped into Lickwind. He'd stuttered in front of Josiah. He'd bent the rules to allow Trieu on his place; and before he could blink an eye, along came Susan. Bad luck plagued the ranch, and the culprit eluded detection. His bank account reflected activity he had no control over. And now his father was in town and going forward in church.

The door to the main house burst open. A small figure in a brown hat came tumbling out and ran toward Thomas.

"Father says," Anna announced regally, "not to even think about climbing on Zeus's back. He says he has his gun, and he'll shoot you in the leg."

Thomas glanced at the house. He could see both Tien-Lu

and Trieu staring at him from the window.

"Tell them I won't do anything foolish." Thomas plucked the hat from Anna's head. "Bertie said to wear this when you're doing homework. Why are you wearing it now?"

"I want to wear what Miss Roberta gave to me."

Roberta.

Thomas glanced at Zeus and plopped the hat back on Anna's head. "Go tell your family that I'll not be doing any riding today."

Roberta.

It was all her fault. It began the moment he climbed off the train, encountered Miss Craig, and stuttered in front of Josiah. He half blamed Bertie for the ease of Susan's entrance to his ranch. And, if Thomas were honest, part of the reason he'd not caught those responsible for stealing and destroying his property was because he spent more time thinking about and worrying about Bertie than he did thinking about and worrying about his ranch.

The only thing he couldn't blame on Bertie was the bank activities and his father's arrival. Zeus snorted one last time and pranced over to where Thomas stood. The horse cocked his head as if confused. Thomas stretched out his hand, wanting to touch the beast on the nose, but the horse backed up.

No, Thomas thought, *nothing has gone as planned from the moment I stepped into Lickwind.*

But he'd never been happier, and it all had to do with the presence of Miss Bertie Craig.

What was it Donald had said? The Craig girls had a reputation for setting their sights on a man and turning his life upside-down until he married her.

Married?

Chapter 8

Thomas had been feeling some camaraderie with Frank Llewellyn as they tried to figure out who was depositing money into his account, but he didn't expect that the banker felt the same. Monday morning dawned without interruption; and before Thomas could down his first cup of coffee, he saw the banker arriving at the ranch. Most bankers didn't make house calls, so Thomas figured something important had spurred the man into riding the hour plus it took to get to the Two Horse Ranch. They sat on Thomas's front porch. Tien-Lu poured coffee, and Frank shared the conversation that had taken place back in town at the restaurant. Thomas had heard it already from both Rex and Davey.

"I believe in your father's innocence," Frank said.

"Why? Because he's claiming to be a Christian or because he's now a sheriff?"

Frank took a deep breath. "Those are both sound reasons, but it's these money transactions. The money your father was given sounds close to what the cattle would have brought at market. Whoever is doing this to you did somewhat the same to him. It has to be an original settler. That narrows it down considerably. The Collingswoods, Kincaid, or Albert Smit."

His father had been given money? None of this made sense, not even the banker's interest. "Why are you so interested?"

"Funny how things work out." Frank fiddled with the top button of his coat. "When them Craig girls first arrived, I agreed with the Collingswood brothers. Lickwind was no place for women. But I admit I was wrong. Them women have turned the place into more than a mud street and a few lost souls. The whole town acts like a community now."

"What's on your mind, Llewellyn?"

"When you came to town, I was back East visiting my sister. She's sick. I went home, put things in order, and returned here."

"And?"

"I recently received a telegram. My sister's dying. I can either bring her three children here or I can go there."

"You're going there?"

"Yes. Watching the way those Craig girls stay together has made me realize that I'm all my nieces and nephews have. I'm putting my family first."

Thomas took a sip of coffee and waited.

"I'm thinking about asking Miss Regina to marry me. She's been taking care of me at the restaurant, always makes sure my coffee cup is full. And, now that she's my housekeeper, I can see the riches having a woman's touch brings to a home. Lately, I've been looking forward to seeing her smile. Plus, the way she always looks out for Walter, no matter the sacrifice, makes me think yesterday morning's service about forgiveness is truer than I ever imagined. If Miss

Regina will have me, I'll take her away from here. Start a bank in my hometown and give us all a fresh start."

There was that word again: forgiveness. He kept hearing it from Scotty, and last week the preacher in town seemed quite taken with the notion of forgiveness. Thomas needed more time. He'd never admired men who made decisions without thinking them through.

"The way I figure it," Frank continued, "there are only two men in Lickwind who have enough money to purchase the bank."

"Me and Josiah Temple?" Thomas guessed.

"I'm not counting Josiah."

"Then who else?"

"Albert Smit."

"Smit has money? Now that's a surprise," Thomas could not help but muse aloud.

Frank agreed. "He doesn't look or act like he has much, but what that man can do with numbers is amazing. He knows when to sell and when to hold off. He's had money in the bank since it opened. Unfortunately, he's barely literate. Owning a bank wouldn't appeal to him in the least."

"You're friends with Josiah. He'd probably love to own the bank, so why are you sharing this news with me?"

"I've built that bank up from nothing. I'm proud of it. For a town with only one street, we have a bank to equal Philadelphia's. I don't want Josiah near it." Frank leaned forward. "The man owns Margaret's bordello, and it's about to go out of business. He'll run the bank into the ground for his own gain. And," Frank admitted, "truth is, Josiah has very little money. Right now he's land rich and money poor. But he'd find a way to purchase the bank, be it honest or not."

So Josiah owned the bordello. Thomas supposed he should be shocked, but he wasn't. "Fact is, as you well know, you can't stop Josiah from buying it if he can get the money. Law says you have to publicly announce that it's for sale."

"That's true, but—"

A horse and rider came over a nearby crest. Frank squinted, trying to make out the identity. Thomas stood. Donald Potter rode into view.

He reined in his horse, slid off in one fluid motion, and said, "I need to speak with you, Thomas."

"Whatever you have to say, you can say it in front of Llewellyn."

Donald didn't look inclined, but went ahead. "You've got trouble, Thomas. Looks like the rustling problem has returned along with your father."

❧

It didn't take long to set up a town meeting in Lickwind, especially when the price of cattle, the state of cattle, or the disappearance of cattle was in question. The town's leaders, except for Josiah Temple, wound up at the Back Porch. Bess, with a I'm-not-in-the-mood-for-nonsense look, told Bertie to stop making moon eyes at Thomas and to start peeling potatoes. All Bertie wanted to do was listen to the men like Bess got to. Distracted, she sliced her finger with the paring knife.

"Oh, Grandmother's bloomers." She stuck the offending digit in her mouth and looked around the kitchen, finally grabbing a clean dish towel and blotting at the blood.

Bess came back, more than a little annoyed. "They're done for tonight."

"I need to know. Is Thomas in trouble? Did his father do

something? What's going on?"

"All I know is that some folks out near Cheyenne are missing cattle. Thomas is getting the blame; and now that his father's here, it's not looking good."

Bertie stood. "Thomas has nothing to do with that."

"I believe that. Oh, Bertie, whatever you're up to, I can't help but think it won't work. Thomas Hardin is not a church-going man. In all good conscience, I cannot permit you to consort with him."

Bertie moved the potatoes from the table into a pan of water. "I love him."

"You're too young to know about love."

"I'm the same age as Adele was when she married Ellis, and I'm the same age Corrie was when she married Brian."

"Adele was born old, and Corrie was born to be a wife and mother. Besides, Thomas Hardin is not a marrying sort of man."

Bertie closed her eyes, the urge to pray strong. "Bess, you know what this conversation reminds me of?"

"I'm almost afraid to ask."

"It reminds me of how you felt when you realized you were falling in love with Gideon. You had the same doubts about his character, about his walk with the Lord. But somehow you knew the true man—just the way I know my Thomas."

Bess's lips puckered, and tears shimmered in her eyes.

"I love him," Bertie repeated.

Bess stood still, so still that only the rise and fall of her chest proved life. "This is my fault. I should have curbed your actions. It's just," her voice broke, "you remind me so much of Papa, always dreaming, always moving, always so full of energy. I thought I was doing right by you."

"You did do right by me."

It didn't matter. Bess was sitting in a chair with her head in her hands. Bertie started to go to her, but Bess held up a hand. After a moment, Bertie quietly slipped out the back door.

The full moon did a good imitation of a lantern as Bertie walked the few feet to Gideon and Bess's home. She let herself in the front door and headed for her room. How silly and young she'd been this morning.

She hung the green dress Matty had sewn for her on a peg and put on her nightgown. Huddled in bed, her stomach and mind flip-flopped with reaction to the day's events.

She loved Thomas Hardin.

She had to tell him.

Chapter 9

"Thomas Hardin!" The cry, actually loud voices blended into one, sounded too close. Thomas let go of the post he was holding and stared at two frowning Collingswood brothers and one visibly irate Gideon Riker.

"Where's Bertie?" Gideon demanded.

Thomas walked to meet the men, giving a backward look at a barn that should have been finished long ago. He was missing about fifteen head of cattle and in no mood to hear about how he wasn't good enough for Roberta Suzanne Craig.

"She's at home with you," he growled.

"No, she left early this morning!"

Luke rubbed a hand across his face, worry lines running deep. "Bess thought you'd eloped."

"What!" Just when Thomas thought nothing else could surprise him, Bertie managed something.

"Bertie definitely insists that she's in love," Gideon said slowly. "Bess caught on yesterday that it wasn't just Bertie making moon eyes." His eyes narrowed. "I agree."

"W—we haven't t—talked m—marriage." Thomas's throat was closing again. Cattle were missing, his father was nearby, and now Bertie was nowhere to be found. He didn't like this. He didn't like it at all.

"Which way do we head now?" Luke asked.

Soon every man from both the Two Horse and the Rough Cs was out looking for Bertie.

❧

Bertie stood behind a cottonwood tree and watched as Josiah Temple and the outlaw moved Thomas's cattle south. She finally recognized the other man. Not an outlaw really, but he'd scared her and Bess a few months ago when he shot up the town after the railroad drove the last stake in.

One of the calves got his foot stuck between two huge rocks. Josiah got off his horse to dislodge the dogie.

Bertie bowed her head. Never before had she felt so sure that God wanted her to call upon Him. "Oh, Father. I need You beside me right now. I am so frightened. Father, I've acted shamefully, disobeying them, coming out here alone when nobody knows where I am. I need forgiveness. You've always taken care of me and blessed me with a family who loves me, yet I blamed You for my sorrows. Father, forgive me now, and help me know if I'm doing what is right. Please let Thomas find me."

The moment she said "amen," she felt better.

She'd come upon the men hours ago—she'd only wanted to go to Thomas, tell him she believed in him—but she'd never ridden so far out of town alone. She'd gotten lost, turned around, and instead of surprising Thomas, she'd stumbled across the real rustler. She'd started to hurry to the Two Horse, but didn't want Josiah to get away.

Bad luck followed the men, otherwise Bertie never would have been able to keep up. First, Josiah's horse threw a shoe. And now one of the cows had its foot firmly wedged between two good-sized rocks.

She was about tuckered out from trying to keep up when another rider joined the men.

The men stopped beside a small stream to rest the horses and talk. Bertie sank gratefully to her knees. Grandmother's bloomers, she never expected anything like this.

Why was Josiah stealing Thomas's cattle? Josiah had tons of money, everyone said. Not that he was a good tipper when Bertie waited on him. He looked different this morning: a little wild and a whole lot scarier.

Bertie crawled to a closer tree so she could see the third man.

At first, she didn't believe her eyes. Josiah patted the older man on the shoulder, laughing.

Albert Smit?

Bertie covered her mouth. Why was Mr. Smit with these men?

No, wait a minute.

Even from a distance, Bertie could hear the ominous sound of Josiah laughing as he knocked Albert to the ground.

Ramon chose that moment to find her. He trotted up, nudged her legs, looked toward the scattered cattle, and barked. Josiah's companion started in her direction.

Bertie took a breath. She was winded, but letting them catch her would not save Mr. Smit or Thomas's cattle.

Wishing she still wore her father's comfortable, worn boots instead of these new ankle boots, Bertie turned around and ran right into Thomas's arms.

❧

Josiah Temple deserved to be the first man to call the Lickwind jail home. Donald Potter looked like he was enjoying himself as he filled out the paperwork that Sheriff Hardin promised to deliver along with the prisoner.

All last night and early this morning, the townspeople had gathered at the Back Porch and put together the pieces to a mystery that started before Thomas and his father had been run out of town. Albert Smit put his hand on the Bible and swore to tell the truth. "I knew all those years ago that Thomas Hardin wasn't responsible for rustling cattle."

Every resident of Lickwind leaned forward. Little Brianne nodded and banged her hand on the clean floor of the restaurant.

"Josiah gambled away the money his father left him. When we first moved out here, I gave him a sizable loan and tried to advise him, but things weren't moving fast enough for him. He started rustling so he could buy more land. At first, I didn't know it was him; and by the time I figured it out, he'd already made it look like Hardin was not only guilty but also rustling from the real crook."

Jim paced the floor and asked, "And why didn't you step forward then?"

Albert hung his head. "He's my brother-in-law. My deceased wife's only brother. I promised her I'd watch out for him, only I've not done too good a job."

Thomas leaned over and whispered in Bertie's ear. "Jim and Luke might very well be the only two men who knew that Albert and Josiah were distantly related. They don't like each other much. Albert didn't even allow his boys to call Josiah their uncle. Yet every time Josiah messed up, Albert tried to fix it. He knew Scotty would keep the men from stringing up my father, and so Albert made sure we had enough money to start over. When I first got here, Albert made no secret of that fact he wanted me gone. He was doing more of the same when he made a fuss about Anna being in school. I figured he was cut out of Josiah's cloth. Turns out he knew I'd spur Josiah into thinking it was safe to rustle again now that there was somebody to blame. Albert's a good man in his own way. Every time Josiah destroyed something belonging to the Two Horse, Albert tried to make up for it by depositing his own money into my account."

"Poor Mr. Smit," Bertie whispered. "Imagine carrying all this on his conscience."

Thomas nodded and looked at his father seated next to him. The two men had started mending the broken fences of their past. Sheriff Hardin waited to escort Josiah on the next train. Rustling was often called a hanging offense, but not in a town where the Craig girls had any say. Plus, Scotty had already made his opinion known. Look at the good that had come from not hanging Sheriff Hardin.

Bertie looked around to see if Bess was looking. Bess and Gideon had not yet given Thomas permission to come calling. Yes, they acknowledged that Thomas had agreed to study the Bible with his father, but that didn't mean anything until he accepted the Lord.

Bertie grinned at the thought of Thomas studying the Bible with his father. After this trial, Sheriff Hardin intended to turn Josiah and his partner over to the proper authorities, then Sheriff Hardin would return to Lickwind. After all, the town already had a jail. It surely needed a sheriff. And a father needed a second chance with his son.

It took hours, but finally all the questions were answered. Bertie left the proceedings and hurried to the restaurant. Seemed a trial was good for business. She quietly tied on her apron. Gazing out the open window of the kitchen, she could see a section of the Union Pacific train track. How much her life had changed since that long-ago day when the Craig girls arrived in Lickwind.

Jim came through the kitchen door chuckling.

"What's so funny?" Bertie asked.

"Your young man," Jim announced.

Bertie couldn't help but smile. She liked the sound of that. Her young man. "Well, are you going to tell me what's so funny?"

"He just offered me a buck-fifty for you. Seemed to think that was necessary." Jim put a hand on her shoulder and said softly, "If that young man of yours ever gives his heart to the Lord, and if you're both ready, I just might take that money."

Before Bertie could respond, Jim disappeared through the door, and Thomas took his place.

A place he'd stay forever—in her heart.

For true.

Epilogue

June 1874

A milling crowd of youngsters slowly sorted itself out around the eight adults assembled in front of the photographer in the parlor of the Rough Cs.

Bertie tugged her renegade daughter closer to her, wiping at the dirt-smudged face. A full inch of lace hung from the four-year-old's hem. "Laura Hardin, look at you!"

Thomas watched the pair, an indulgent grin on his face. Not long after he made peace with his father, he'd also made peace with his heavenly Father. He'd carried that spiritual contentment into his marriage to Bertie. "I'm sure your mother never looked like that," he informed three-year-old Robert, standing proudly beside him.

"Oh, I couldn't count the times." Bess Riker sighed.

In front of her, three-year-old Kate Riker pulled on her four-year-old brother Stanley's arm. "Stand up stwaight," she ordered.

Bess and Gideon exchanged laughing glances. "Someone else is just like her mother," Gideon teased. Bess only smiled and looked content.

Her husband slipped his arm around her. "Quite an honor, having our pictures taken with Lickwind's next mayor."

"I haven't won the election yet," she reminded him.

"You will."

Seated on a nearby chair, Corrie Collingswood pulled squirmy one-year-old Daniel onto her lap to hide the bulge of her fifth child on the way. Beside her, Luke stood proudly with three-year-old Mark on his arm and the five-year-olds, Brianne and Madeline, in front of him. The growing family still lived in the ranch house, which had been expanded twice in the past five years to accommodate both Collingswood clans.

Matty waded through the knot of children as Jim called, "Kids, hurry."

Five-year-old Matthew stood on Matty's left; Bess arranged two-year-old Jamie on Matty's lap; and Jim grabbed almost-four-year-old Corliss away from Corrie's twins.

As soon as the photograph was done, Matty tugged urgently on Luke's sleeve. After a pause, during which she bit her lip as though holding back a cry, she said, "Did you take care of things?"

Luke shot Jim a repentant grin. "Ahh, big brother, you might want to tote your wife upstairs. I sent Scotty for Doc Wilson."

"Why?" Realization dawned, and Jim's hazel eyes widened. "Today?"

"Now, Sweetheart." Matty winced and rubbed her big tummy as Jim took the stairs two at a time with his wife in his arms.

Bess dashed past them, and Corrie followed as quickly as her girth would allow.

Matty had one more request before her husband deposited her on the bed and permitted her sisters to take over her care. "Tell Bertie to make the photographer stay. I won't be long, and I want pictures of these twins who are about to make their appearance."

Downstairs in the parlor, Madeline requested, "Auntie Bertie, tell us again about the big mistake that made you brides."

"It wasn't really a mistake, Honey," Jim called as he returned downstairs to await the newest arrivals. "It was the beginning of countless blessings."

BUTTER BUDS

2 ½ cups flour
1 cup brown sugar
2 beaten eggs
1 cup butter
2 tsp vanilla
1 tsp baking powder
¼ tsp salt

Cream butter and sugar. Add eggs and vanilla. Sift in
dry ingredients and mix until like soft dough. Pinch
off pieces. Roll in hands; then press down with form.
Bake in 350–375 degree oven.

PAMELA KAYE TRACY

Pamela is a new bride living in Arizona, where she teaches at a community college. Pamela had her first novel of inspirational fiction published in 1999 by Barbour Publishing's **Heartsong Presents** line. She has been a cook, waitress, drafter, Kelly girl, insurance filer, and secretary; but through it all, in the back of her mind, she knew she wanted to be a writer. "I believe in happy endings," says Pamela. "My parents lived the white picket fence life." Writing Christian romance gives her the opportunity to let her imagination roam.

A Letter to Our Readers

Dear Readers:

In order that we might better contribute to your reading enjoyment, we would appreciate you taking a few minutes to respond to the following questions. When completed, please return to the following: Fiction Editor, Barbour Publishing, Inc., P.O. Box 719, Uhrichsville, OH 44683.

1. Did you enjoy reading *A Bride for a Bit?*
   - ❏ Very much—I would like to see more books like this.
   - ❏ Moderately—I would have enjoyed it more if _____
   _____
   _____

2. What influenced your decision to purchase this book? (Check those that apply.)
   - ❏ Cover
   - ❏ Back cover copy
   - ❏ Title
   - ❏ Price
   - ❏ Friends
   - ❏ Publicity
   - ❏ Other

3. Which story was your favorite?
   - ❏ *From Halter to Altar*
   - ❏ *From Pride to Bride*
   - ❏ *From Carriage to Marriage*
   - ❏ *From Alarming to Charming*

4. Please check your age range:
   - ❏ Under 18
   - ❏ 18–24
   - ❏ 25–34
   - ❏ 35–45
   - ❏ 46–55
   - ❏ Over 55

5. How many hours per week do you read? _____

Name _____

Occupation _____

Address _____

City _____ State _____ Zip _____